D0961327

RED WOLF

OTHER YOUNG ADULT NOVELS
BY RACHEL VINCENT

The Soul Screamers Series
The Stars Never Rise duology
The Brave New Girl duology
Every Single Lie

RED WOLF

RACHEL VINCENT

An Imprint of HarperCollinsPublishers

HarperTeen is an imprint of HarperCollins Publishers.

Library of Congress Cataloging-in-Publication Data

Names: Vincent, Rachel, author.
Title: Red wolf / Rachel Vincent.
Description: First edition. | New York, NY : HarperTeen, an imprint
    of HarperCollins Publishers, [2021] | Audience: Ages 14 up. |
    Audience: Grades 10-12. | Summary: When fulfilling her duty as
    a shapeshifting guardian for her village means abandoning the
    young man she loves, the future she imagines with him, and her
    values, sixteen-year-old Adele must decide how far she is willing
    to go to keep her friends and neighbors safe.
Identifiers: LCCN 2020044127 | ISBN 978-0-06-241162-4
    (hardcover)
Subjects: CYAC: Werewolves—Fiction. | Monsters—Fiction. |
    Responsibility—Fiction. | Betrothal—Fiction.
Classification: LCC PZ7.V7448 Re 2021 | DDC [Fic]—dc23
LC record available at https://lccn.loc.gov/2020044127

Typography by Corina Lupp
21 22 23 24 25   PC/LSCH   10 9 8 7 6 5 4 3 2 1

First Edition

For Jennifer Lynn Barnes, who reminded me
how much fun it can be to return to your roots

ONE

The dark wood moaned—a deep, eerie sound that was more than just the groan of shifting tree limbs. I turned, and my empty basket swung in the crook of my right elbow as I stared into the wooded expanse that enclosed most of Oakvale. My breath hovered in front of my face in a little white cloud. It was always chilly near the woods, even in the height of summer, but on a clear winter day like today, just staring into the unnatural darkness was enough to send a fresh chill skittering up my spine.

To my right, a torch crackled, its flame flickering at the top of a post driven deep into the frozen ground. Beyond that, another torch glowed a few feet away, and beyond that, yet another. There were hundreds of them forming a ring around the village, a protective halo of light that the village watch kept burning at all hours. In all weather.

Because the woods were full of monsters, and monsters were afraid of light.

My delivery to the Bertrand cottage hadn't required me to go near the forest. Still, on my way home I'd found myself drawn toward the trees, walking the outer perimeter of the village, beyond the pasture and the fallow fields instead of taking the shorter path straight through. Ever since I was a small child, the dark wood had called to me, its eerie voice half seduction, half warning. I had no intention of answering. Yet I couldn't seem to stop myself from *listening*.

A slithering came from deep within the forest, accompanied by the dry rattle of skeletal branches. Then I heard my name, a soft plea carried on a cold breeze from the depths of the woods.

Adele. Help me.

An old ache gripped me. That was my father's voice.

My father had died eight years before. I *knew* that wasn't him calling from the forest, but knowing that didn't make the voice any easier to ignore.

Unsettled, I turned away from the trees to head home, suddenly aware of how long my circuitous detour had taken, and as I crossed the empty pasture, I heard footsteps at my back.

"Adele."

Startled, I spun to find Grainger Colbert behind me. I couldn't resist a smile. His grin developed more slowly as he closed the distance between us, his blue-eyed gaze studying me. I could feel my face flushing from his attention. He looked handsome in his leather vest and boots, his sword hanging from a scabbard at his waist, and the knowledge that he had eyes only for me made a delicious warmth blossom in the pit of my stomach to chase away the chill of the day. Of the forest.

He reached out to tug playfully at the hem of my worn brown cloak. "Making deliveries?"

"I've just finished."

"Then you might have a moment to talk?"

In my dreams, I had all day to talk to him. All night. But today . . . "Maybe *one* moment. Tonight's the full moon, so—"

"You're going into the dark wood again?" His smile faded into a look of concern.

"I'll be with my mother. Gran depends upon our deliveries."

He stepped closer, staring down into my eyes, making my pulse race. "Your grandmother should come stay in the village. It makes no sense for anyone to live alone out there, much less a woman of her age."

"I've been telling her that for years. Maybe today she'll listen." But I had no real hope of that. My grandmother had lived alone in the dark wood since before I was born, surviving by rarely venturing far from the clearing where her cabin sat—an island of daylight in a sea of shadows.

It was the journey that held most of the danger.

"It isn't safe in the woods for two women alone." Grainger leaned closer and gave my cloak another little tug, his nose brushing my hair as he whispered, "When we're married, *I* shall accompany you, if you insist upon visiting your grandmother out there."

My pulse raced so fiercely I was certain he could hear it. "You would come with me?"

His hand went to the pommel of his sword. "The village watch protects all of Oakvale." And when his father retired, someday, Grainger would be the head of the watch. "Do you think I would do any less for my own wife?"

Wife. The thought drew my lips into another smile as I gazed up at him. I'd been in love with him since I was twelve years old, when he'd run off the Thayer brothers, who had cornered me behind the mill and were taunting me about my red hair. Grainger had said my hair was beautiful. Then he'd stolen a kiss and sworn that someday he would marry me.

Since then, he'd been a constant fixture at my side, sweetly eager to make his claim known, even though no one had challenged him for my affection. And yet, that little thrill had not begun to fade with familiarity. It sparked anew between us every time his hand brushed mine or his gaze settled on me. Every time he stole a kiss . . .

"It's been a month since I asked for your hand. I must admit, I'd hoped to have an answer by now."

"And I'd hoped to give you one." I pulled my cloak tighter against the cold. "Yet every time I try to talk to my mother, she's too busy to speak on the matter."

"I will ask my father to press the issue."

"No, don't." Though she'd always been gracious to him, and he to her, my mother was privately wary of the head of the watch. She'd never said why, exactly, but I'd always suspected it had to do with my father's death. "I'll talk to her on our way to Gran's cabin. She won't be able to avoid the subject, when there's only the two of us."

Grainger nodded. "You'll both be careful out there?"

"And we won't veer from the path. Or stop. It isn't our first trip into the dark wood." I rose onto my toes to press a kiss to his cheek. "And if you come by later tonight, I'll recount our entire adventure for you. It will be as if you were right there with me."

"I look forward to that." He caught me around the waist before I could drop back onto my heels, and he claimed a kiss boldly from my lips. "I've just finished maintaining the torches, and I'll be on patrol until dusk, hoping to lay eyes on the fox that stole one of Madame Girard's eggs. Expect me once the sun has gone down."

"You checked the torches alone?"

When I was born, the unnatural forest had only bordered two-thirds of our tiny village, but in the sixteen years since, it had swelled to surround Oakvale entirely, except where the river formed the northern border. Which meant there were many more torches to maintain now than there were when Grainger's father took over the village watch, when we were little.

That task seemed impossibly large for one man.

"No, I was only responsible for the east half of the halo. Yet that still took all morning."

"Did you hear anything from the woods?" He wouldn't have been able to see more than a few feet into the forest, but the dark wood was rarely quiet.

"Just howls and snorts today. The deep, angry kind, as if a bull were about to charge from the darkness." Grainger knew that wouldn't happen, thanks to the torches, yet the thought obviously made him uncomfortable. "But a couple of days ago, I heard my uncle call out."

Rufus Colbert had been a member of the watch, like his brother and nephew. But he died two years ago.

"I know it isn't real," he continued, his frown deepening. "Yet it gives me chills every time."

"Yes, it does. Today I heard my father's voice." Again.

I shook off that memory, choosing to focus on the man in front of me instead. On the promise of the future, rather than the sorrow of the past. "Well, on behalf of the entire village, I thank you for maintaining the torches." That was a tedious but vital part of protecting Oakvale, and pride swelled within me for his part in the effort. For his dedication to protecting the village. Grainger was a good man. Strong, and gallant, and honorable. And handsome enough to keep my thoughts as occupied as my hands during hours spent kneading dough at the bakery. *Speaking of which* . . . "My mother's expecting me, but I promise we'll be back before nightfall."

"I'll see you then." His focus lingered on my mouth, and I felt the ghost of his lips there.

"I look forward to that."

Grainger gave me a smile that lit my insides on fire. "Have a pleasant afternoon, Mademoiselle Duval," he teased.

"And you, Monsieur Colbert," I called playfully over my shoulder as I turned to head into the village. I could feel his gaze on me until I rounded the community barn.

On the way home, I strolled past two dozen small cottages with thatched roofs, several of which I'd made deliveries to that morning from my mother's bakery. Most families on the edges of the village could only afford a standard order of rye, but those deliveries were my favorite—simple bread for people who were happy to have it.

Closer to the center of the village, the larger, sturdier structures were home to customers who placed more expensive orders, then complained about the size, or the cost, or the quality. Their real objection, though, was that the only bakery in Oakvale was run by the Duval women.

Redheaded witches, they whispered when they thought we weren't listening. Or, sometimes, when they were sure we *were* listening.

I passed those houses with my head held high, then I crossed the broad, muddy lane leading to the manor held by Baron Carre, the local lord, and his household. The grand house was vacant at the moment, of course, because the baron had other homes, and because anyone with the means to leave Oakvale during the harshest winter months would do exactly that.

With our village surrounded by the dark wood, except where the river cut through it, regular trade and travel had to be conducted by boat, which was the only safe way in or out of Oakvale. But during the heart of winter, the river froze over, almost entirely isolating our little village until the spring thaw.

Baron Carre and his household had abandoned the village more than a month ago, just days before the hard freeze, and we wouldn't see them—nor would we benefit from their patronage—again until spring.

We wouldn't see many visitors or traders either.

Past the baron's estate, I continued down the muddy path until I stood in the broad square—really more of a rectangle—at the center of the village. The square was presided over at one end by the church, built of hand-hewn wood planks the year I was eight. The year my little sister was born. At the other end stood the Laurent house, the second largest in the village and the only one built entirely of stone.

I crossed the square quickly, holding my breath as I passed the thick post mounted in the center, surrounded by stones set into the ground. Ash had long ago been washed from the stones, but the old, scorched post would forever bear the scars of every fire it had endured. Of every man and woman burned at the stake in order to protect the village.

Looking at the post chilled me almost as deeply as standing

on the edge of the dark wood. So, as usual, I averted my gaze, and swift movement caught my attention. There was a boy—no, a man—walking quickly across the square.

"Simon!" I called, and the oldest of the Laurent boys turned. When he saw me, a smile beamed from his face, bright enough to light up this entire muddy hamlet. "What's the hurry?"

"Good news today, Adele!" he called, walking backward now to keep me in sight.

"Well then, don't keep it to yourself!"

He laughed. "You'll hear soon enough. I'll see you tonight!"

"Tonight?" I asked, but he'd already turned and was jogging toward his house.

Smoke billowed from the chimney of my home, the smallest structure bordering the village square, carrying with it the scent of fresh bread. I couldn't resist a smile as I approached, because through the small front window, its wooden shutter propped open, I saw my mother at the table in the center of the room, kneading dough with both hands, sending up little puffs of rye flour as she sprinkled it over the work surface.

Our cottage might not have been large like the Laurents' home, but unlike the smaller structures on the edges of the village, it had a separate room in the back for sleeping, made necessary by the large oven and table taking up most of the main room. I loved our little cottage because in addition to that back room, there was enough space in the front for us to host the occasional customer who wanted to rent space in our oven, rather than buy our bread. The chance to gossip with a neighbor while I worked was easily the highlight of any week, especially during the long, cold winter, when we spent much of our time cooped up inside.

The heavy wooden door creaked as I pushed it open and stepped into my home. The scent of minced beef wafted over me, making my mouth water.

"Adele!" Sofia squealed as I pushed the door closed, cutting off the winter chill. My eight-year-old sister stood from her stool at the smaller kitchen table and dropped a handful of dough on the floured surface. "I'm making a meat pie for our lunch!"

"For *your* lunch," my mother corrected her with an indulgent smile. "Adele has one more delivery to make."

"A meat pie?" I arched one brow at my mother, then my gaze slid toward the pot bubbling over the fire. As usual, today's orders were all for simple flatbread, made either of rye or barley. When I'd left to make my morning deliveries, there'd been no sign of fresh beef or of the rich pastry crust my mother was now making. In fact, we hadn't eaten meat, other than smoked fish from our small store of preserved trout, in more than a week. "What's the occasion?"

"The Laurents and the Rousseaus finally came to an agreement."

No wonder Simon was all smiles!

My mother's gaze lingered on my face as she studied my reaction.

10

"How wonderful for Elena!" I set my basket on the other end of the table, hiding my frustration on my own behalf behind a bright smile.

Why was my mother so interested in my response to my best friend's engagement, when she'd refused to even discuss Grainger's request for my hand?

She went back to her kneading. "There's to be an engagement ceremony tonight." Which would mean a village-wide celebration. "Monsieur Laurent has placed a large order. When the meat pies go into the oven, I have to start some more raisin bread and an apple tart. In addition to the flatbread."

I could only stare at my mother. "An order like that will deplete most of our stock of honey, and there will be no new shipment until the spring thaw."

"I am aware, Adele. But the fee for such an extravagant commission will be a blessing in the middle of winter."

I removed the cloth covering my basket. "Madame Bertrand sent half a pound of salt pork, and she thanks you for the rye disks." Others had made payment in the form of smoked meats and winter vegetables like turnips, cabbage, and potatoes. "Do you think you can spare me for a moment, if I promise to start the tart as soon as I get back? I want to congratulate Elena."

Elena Rousseau had been my closest friend since we were old enough to run through the pasture on the western edge of town, clutching our rag dolls. She was the sweetest girl in the village, but also the shyest and most timid, and as badly as I

11

really did want to congratulate her, I also wanted to seize a quiet moment in which to assure her—again—that Simon would make her a wonderful husband. He was a good man. One of the few, like Grainger, who was not suspicious of my red hair or prone to spreading baseless rumors about my family.

He would care for her and about her. Other than Grainger, a better man could not be found in the village of Oakvale.

"That'll have to wait until tonight." My mother sprinkled more flour onto her dough, to keep it from sticking to her hands, and Sofia mimicked her technique at the smaller table. "I've wrapped some raisin bread and a rye loaf for your grandmother." She pointed with one flour-coated hand at two cloth-wrapped bundles on the mantle. "Go straight there, and don't veer from the path."

The path. In the woods.

My heart pounded. "You want me to go to Gran's by myself?"

"I think you're ready, Adele." The tension in her bearing belied the calm smile she gave me.

"I want to go!" Sofia dropped her dough on the table with a soft thud. "I'm ready too!"

My mother looked up sharply. "No."

"But I'm not afraid!"

That was true. Nothing scared my little sister, probably because she'd been an infant when our father died. She had no memory of him. She hadn't seen him carried out of the forest by the village watch, his left arm and leg shredded by the wolf that had attacked him. She was spared the brutal mercy my mother and I witnessed, a trauma that had impressed upon me at an early age that the threat of the dark wood extended well beyond its border.

Making it out of the forest was not enough; one had to make it out *unscathed*, or the villagers of Oakvale—our neighbors— would finish the job, for the good of the entire community.

In the eight years since our father's death, Oakvale had lost only a handful of villagers to the dark wood—all careless souls who'd veered from the path—which had left Sofia with no clear understanding of how dangerous the forest was. What she knew was that Gran lived in the dark wood and that our mother survived a trek through the forest every month to take her a basketful of baked goods, help with any necessary repairs to her cabin, and catch her up on news from the village. She knew that I'd recently started going with our mother, and that Gran would feed us, then send us home with enough fresh game to get us through the month.

Yes, she also knew about the vines, and the voices, and the eerie footsteps in the dark, as did everyone else in the village. But those terrors seemed to fascinate her, rather than spook her, which frightened my mother endlessly on her behalf.

That frightened me too, because I understood her fascination with the woods, and I worried that she felt drawn toward the forest just like I did. That some day, she might answer that call.

"You're too young," I told Sofia. "And, Mama, you'll need

my help with the tart." The Laurents' order would be difficult to fill even with both of us working.

"I can make the tart!" Sofia pounded one small fist into the scrap of dough intended to keep her busy.

"You can help me prepare the apples," my mother conceded. "But not until you've finished your meat pie."

Sofia's green eyes lit up, and she pushed a lock of copper-colored hair over her shoulder as she turned back to her task.

"Surely Gran's delivery can wait until tomorrow." I removed the smoked pork from my basket and set it on the shelf above the brick oven. "She'll understand, once she hears about Elena's engagement."

"Tonight's the full moon, Adele." The day we were expected every month. "If neither of us arrives, your grandmother will think something's wrong. I can handle the orders." The tone of her voice suggested that I would not win this argument. "You'll see Elena tonight. Go deliver Gran's bread and make sure she feeds you something warm before you head back. It's a long walk."

It certainly *felt* like a long walk, anyway. Even with my mother at my side, I usually had to remind myself to breathe, and now . . .

"There's a lantern hanging out back." My mother wiped her hands on her apron as I packed my grandmother's baked goods into my basket and draped a fresh cloth over the whole thing. The raisin bread was still warm, and it smelled delicious. "Adele." She took me by both shoulders, and the concern swimming in her eyes fed my self-doubt. "Be careful. Stay on the path and don't stop until you get to the cottage."

"I know."

"The lantern will keep you safe."

"I know, Mama." Monsters hated light, and they feared fire.

I reached for my threadbare brown cloak, but before I could lift it from its hook, my mother shook her head.

"You'll need something thicker than that." She motioned for me to follow as she pushed past the curtain into our private room at the back of the bakery, where she knelt to open the trunk at the end of her low straw mattress, opposite the one Sofia and I shared. "This will keep you much warmer." She stood, shaking out a lovely red wool cloak.

That crimson fabric had been folded up in my mother's trunk for as long as I could remember. When I was a child, I would run my hands over it any chance I got, before she shooed me away and closed the lid. Yet in all those years, I'd never seen her take it out of the trunk. In fact, I'd had no idea it was a cloak until that very moment.

I frowned at the beautiful garment. "Aren't you saving this for something special?" Why else would she have had it all this time? The cut was simple and functional, and the material would be warm without adding too much weight. But the color was extravagant—a deep red hue she'd once said was made from berries grown in the forest.

"It isn't mine, Adele. It's yours. Your grandmother made it

15

the year you were born, and I think you've finally grown into it." She turned me by my arm and draped the cloak over my shoulders.

For a moment, my surprise was enough to overwhelm the nervous buzzing beneath my skin at the thought of stepping into the woods by myself. Of facing a darkness that daylight could not penetrate.

Because the cloak fit perfectly. The rich fabric fell to my ankles, draping over both of my arms, as well as the basket. And it was warm. Almost too warm to wear inside, with the heat leaking beneath the curtain from the oven in the main room.

"I can't believe how quickly these last sixteen winters have gone. You were born on a day very much like this one. Cold and clear." She turned me to face her again, and there was something odd in her eyes. Something both assessing and nostalgic beneath the warmth of her gaze, as if I somehow seemed different to her today. "You came into the world just hours before the full moon rose."

She tied the cord loosely at my neck, to keep the cloak from slipping off, then she lifted the hood to settle it over my head, framing my face. "Beautiful," she declared as she stepped back to look me over.

"Gran really made this for me? Why didn't either of you ever tell me?"

"Because that would have ruined the surprise. She'll be thrilled to see you in it." My mother pulled me into an embrace

16

that lasted a little too long. Then she turned abruptly toward the front room again. "You should get going, if you want to be back in time for the celebration. Don't forget your lantern."

I pushed the back door open and grabbed the lantern hanging on the wall. The candle inside the simple metal frame was short, but it should be enough to get me through the trip.

"Pretty!" Sofia jumped up from her stool the moment I stepped back into the front room. "Where did you get the red cloak?"

"It's a gift from your grandmother," Mama told her. "Adele is sixteen years old this season, and it's time for her to start thinking about adult things."

The flush that rose in my cheeks had nothing to do with the heat from the oven. She wanted me to think about "adult things," yet she wouldn't even discuss Grainger's request for my hand. A refusal that made even less sense to me than her wariness around his father.

"Hurry," she said as she went back to her dough. "And do *not* stop on the path."

"I won't." I gave Sofia a smile as I lit the lantern, then I pulled the front door closed behind me.

On my way west through the village, I passed the blacksmith, the candle maker, the fletcher, and the spinster, who all looked up from their work to compliment my new cloak. I nodded to Madame Gosse, the potter's wife, and after returning my polite nod, she stopped to observe to the spinster that perhaps red was not *precisely* my best color, considering the strong coppery cast of my tresses.

I gave them both a friendly smile and kept walking.

I passed the sawmill, the fallow fields, and the empty pastures, and as I approached the path leading into the forest, I saw a group of villagers gathered at the edge of the wood, working in the light from the halo of torches, which penetrated into the forest where daylight refused to fall. Half a dozen women with baskets were gathering acorns, while three men from the village watch stared out into the forest with their hands on the pommels of their swords, ready and willing to take on any beast that might lurch from the inky darkness.

But only one kind of monster ever ventured from the dark wood—the same species that had cost my father his life.

Loup-garou. Werewolf.

They looked normal in their human guise, but *loup garou* were enormous and bloodthirsty in wolf form. Though my father had survived the initial attack from a werewolf, I'd seen the remains of other victims ripped limb from limb. Twice, when I was a small child, the village watch had recovered little more than a leg, still wearing the shredded scraps of a pair of trousers.

Werewolves were the reason for the halo kept burning around Oakvale—*loup garou* were afraid of fire.

A few yards to the east, the Thayer brothers were hard at work with their axes, chopping new-growth trees from the perimeter of the forest. The woodcutters worked daily to keep the woods from encroaching any farther upon Oakvale, yet they never managed to actually push it back. And as grateful as I was for their service—which they profited from by selling the trees to the villagers as firewood or to the sawmill to be split and planed into lumber, then sold down the river—I found the brothers themselves to be unpleasant, at best, and occasionally an outright menace.

"Adele!" a familiar voice called as I approached the wood, and I realized that Elena was among the women gathering acorns. She broke from the group and raced toward me.

"Congratulations!" I pulled her into an eager embrace. "But shouldn't you be getting ready for the celebration?"

She shrugged, chewing on her lower lip. "You know what the priest says about idle hands. And I needed a distraction." Elena stepped back to look at me. "What a beautiful cloak!" Then her focus fell to my basket. "You're going to see your grandmother? Alone?"

"She won't be alone for long," Lucas Thayer called, his ax propped over one thick, broad shoulder. "If Adele goes out there, she'll soon be joining her father."

"Shush!" one of the ladies scolded, rising from a kneeling position to glare at him. "Leave the poor girl alone. She ought not go on her own, but it's her choice."

Noah Thayer snorted. "Who do you think the watch will recruit to help find her body and drag it from the woods to be burned? She shouldn't be allowed out there. Neither should her grandmother. Emelina Chastain is a witch, and you all know it. How else could an old woman survive in the dark wood all on her own?"

"She isn't on her own," I snapped at him as my temper flared. "My mother and I bring her supplies every month. And I've never known either of you to turn down her venison."

Our errand was as important for us as it was for my grandmother. For the most part, villagers were unable to hunt in the dark wood, even when they could afford to pay Baron Carre for the privilege, but deer often wandered into the clearing around my grandmother's cabin, and she always seemed to be waiting for them with an arrow notched in her bow.

And not even the neighbors who whispered "witch" behind our backs had ever turned down the fresh game she sent for my mother to trade for ground grain, honey, salt, and ale. They were willing to deal with the redheaded Duval women and their mad, reclusive matriarch, as long as those dealings filled either their bellies or their purses.

"Mark my word," Lucas Thayer said as I settled my basket into the crook of my arm and stepped back onto the path, my spine straight and my head high. "That girl will come back in pieces."

The dark wood was alive. That's how it had always felt to me, anyway. As if every breeze that skimmed my skin were a breath from the forest itself, blowing over me. As if I'd marched into the belly of some great beast.

As if I'd been swallowed whole.

My heart pounded at that thought, but I sucked in a deep breath and kept putting one foot in front of the other.

Stay on the path. Don't stop. Hold your lantern high.

Nothing could hurt me if I followed the instructions. Right? Yes, there were monsters in the woods. But they were afraid of light. Of fire.

I would be fine, as long as I had my lantern.

Within a few steps, I lost sight of the light from the village, and a few steps beyond that, I could no longer hear the thunk of the Thayers' axes or the women talking as they gathered acorns.

Every step carried me deeper into the darkness, and I could feel the chill of the frozen earth through the leather soles of my shoes. The forest swallowed the light from my lantern just a few feet from the source, leaving me isolated in a bubble of weak firelight, staring out into impenetrable gloom.

I'd never been alone in the dark wood before, and I felt my mother's absence like the loss of a limb. She'd grown up in my grandmother's cabin, though back then, before the forest had encroached so boldly upon Oakvale, it was just inside the dark wood. So she was far more familiar than I was with the dangers and with ways to avoid them.

Though I could only see the path beneath my feet and the occasional branch that dipped into view over my head, I could feel the woods around me. And I could hear . . . things. An unnerving slithering that seemed too loud and too late in the season to be snakes. A series of wet snorts. The crack of twigs beneath a foot too heavy to be human. The dry clatter of dead branches crashing into one another with every breeze.

Just keep walking.

A sudden gust of wind lifted the edge of my cloak, and I shuddered as cold air wafted up my skirt. My arm began to shake, and the bubble of light around me trembled. The shadows overhead danced.

I dropped my basket. Then the wind gusted, and my lantern blew out.

TWO

Terror clutched me like a fist squeezing my rib cage. I froze, afraid to take another step because I could no longer see the path in front of me, and that was when I realized I'd broken two of the rules. My lantern had gone out *and* I'd stopped walking. But if I kept going without being able to see the path, I might accidentally deviate from it. And if that happened, getting lost would be the least of my worries.

Turn around, Adele. I picked up my basket, fumbling in the dark, and stood slowly. *Just turn around and walk in a straight line until you hear the axes. Until you come out of the forest.* That would be much safer than pressing on toward my grandmother's cabin in absolute darkness. So I carefully turned, feeling with one foot for the edge of the path. Then I started walking.

I didn't realize I'd veered off course until my foot struck something. I screamed as I fell forward, arms flailing. I dropped the lantern. My hands slammed into the ground. Twigs bit into my palms and pain shot through my wrists and shoulders.

My basket landed somewhere to my left. The scent of raisin bread suddenly wafted over me as the cloth-wrapped bundle rolled away, crunching over dead leaves.

I sucked in a deep breath, the cold air scraping my throat raw as I fought panic.

Get up! Run!

No, call for help and wait for someone to find you!

Seconds slipped past as I tried to decide which would be least likely to get me killed. The Thayers and the watchmen might still be close enough to hear me scream.

But the monsters might be closer. My initial scream might have alerted them to my presence, and shouting for help might only draw them to me.

Something slithered over my ankle and a shriek ripped free from my throat. My jaw snapped shut, cutting off the sound, but it was too late. I could feel the forest closing in on me with a cacophony of soft, unidentifiable sounds. I slapped at my leg and the vine released its grip on me then rustled through dead leaves.

I sat up and concentrated on my breathing, trying to slow my racing heart. To hear something other than the rush of my pulse and the rasping sound of my own panicked inhalations. The quieter I managed to make myself, the more I could hear from the forest around me. Twigs snapping. Branches swaying.

The rustling of what sounded like leathery wings. The wet sound of something large breathing. Snorting.

Two points of light appeared to my right, and I gasped. They blinked. Then blinked again. My heart slammed against my ribs with the realization that I was looking at a glowing set of eyes. And that they definitely were not human.

The beast took a breath, and the wet, rasping sound seemed to last forever, as it filled its huge lungs. The soft rumbling swelled, and I realized I was hearing a growl.

A wolf.

Not a normal wolf. *Loup garou.*

Fear washed over me like a bucket of frigid water, leaving goose bumps on every inch of my skin. My stomach twisted as I watched those two points of light. They blinked again. Then I heard a soft *oof* of breath and the pounding of massive paws in the underbrush as the wolf lunged.

Every muscle in my body tensed. I swung the lantern, aiming at those bright eyes as they raced toward me.

A scream tore from my throat as the lantern crashed into the wolf's skull, little more than an inky blur against the greater darkness. The metal frame broke in my hand. Something warm and wet splattered my face, accompanied by the scent of blood. The wolf whimpered—a sound like the fletcher's dog makes when he kicks it—and I heard the beast stumble to the side.

I shoved myself to my feet and took off running, still clutching the broken lantern. Unseen branches slapped my face and arms. Roots and vines snagged my feet, as if the forest floor were trying to trip me. I stumbled several times, but I kept going, tearing through the woods as quickly as I could. I had no idea where I was headed. But I was headed there *fast*.

My legs felt oddly powerful, propelling me through the woods at a speed I'd never attained before, and what should have felt like an abuse of my muscles suddenly felt like a relief. Like scratching a desperate itch.

My legs *wanted* to run.

My arms pumped at my sides now, maintaining the rhythm of my stride. Aiding my balance. My lungs expanded easily, fueling my body so efficiently that even though I'd never moved that fast in my life, I wasn't huffing. The speed felt natural.

I felt like I was born for this.

Yet despite my speed, within seconds, I heard the wolf crashing through the forest behind me, so close I could practically feel its breath on my neck. Fresh terror fueled my muscles, and my legs gave me another burst of speed, carrying me even farther from the path. Even deeper into the dark wood.

And suddenly I realized I could see.

The trees were little more than skeletal shadows, some of which actually seemed to be reaching out for me, but I could *see* them. Which meant I could avoid them.

For the first time in my life, the impenetrable darkness of the forest had begun to loosen its grip. But the wolf was gaining on me at a terrifying pace. I would not be able to outrun it.

I would have to fight.

That realization should have sent me screaming in terror, yet it seemed to calm me. To focus my thoughts. I squinted into the dark as I ran, looking for . . .

I had no idea what I was looking for, until the moment I saw it. A fallen tree. A big one, with a trunk broad enough to shield me for a second. I swerved to the right and leapt over the trunk as if I'd grown up jumping hay bales with the village boys, then I hunched down against it, my red cloak bunched up behind me. I shoved my hood back and as I lifted the broken lantern, I realized I could see better with every passing second, even without a light.

Something was happening to me. Something strange and *miraculous.*

The lantern was suddenly nearly as visible as it had been before I'd stepped into the forest. Though it was useless now. The metal frame had come apart, and—

One thinly hammered metal panel had come loose, exposing a sharp, wickedly jagged edge.

As the wolf thundered toward me, its huffing breath growing louder with each passing second, I ripped that small panel from the frame and clutched it in my right hand, ignoring the pain as an edge bit into my skin. Distantly, I realized I could smell my own blood as it rolled down my palm.

An instant later, the fallen tree rocked against my back as the wolf launched itself off the trunk. The beast flew over me to land in the underbrush a few feet away, and as it spun to face me, I got the first good look at my opponent.

It was huge, its narrow muzzle pulled back in a snarl, revealing sharp teeth I could see alarmingly well. Its claws gripped the dirt as it prepared to leap. Its fur was like fresh snow, pale and gleaming.

The wolf pounced, driving me to my back in the dry underbrush. I screamed as massive paws landed on my shoulders, claws digging into my skin through the thick wool of my cloak. My pulse raced fast and loud, and my vision swam. The wolf snarled, and the odor of rot on its breath wafted over me. Then its massive muzzle opened, and the beast lunged for my face.

I shoved the metal panel into its neck.

Sharp teeth froze inches from my nose. Saliva dripped from its muzzle, and I turned my face so that it hit my cheek instead of trailing into my mouth.

The wolf tried to back away, and adrenaline surged through me. My left arm shot out, clamping around the beast's neck out of some instinct I couldn't fathom. I rolled to my right, throwing the wolf onto its side. My right hand twisted the hunk of metal buried in the monster's neck, dragging the makeshift blade through its flesh. Across its furry throat.

The beast made a strangling sound as blood sprayed from the wound. I scrambled to my feet, trying to escape the mess, but a warm stream hit the side of my face and splattered the front of my dress through my open cloak.

For a moment, I stood, stunned and gasping for breath.

Then a vicious cramp seized every muscle in my body at once, drawing my arms and legs into unnatural positions. I collapsed into the dirt on my side, twitching, trapped in mute horror as my entire body became one excruciating injury. My bones ached cruelly. My joints popped. My skin—every square inch— was assaulted with a vicious itch.

I felt like I was being pulled apart on the rack and stitched into a new shape.

And as suddenly as the whole thing had begun, it ended.

I sat up, perplexed, yet panting with relief from the fading pain. And with a start, I realized that the world looked brand-new.

I'd been able to see better in the woods than ever before since the wolf had attacked me, but suddenly I could see as if it were broad daylight. A hundred different hues of fallen leaves, from crunchy brown to black and rotting. Every crevice on the bark of every tree within sight. Thick, gnarly woody vines, the grayish brown of tree trunks. I processed all of it with an eerie clarity.

WELCOME, CHILD.

I flinched, startled by a message that seemed to have bypassed my ears entirely, to be spoken directly into my head. I'd heard my father's voice in the woods several times since his death, but this was no voice I recognized. It didn't sound human.

This was different than the dark wood's normal manipulation.

It was more of a . . . greeting.

I looked around, searching warily for the source, and instead, my gaze snagged on the white wolf lying in a pool of its own blood, staring sightlessly at the fallen tree behind me. Its throat was a gruesome wound, still oozing blood into a puddle soaking into the ground. A foot away lay the pane of metal that had ripped open a grisly gash in its fur.

I'd done that.

I reached for the metal, but the hand that stretched into my sight wasn't a hand at all. It was a paw. A wolf's paw, with thick, rust-colored, wiry fur that looked nothing like the beautiful snowy fur of the wolf I'd killed.

Terror fired through me, tightening my throat. Racing in my pulse. I tried to clench my right fist, and the rust-colored paw curled inward, claws curving toward the ground.

I rose, and I found myself standing on *four legs*.

As panic gripped my chest—as I sucked in rapid, shallow breaths—a frightening comprehension settled into my bones. I was a wolf.

This isn't possible. Yet my body welcomed the new form as if it were an old and comfortable dress. The night was freezing, yet I felt warm, insulated by the fur covering my skin. I could easily distinguish a myriad of individual scents. Rotting leaves. My own blood. The burnt wick from my extinguished candle. The musky scent of the wolf lying dead in front of me.

I'd feared death in the dark wood, yet I'd succumbed to an

even worse fate. I had become a monster.

Noooo. A lupine whine leaked from my throat.

I'd been infected. But how? The wolf hadn't bitten or scratched me. It hadn't broken my skin. Yet there I stood, in a form that would terrify my neighbors.

When I was eight, my father was burned alive in the village square, while my mother and I watched from the crowd, because my neighbors *suspected* he might turn into a werewolf, after being attacked by one.

Now I had become, without any doubt, the very beast they'd believed him to be.

And yet, I didn't feel like a monster. Or, how I imagined a monster must feel. I had no urge to spill human blood. To consume human flesh. Still, when the rest of Oakvale discovered what I had become, my fate would echo my father's. My mother would lose me like she'd lost him, and this time Sofia was old enough to be scarred by the ordeal, just like I'd been eight years ago. The charred post in the village square would haunt her like it haunted me.

This can't be happening.

I backed away, shaking my head in mute denial, and my paws got tangled in something. In a mass of material.

I was caught up in my own dress—or maybe in my cloak. I backed up, tossing my head, trying to fight my way free from the cocoon of cloth, but that only seemed to further entangle me.

"Adele."

I froze at the sound of my name, and it took me a second to realize I recognized that voice. And yet another second to realize that the speaker shouldn't have recognized *me*, as I currently stood.

Gran? But the word came out as another hoarse whine.

"Calm down, *chère*. Everything is okay," she assured me as I nudged my way forward to peek from beneath the hood of my new cloak. "You did very well."

I . . . *what*?

"Your mother will be so proud."

My mother would be *proud* that I'd become a monster?

I tossed my head, and the hood flopped to the right, revealing the forest to me again. And there stood my grandmother, straight and tall in a bright red cloak virtually identical to mine, except for a beautiful white fur trim.

I'd never seen her wear that cloak before.

She knelt in front of me, unfazed by the dead wolf, and untied the cord holding my cloak closed. Then she pulled it aside to loosen the bodice beneath. "Come on out of there, child."

Finally free, I crawled out of the ill-fitting garments and stood in front of her. Something swished in the underbrush behind me, and I spun around, on alert for the new threat, only to realize that I'd heard my own tail swishing through a bed of dead leaves.

Because I had a tail.

My grandmother laughed. "That takes a little getting used

to. But your instincts are good—there is much to fear in the dark wood, even for us. Be still for a moment. Close your eyes and listen, and you'll see."

I didn't want to be still. I didn't want to close my eyes. I wanted answers. But I couldn't ask any questions, in my current form.

"Go on, child. Close your eyes," my grandmother insisted. So I did.

At first, I heard nothing but my own breathing. My own heartbeat. Then slowly, I became aware of a subtler sound. A soft sliding, like a snake slithering through the underbrush toward me, from the left. Only it was much too cold for snakes.

My eyes flew open. My front left paw slammed down on something long and round. Something about the thickness of two of my fingers. It was a woody vine, which had been heading right for me—moving all on its own—until I'd pinned it. And even as I stared at it, the vine began to curl upward on either side of my paw, slowly winding around my wrist. Or, what would be my wrist, if I hadn't become a monster.

"Good." My grandmother gave me an approving nod, and I whined, puzzled by how pleased she seemed about the horrific change in me. "But that's only the beginning. You're more prepared, now that you can see in the dark wood, but that doesn't make you safe. Reassume your human form, and let's get you cleaned up."

I could only cock my head to the side, hoping the gesture

communicated a question I couldn't actually ask.

She smiled as she knelt in front of me, her joints popping in protest. "You only have to want the change, to make it happen. Think about your human form. Focus on reclaiming it."

I blinked at her, then I turned to assess the threat from more vines slithering slowly toward us. Beyond those, I heard a symphony of other sounds, and I realized that the monsters— and maybe the dark wood itself—were closing in on us. We should go. Surely I could reassume my human form in a safer location.

Another whine leaked from my throat with that thought.

"I'll watch over you, child." My grandmother stood and tucked back one side of her cloak, revealing a hatchet with a distinctly sharp blade, hanging from a belt buckled around the waist of her dress. "Get going, now."

So I closed my eyes and thought about my human form—the only form I'd ever known, until a few minutes ago. I visualized my feet, with high arches and long second toes. I remembered my arms, my somewhat bony wrists, and the narrow fingers that had grown adept at kneading dough. I thought of my face. Of the sprinkling of freckles across the bridge of my nose and the highest part of both cheekbones. And of my hair, long and strawberry blond, which shone like copper in bright sunlight.

Suddenly that full-body cramp enveloped me again, and I fell to the forest floor, writhing as my joints popped and my bones ached. As my skin itched viciously and my muscles contracted painfully.

Less than a minute later, it was all over, just like before. Only this time, I found myself curled into a ball on a bed of dead leaves and sharp twigs, naked and shivering. But in my own human skin.

"Gran?" I sat up, knees tucked to my chest, trying to ignore the way that bits of the forest floor were poking my bare backside. "What's happening? The wolf didn't bite me. How could I be infected?"

"Get dressed, *chère*. I'll explain on the way to my cabin."

Shivering violently, I looked around as I pulled my clothing closer and was disappointed to realize the dark wood was once again a land of murky shadows. That was still much better than I'd ever been able to see in the dark wood before, yet a far cry from the clarity I'd had in that inexplicable wolf form.

"Hurry, Adele," my grandmother urged, and I pulled my dress over my head as fast as I could, trying to push back the feeling of exposure and vulnerability that my own nudity inspired. "Stand and turn," she said, and when I had, she tightened the laces of my bodice, then tied them. Gran snatched my cloak from the ground and shook it free of leaves and twigs, then she draped it over my shoulders.

"This way. You strayed quite a bit from the trail." She took off in a direction I couldn't identify without the sun visible overhead, and I bent to grab my broken lantern.

"I—Gran, I didn't stray from the trail. I was *chased* from it by a huge werewolf!" I turned to stare down at the dead wolf. "What about . . . that? We're just going to leave it?"

"I'll come back for what can be used. The forest will dispose of the rest," my grandmother insisted, gesturing for me to follow her. "The dark wood is full of monsters, you know."

I nodded as I followed her deeper into the forest. "Everyone knows that."

THREE

"I'm sure you must have questions," my grandmother said as I trailed her through the dark wood, my gaze constantly roving, on alert for threats.

"Just a few."

Her soft laughter floated back toward me as I took in my surroundings, and the thing that most struck me, now that I could actually see in the dark wood, was the fact that the forest itself *truly* seemed to be alive. While I'd had that feeling before, experiencing it up close was entirely different.

Unless she was asleep, my sister, Sofia, was constantly in motion, as if she just couldn't sit still. The dark wood moved like that. As if it were breathing. Fidgeting. Waiting impatiently to be given something to do.

Or someone to eat.

Vines slowly coiled, wrapping around branches or twisting

their way toward the ground. Limbs swayed without the aid of the wind. Branches seemed to grasp for me as I walked, like hands reaching out from the darkness. But for the first time in my life, I could see well enough to smack at fluttering, stick-like bugs the size of my palm when they tried to land on my arms and shoulders. I could sidestep a deep shadow blinking at me from beneath a clump of underbrush—a shadow that appeared to have *teeth*.

"Adele?" My grandmother turned to look back at me, and I scurried to catch up.

"Sorry. I don't understand what's happening. I'm a werewolf?"

"Yes."

"*How* is that possible, if I wasn't scratched or bitten?"

"You were not infected by the beast you killed. However, your transformation *was* triggered by your contact with it. The wolf has always been in your blood. This has always been your fate."

"What does that mean? And how did you know that was me?" I gestured, one-handed, in the direction of the spot where she'd found me. "How did you know I would be out here?"

Her smile felt strangely reassuring. "Tonight is the full moon, child. You were born under this moon, sixteen years ago." She stepped over a thick root as it rippled up from the dirt in her path, moving with the ease of a much younger woman. With more grace and quicker reflexes than I'd ever seen from her. "Your mother and I have been planning for this day for a very long time."

"You planned for my candle to go out on the path? For me to be attacked by a—?" And suddenly I understood. "You made this happen. Why? *How?*"

"Your mother rigged the lantern. I released the wolf."

"I—what?" I stopped, and when she realized—again—that I wasn't following, my grandmother turned, impatience flickering behind her pale eyes. "Where did you get a werewolf? Why would you send him after me?"

"Her," Gran corrected. "I tracked and captured her this morning. Unfortunately, I was too late to stop her from attacking a merchant wagon." Her shoulders slumped beneath the weight of a failure more profound than anything I could imagine. "I think it was on the way from Oldefort. The driver and his wife both lost their lives."

"We weren't expecting a merchant." They were few and far between in the winter months, and when Oakvale *was* forced to send people through the forest for emergency supplies during the harshest part of the year, the village watch always sent an escort with them. The group invariably left in the middle of the day, heavily armed, carrying torches and lanterns. We hadn't lost any merchants in several years.

Oldefort, evidently, was not so fortunate.

Gran nodded gravely. "My greatest sorrow is that I cannot protect the ones I don't know to expect."

"Protect them? How would you protect a caravan, alone in the dark wood? And how did you capture a werewolf?" I blinked at her in the shadows. "I don't understand how any of this is possible."

Gran glanced pointedly at the ground near my feet, and I looked down to see another woody vine reaching for my ankle. "They aren't always that slow," she said. "They're still testing you."

"They're testing me? The *vines* are testing me?"

"Twice in my tenure as a guardian, I've found villagers hanging from vines draped over tree branches, as if from a gallows. You should not get in the habit of standing still for long out here."

"Considering that I don't plan to *be* in the dark wood very often—"

"You will be." The gaze she turned on me felt heavy. "You *must* be, Adele. Come. There's the path."

I looked in the direction she pointed, and I saw the path worn into the forest floor by years of traffic—foot, hoof, and cart wheel. I'd never had a clearer view of it. And there, just a few feet away, lay the basket of bread I'd dropped.

"I'm sorry, Gran." I knelt on the ground next to the loaf of raisin bread, which sat on its side beneath a broad fern leaf. "It's ruined." The rye bread hadn't fared much better.

"Don't fuss over the bread, child. It was only an excuse to send you out here."

But she loved sweet breads, and raisins were too costly to waste. And yet, despite the squandered expense, bread *did* seem like a pointless thing to fret over, considering that somewhere out there in the forest, a merchant and his wife had lost their lives. That moments before, I'd stood on four legs, just like the beast that killed them.

A fresh bolt of fear crashed over me as that understanding finally seemed to settle in. "Gran, how are you so calm? They're going to *burn me alive* in the village square, just like Papa."

"They're not going to burn you." She waved away my fear with an off-hand gesture. "No one's going to know about this."

"Of course people will know! How could I possibly keep them from finding out?"

"You will keep your secret the same way your mother and I have kept ours."

"You . . . ?" I blinked at her. "And Mama? What . . . Gran, what's *happening*?" I demanded softly as I picked up my empty basket and shook off the cloth covering, trying to hide the tremor in my hands.

She stepped onto the path and tugged me forward with her, and finally I regained my sense of direction. Her cabin was directly ahead. "You are becoming what you were always meant to be. You and Sofia are descended from a long line of women gifted with great abilities and burdened with an even greater responsibility."

I stumbled to a stop on the path, frowning at her. "This is

how you can live alone in the dark wood?" How she could see so well and move so lithely through the forest? "We're all . . . What are we?" Werewolves, obviously. Yet not infected. Not snow-white, like the beast I'd killed.

"There are many words for what we are, child, and you've heard most of them. Yet they all fall short of the truth."

"Monster," I said as a chill worked its way across my flesh. "We're monsters."

"Yes." She nodded firmly, and I felt a little sick at the admission. I'd expected her to deny it. "Never doubt that we are monsters, Adele. But that is perhaps the vaguest of all the descriptors. We are werewolf. *Loup garou*. Lycanthrope. Every region has its own name for us, and none is more common than simply 'witch.' Because your neighbors' superstitions are rooted in truth; what we do—what we *are*—relies on a very particular and ancient kind of magic. An ability to alter our forms and a set of skills that are just as natural to the women of our line as any of your human abilities are."

"Werewolves." My voice echoed with shock. "We *are* monsters."

"Yes. But of a kind unlike any other. The wolf you killed—*she* was a beast. A whitewulf. They are destroyers. Indiscriminate slayers. Consumers of human flesh."

"And we are not?" The tension in my voice begged her for a word of solace.

"No, child." Her gentle smile did more than her words to

ease my mind. "We are redwulf. We are guardians. You are destined to protect your village, as your mother has for years. As I did, before her. As Sofia will, some day. And as your own daughters will."

Confusion and fear battled within me, but before I could ask the rest of my questions, my grandmother pointed at a familiar landmark: a narrow, subtle fork in the path, where it turned toward her cabin. "This way."

Her clearing appeared within minutes, an oasis of light in a sea of darkness, and a comforting sight that had never failed to make me smile. As far as I knew, this was the only place in the entire dark wood where daylight ventured. And for the first time in my life it occurred to me to wonder why.

"This place is special, isn't it?" I felt that today, in a way I'd never been able to before. "Why is there light here? *How* is there light here?"

"There is light here because I persist against the darkness," she said as we stepped into the clearing. "The forest continually encroaches, but just like the village woodsmen do for Oakvale, I chop the trees down when they intrude upon my clearing. I cut the vines. I beat back the brush and the roots. I fight for this land, to keep it from being swallowed by the dark wood, as my mother did before me. As your mother will, soon. Your ascension has come just in time, because I cannot fight this battle forever. I am an old woman now."

Yesterday, I would have believed that. But today . . . "You

just told me you tracked and captured a wolf. A whitewulf," I corrected myself, before she could.

"Yes. And if my strength holds out, I will be able to do the same for Sofia in a few years. If not, that will be up to your mother. And to you." As if to punctuate her point, my grandmother pulled the hatchet from her belt, and as we approached her cottage, she bent to swing it at the ground, where a woody vine was coiling almost leisurely toward her foot.

Her hatchet cleanly bisected the vine. The amputated bit went still, seeming to shrivel right before my eyes, while the rest slithered back into the woods faster than I'd ever seen a vine move. Before today, I'd only ever seen them writhe slowly, and that had been eerie enough.

"Persistence," Gran announced as she slid the hatchet back into the loop on her belt.

On our way across the clearing, she stopped at her small stone well and pulled up a bucket of water, which she hoisted off the hook and handed to me. I took the heavy pail and followed her up three steps into the main room of her small but cozy cabin.

A fire blazed in her hearth, a pot of stew suspended over it.

"First, wash your face." She handed me a rag as I set the bucket on the table. "Then change into that, and I'll work on your dress." Gran waved one hand at the nightgown draped across her bed, and I realized she'd laid it out for me.

"You knew I would arrive covered in blood?"

"I certainly hoped so. The first kill is important. Without it, you would never have been able to claim your wulf form. To ascend to your role as a guardian."

I wiped my face thoroughly, and the rag came away stained red. "So, if I'd been unable to kill that whitewulf, I wouldn't have turned into a redwulf?"

Gran took a wooden bowl from a shelf on the wall and filled it with a ladleful of stew from the pot. "If you'd been unable to kill her, you would be dead."

Horror washed over me. "Has that happened? To someone in our family? To one of the other . . . guardians?"

"A few times. Most recently to my sister. Margot. She died during her trial."

"Is that what this was?" I scrubbed my face one more time, then I laid the rag over the back of a chair to dry. "A trial?"

"Yes. Your mother has been terrified of this day for years, so let's get you cleaned up as quickly as possible, so we can send you home and put her mind at ease." She glanced pointedly at the nightgown again.

I took my cloak off and hung it on a hook by the door, where my grandmother had already hung her own. "This trim . . ." I ran one hand over the fur edging her hood. "Is this whitewulf?"

"Of course. Tonight, I'll go back for the fur from your first kill, and on your next visit, I will adorn your cloak with it. As is tradition."

I wasn't sure how I felt about that. Fur was used as a warm lining in everyday clothing and as a decorative edging—a *purfelle*.

But I'd never seen anyone in the village wearing fur with as fine a pelt or as pure a color as the trim on Gran's cloak. My new trim would not go unnoticed.

Maybe people would think it was rabbit fur, from a distance.

"I need your dress, Adele." Gran sank into a chair in front of the fire with the bucket of fresh water at her feet and a scrub brush in one hand.

"Sorry." I reached back to untie my bodice and loosen the laces, then I pulled the dress over my head, careful not to smear any more of the blood on my skin. I stepped into her nightgown and handed her my dress.

"Next time, fasten your cloak at the front, and with any luck, your dress will be spared." She dipped her brush into the bucket, then she began scrubbing at my clothing. "Eat, child. You must be famished, after your first change."

I was. So I sank into the chair at her small table and dug in to the stew. "How did this happen?" I asked around a bite of potato and carrot. "How did we come to be guardians?"

"For as long as Oakvale has been threatened by the dark wood, the guardians—specifically, women descended from our bloodline—have defended it. Most other villages in the path of the unnatural forest have their own guardians. Heaven help any that don't," she muttered beneath her breath.

"Why have I never heard this? Why has *no one* ever heard this?" Yet I knew the answer before I'd even finished asking the question. "Because monsters are burned. Like Papa."

She nodded. "Because the village would believe the same thing of a redwulf as it would of a whitewulf—that we are monsters."

"And they're not wrong." That understanding bruised me deep inside. I shifted in my seat, trying to alleviate the sudden feeling that I didn't fit properly inside my own flesh. That I no longer knew my own body.

"No. But they're not entirely right, either. We are much more than just monsters."

"We're guardians. But . . . what if I don't want to be a guardian?"

Gran looked up from her work, her gaze settling on me with an almost palpable weight. "That is your choice. But know that if you choose to stand by when you could fight, people will die. I know this is a lot to process at once. And I know it's quite a burden to lay on a girl's shoulders. But please believe me, Adele—there is no greater regret in the world than knowing you *could* have saved a life, yet you chose not to."

"I . . ." I exhaled slowly. "I don't want to shirk a duty. It's just that . . ." This wasn't how my life was supposed to go. I was supposed to marry Grainger, and *he* was supposed to protect the village. *I* was supposed to work at the bakery with my mother and live in a little cottage next door to Elena and Simon, where our children would grow up to be the best of friends.

This—whitewulfs, and guardians, and the dark wood— wasn't a part of the plan. In my wildest dreams, I never could have imagined all of this, yet Gran clearly expected me to leave her cabin in my red cloak, having ascended to a position and a responsibility I never asked for. I never wanted.

Did my mother truly expect this of me too?

"Eat." Gran dipped her brush into the bucket again. "I know it's a lot. But the more time you spend in the dark wood, the more natural it will all feel. Of course, that's a double-edged sword."

I took another bite and made myself swallow it. "Why are guardians needed, when we have the village watch? Grainger is a skilled fighter, and he'll take over for his father someday."

"Grainger, and his father, and the rest of the watchmen can't see in the dark wood, child. There is little they can do in the forest beyond the fall of whatever light they bring with them. The watchmen need us, though they don't even know we exist."

No one knew. Yet if I were going to marry Grainger . . .

"Gran, if we tell them—if we *show* them—we could work together. We could—"

Her chair creaked as she stood to scowl at me, my dress hanging from her white-knuckled hands, splotched with water from her scrubbing. "Do you remember what it was like to watch your father burn?"

Pain gripped my chest. "Of course I remember." There was no clearer image in my memory, and it haunted me every single day. Every time I passed the scorched post in the village square.

"*Do not* speak of the guardians to Grainger Colbert, child.

Nor to anyone else. Not if you value your own life. Or your sister's. Or your mother's. Promise me."

"I . . ." Her fierce expression gave me no other choice. "I promise."

"You will have to be wary of him, Adele. Your duties will overlap his, but he must not know this. He must not see you go into the forest at night. He must not see you return. He must not find blood on your clothes, or weapons on your belt, or leaves in your hair. I know you care for him, but it is *dangerous* for a guardian to be so familiar with a watchman."

"He would never—"

"He *would*," she insisted as she sank into her chair again, with another pointed look at my stew bowl. "Watchmen burn monsters, child. So you *must* keep your word."

"Of course." I ate several more bites in silence, my thoughts racing along with my heartbeat. I intended to marry Grainger. How was I supposed to keep such a secret from my husband?

"What are my duties, Gran? Am I to patrol the dark wood, like the watch patrols the village?"

"No, the forest is much too big for that. You can see in the unnatural darkness, now, but you are not the kind of monster that truly belongs in the dark wood. Your job is to hunt the beasts. To cull their population, particularly where they venture near Oakvale. A guardian protects her village at all costs, in both the town and the woods. But she does it in absolute secrecy. So you will hunt, and you will patrol the path where it runs through

49

the forest, especially on rare occasions when there are villagers to guard. When a caravan heads out or an emergency messenger is sent through the woods."

That only happened during an outbreak of illness, fire, or famine, in the winter months when the river could not be traveled—rare occasions indeed.

"But the watch accompanies anyone sent into the woods. To protect the travelers."

My grandmother heaved an unladylike snort. "And who do you think protects the watch? We guardians chaperone them from the shadows, making sure those men with their swords have little to protect the travelers from. That nothing attacks the caravan, if a torch goes out. You will be there, watching to see that no one strays from the path. You will protect them from the darkness. And they must have no idea you are there."

"You do that, now?"

Gran nodded. "As does your mother, when she can get away from the bakery without suspicion." And, like the rest of the village, I'd had *no* idea. "She and I are the reason Oakvale hasn't lost a citizen in the dark wood in years. Though she's been able to do less of that, with two girls to care for."

"One, now." I chewed into a bite of venison. "Since I passed the trial." I was old enough to marry, and I'd been working alongside my mother in the bakery for years. Now, evidently, I would be working alongside her in the dark wood as well.

To my surprise, the jolt that thought sent through me was part terror, and part . . . anticipation. Curiosity.

Gran huffed. "Your ascension was only the start, child. But you will grow stronger and faster with time. With experience. With training." She stood again, holding my dress up. The front was wet, from her scrubbing, but the splattered drops of blood were gone. "Change again and come eat in front of the fire. Your dress will dry faster that way."

As I changed out of the nightgown, Gran set my chair next to hers and scooped out a bowl of stew for herself. "You have more questions?"

"Was it a whitewulf that attacked my father?" I asked as I sat next to her.

"Yes, though most people don't know that term. Or that there's more than one kind of werewolf. And there are much greater dangers, deeper in the wood."

"Then why do you live out here? Why don't you come stay in the village with us?"

She blotted the corner of her mouth with a clean cloth. "Because I refuse to give up any more ground."

"What do you mean?"

She leaned forward, slowly stirring her stew with a wooden spoon. "When my father built this cottage for my mother, it was not in the dark wood. Back then, the wood was a more distant menace, slowly creeping across the land. Over the course of

51

several years, my mother saw that it was headed this direction, so she came here to keep up with the threat. To protect the handful of cottages that would become Oakvale. By the time I was born, the dark wood had overtaken much of the landscape, save for this clearing my parents kept safe. But after her ascension, my Celeste didn't want to raise her family in such isolation, so she and your father settled in the village."

"Papa." Suddenly everything I'd thought I'd known about him—about his death *and* his life—felt like a half-finished story. "Did he know about the guardians? About . . . us?"

"Yes." Gran held up one finger, cutting off my next question before I could ask it. "Your father wasn't a watchman, Adele. He was never the danger to your mother that Grainger Colbert is to you. Quite the opposite, in fact. He was a very special man, particularly suited to your mother, and to her calling as a guardian."

"And yet, she let them kill him." I bit my lip, but it was too late to take the words back. It wasn't fair of me to blame my mother for my father's death, so I'd always kept that thought locked tightly within my own heart. But knowing what I knew now?

I wasn't supposed to see it. My grandmother was watching Sofia and me that day, but the bakery is right on the edge of the village square, and while she was busy with my baby sister, I snuck outside and—

"She just watched, while they tied him to the stake and set

him on fire, because they thought he was a monster. But *she* was the monster. We *all* are."

"She had no other choice, child. He was infected. It broke her heart to watch him suffer and die, but if he'd lived, he would no longer have been your father. Her husband. He would have become a whitewulf. He would have terrorized the village, and it would have been up to your mother to protect Oakvale, even against her own husband. And your *maman* . . . she would never have let me spare her that burden. She would have done her duty herself, but she never got that chance, because he was pulled from the woods by the watch before she even knew he'd gone into the forest."

"But surely she could have *tried* to save him." I knew I was wrong, even as I said the words. I understood that now better than ever before, having seen a whitewulf for myself. But my heart could not admit what my head knew to be true. I could not think of my father as a danger to *anyone*, much less to an entire village.

"Suspicion would have been cast upon her, if she'd tried to defend him. People would have believed her to be infected too, because who would defend a werewolf but another werewolf? And that was too close to the truth to risk. She had to protect you girls. And your father understood that. He never fought his sentence."

My hand clenched around my stew bowl, while I tried to accept what I was hearing.

My father believed he had to die. And my mother let it happen.

"Now that you know who you really are, you should have a long talk with your mother. Find out who *she* really is. And who your father was. But make sure Sofia is not listening. Your sister cannot know about any of this until she's older."

"Can't you tell me about them?"

"I could, but your mother deserves to tell her own story. I *can* tell you about my own life, however." Gran spread her arms wide, her bowl gracefully balanced on one knee. "Over the years, I've watched this unnatural forest swallow Oakvale like it swallowed this clearing, isolating our little village, except where the river borders it. I have fought against the dark wood my entire life." Firelight flickered in her eyes. "And I will continue to do that until the day I die."

FOUR

When I'd been fed and washed clean of blood, I donned my red cloak while Gran packed a venison roast into my basket, next to the remains of my broken lantern. "Stay on the path," she warned. "Go straight home."

I had no plans to stray from either the path or her instructions, but . . . "I can see in the dark wood now. I can see the monsters. Right?"

"Yes. But the monsters can see you too, Adele. And one kill to your credit does not make you a threat to most of the things that go bump in the dark. You have a lot to learn before you're ready to veer from the path on your own. Swear to me you will go straight home."

"I swear," I said as she slid the handle of my basket over my left arm.

"And that you will not listen to anything you hear from the forest on your way to the village."

"I know about the mimics, Gran." There were creatures out there that could sound like other things. That could pull voices from one's memory and call out in the guise of a trusted loved one. "I often hear Papa's voice." But like all children of the village, I knew not to trust the voices.

She gave me a grim nod. "But I'm not just talking about mimics. The dark wood has been waiting for you, Adele. It has sensed your ascension coming, and it knows you cannot be snared as easily as other prey, so it will try harder with you. It will speak to you directly, in a voice of its own. You cannot believe what you see or hear when you're alone in the dark wood. Promise me."

"I promise."

"I have one more thing for you, before you go. Do not let Sofia play with this. It is not a toy." Gran turned from the trunk against one wall, and I saw that she was holding a leather belt similar to her own. Hanging from a loop on the right side was a hatchet with a polished wooden handle, wrapped with a leather grip.

She held my cloak up while I buckled the belt. The new weight felt odd, but it also felt *right*. Comforting.

"Keep it covered," she reminded me as she pulled my cloak closed over my dress, fastening a button-and-loop I hadn't noticed before. "There's no reason for a girl your age to be carrying a hatchet. And—"

"And stay on the path. I know."

"Come back next week, when you can, and I'll take you farther into the wood. It is time to familiarize yourself with the things that live in the dark."

I nodded solemnly, dread and excitement warring within me.

"Before you go . . ." Gran gave me an almost mischievous smile I recognized instantly. "Is there any news from the village?"

And by news, she meant gossip, the only thing she truly seemed to miss about communal living.

"Oh! Yes, I almost forgot. Elena Rousseau got betrothed today. To Simon Laurent. There's a celebration tonight."

My grandmother didn't smile. She seemed to be assessing my reaction, much as my mother had. "Elena will be the first of your friends to wed?"

"Yes. And she's a month younger than I am."

She was quiet for the span of several heartbeats. "There's no hurry, child."

"I know. But has Mama told you that Grainger asked for my hand? That he's been waiting a month for an answer?" What if he grew tired of waiting, and his eye began to wander?

Gran sighed. "She did tell me, and surely you understand her hesitation now. He is not a good match for you, Adele. He's dangerous to our entire family."

My hope wilted like a cut flower. "How can you know that, without giving him a chance? He cares for me, Gran."

"Yet if he *truly* knew you, he would fear you, and a man

with a weapon in his hand and fear in his heart is a danger to everyone."

Frustration drew my lips into a frown.

"I'm sorry, *chère*. I know that's difficult to hear."

I nodded. I felt confident that I could convince both my mother and grandmother that they were wrong, but that would probably take more than words. They would have to *see* that Grainger would never hurt me.

"Give my love to your mother and sister." Gran planted a kiss on my forehead, then she opened the front door, and I accepted the well-wishes as a cue to take my leave. But when she remained standing on the top step, rather than retreating into the warmth of her cabin, I realized she intended to watch me until I passed out of sight.

I managed to stay focused on the task at hand—sticking to the path—even as my initial shock and acceptance of everything I'd just learned gave way to a stunned numbness. To a thousand questions I hadn't thought of when Gran had been around to answer them. In part, that was because my feet knew the way. However, it was also easier than ever to stay on the trail now that I could see it properly, even without a lantern.

Until a high-pitched wail nearly startled me out of my skin.

My feet froze on the path. My right hand slid beneath my cloak to grip the head of my new hatchet, evidently ready to wield it through some brand-new instinct, even though I'd never used a hatchet for anything other than chopping firewood.

I turned warily toward the sound, just as the screeching wail shattered into bouncing sobs. Someone was crying. Someone young. Out there in the forest.

There was a *child* in the dark wood. A lost—maybe injured—child. At least, that's what the dark wood wanted me to believe. But what if that sob, like my father's voice, was bait on the end of a fishing line, intended to lure me to my death?

I turned my back on the heartbreaking sound and kept walking.

The crying continued, sobs echoing toward me from the darkness. Twisting my heart into pulp within my chest. The child sounded like Sofia. Yet it *wasn't* Sofia. I didn't recognize the voice, which meant the dark wood wasn't drawing it from my mind. Which meant it *could* be real.

What if there truly *was* a child in need of help out there? Gran had said her greatest sorrow was that she couldn't help people she didn't know to expect in the forest. She would never leave a defenseless child all alone out there. And neither could I.

I stepped off the path, following the sobs. Vines slithered toward my feet, faster than before. Branches reached for me. And twice, I heard the snort of something large, off in the distance. But I kept going until finally I saw a small form standing in the underbrush, in dead leaves up to his little ankles. He was small and pale, with a shock of blond hair, and despite the cold, he didn't have a single stitch on.

Small children went naked in the village all the time in the warmer months, but in the heart of winter? In the middle of the forest?

In the distance, I could see the silhouette of a wagon among the trees. It could only be the one attacked by the whitewulf. The one my grandmother had been too late to save.

Mon dieu, the merchant and his wife had a son. Somehow, he'd survived the whitewulf. He must have been hiding, too scared to come out, even when my grandmother captured the wolf.

"Hey!" I whispered as loud as I could, hoping to catch his attention without alerting any nearby beasts.

The boy spun toward me, startled silent. Tear tracks cut through the dirt on his face, and I could see from here that there were twigs tangled in his hair and grime caked on his bare legs.

"Are you okay?" I stepped over a twisting vine and shoved aside a branch that seemed to be grasping for my hair. "Hey! Little boy!"

He stared at me, wide-eyed, as I made my way carefully toward him, one hand gripping the handle of my hatchet beneath my cloak. For a moment, I thought he would flee. But he only sniffled as he watched me approach.

"I just want to help you. Are you hurt?"

The child didn't answer, but by then I was almost close enough to touch him. Instead, I knelt in front of him, trying to ignore the vine snaking its way toward us across the ground.

"I'm Adele. What's your name?" I asked, but again, no answer came. "How old are you?"

He didn't respond to that either, but he couldn't have been any older than five or six. He was smaller than my eight-year-old sister, and his cheeks were fuller. His teeth smaller. He didn't seem to have lost any of them yet.

"Are you from Oldefort?" That was a day's journey down the river during the warmer months and easily a three-day walk on foot, once one made it through the dark wood. Not that I'd ever been on the other side of the forest surrounding our little village. "Did you come here with your parents? Are they merchants?" *Were* they merchants?

The child remained silent, and I regretted asking about his parents. He'd probably seen them slaughtered. No wonder he wouldn't speak.

"Well, you must be freezing." That vine slithered closer, and I slowly pulled my hatchet from my belt. "Come with me, and we'll get you something warm to wear and something good to eat. Okay?"

The vine reached for my ankle, and I swung the hatchet at it. My new blade sank through the woody rope with a satisfying thunk, and the child flinched, even as what was left of the vine retreated into the shadows, rustling dead leaves on its way.

"Come, *mon loulou*," I said, addressing the nameless boy as I might one of the boys from the village. How had a child survived out here on his own, even for a few minutes?

61

I dropped the hatchet through the loop on my belt and held my hand out again, and this time the boy slid his grimy little fingers into my grip. His trust was a warmth blossoming inside me, in spite of the cold, and suddenly I *truly* understood what Gran had been trying to tell me. I could make a difference. And I wouldn't be able to live with myself if I turned my back on such a responsibility.

I gave the child a reassuring smile, pushing back my own fear as I turned and led him in the direction I'd come from.

We came out of the forest exactly where I'd entered it hours before, on the path that led between the fallow rye field and the empty bean field. Several boys from the village ran by in a little pack, scaring crows from what was left of the dried-up stalks. The boy in my care canted his head to one side, watching them play.

Before we'd made it more than a few feet from the tree line, footsteps thumped toward us from the east, on the dirt path that ran around the outside of the village. "Adele!"

I turned toward Grainger's voice, relieved for a second before I remembered to close my cloak. To hide my hatchet.

To hide myself.

"What—?" He stopped a few feet away, frowning down at the naked child. "Where's your mother? And who's this?"

"Mama's busy with the Laurents' order."

"You went into the dark wood alone?" Grainger frowned,

his voice gruff with concern. "If I'd known, I would have come with you. It's the watch's *duty* to escort people who have business traveling in the dark wood."

"I know. But Gran's cottage is only a half hour's walk, and I've been many times. And look!" I glanced down at the child whose hand I still held, hoping the distraction would keep Grainger from noticing my broken lamp. From asking questions I couldn't answer. "I found him in the woods, but he hasn't said a word so far."

"You found him in the *dark wood*?"

"Yes. Near a merchant's wagon. I think it belonged to his parents. And I don't think they made it," I added in a whisper, trying not to choke on all that I was concealing from him.

Grainger knelt in front of the boy, his sword clanging as it grazed the ground. "What's your name, little one?" But the child only stared up at him with pale blue eyes. "You must be cold. You're covered in goose bumps."

Finally, the boy nodded.

Grainger removed his leather cloak. "Is it okay if I wrap you up in this? Bundle you up like a loaf of Adele's bread?"

The child gave him another mute nod, and I couldn't resist a smile when Grainger draped his cloak around the boy's shoulders. It trailed over the grass behind him for at least a foot, but Grainger only tugged the cloak closed and buttoned it, as if the fit were perfect. The child smiled up at him, clearly enamored of the fine garment.

"I'm going to pick you up, okay? If I carry you, we can get you inside faster." The boy nodded, and his gaze tracked Grainger as he stood. Then Grainger carefully lifted the child into his arms, as if he were carrying a very delicate bundle of firewood. Or a baby.

I tucked the ends of the leather cloak around him, which was when I noticed several spots of blood on the soles of his bare feet. "He's a little cut up," I said as I covered them. "But not as much as I'd expect, considering."

"Where are his clothes?" Grainger asked as we set off down the dirt path into the village.

"I don't know. He was like that when I found him. Crying. Alone in the dark wood."

Grainger's brows drew low over eyes a darker shade of blue than the child's as we passed the miller's workshop. "Poor kid. We probably won't be able to get him back home—wherever that is—before the thaw."

"I know."

As we approached the first of the cottages, Madame Gosse, the potter's wife, paused in her conversation with the thatcher's wife, Madame Paget, and they turned curious gazes our way.

"Grainger! What have you there?" Madame Paget asked as both women headed for us.

"Adele found a child in the forest," Grainger said, and I pulled back the hood of his cape to reveal the boy's face.

"In the dark wood?" Madame Gosse asked. As we might

64

possibly have meant another forest. "What were you doing out there?"

"I was taking a delivery to my grandmother."

Madame Gosse's scowl said exactly what she thought of a woman living alone in the woods, and I bit my tongue to keep from defending Gran, who—as it turned out—was perfectly capable of defending herself.

"What was *he* doing out there?" Madame Paget frowned as Grainger's cape fell open, and she realized the boy was unclothed. "And bare as the day he was born, in this cold. He was alone?"

"Yes. He hasn't spoken a word," I told her. "But I found him near a merchant's wagon. I don't think his parents made it, but there doesn't seem to be a scratch on him."

"Well then, I'd say he's blessed beyond reason. A shame about his parents, though." Madame Paget heaved a grim shrug. "Bring him to my cottage, Grainger. I'll see that he's fed and clothed."

We followed Madame Paget to her cottage next to the church, where she opened the door to let us into the small, warm space. Her home was modest, but it was roomier than mine, because in addition to the room in back where the thatcher and his wife slept, there was a loft where little Jeanne and Romy shared a bed, over the main room.

Jeanne was just a year younger than my sister, and Romy was five. When we came in, both girls looked up from the poppets they were playing with near the hearth, and the moment she saw what Grainger was carrying, Jeanne jumped to her feet, her doll forgotten. "Who's that, Mama?"

"He hasn't yet told us his name." Madame Paget headed straight for the hearth and added a log to the fire. "Jeanne, go get a bucket of water. Take your sister with you."

Jeanne grabbed a bucket and herded her sister outside.

Grainger set the boy down in front of the hearth, and Madame Paget removed the cloak and handed it back to him, so she could examine the little boy. He shied away from the roaring blaze while she ran her hands down all of his limbs. "He's frightfully cold, but you're right—he doesn't appear to have any injuries. And he doesn't look sick. Are you hungry, child?"

The boy nodded, eyes wide as he took in all the adults staring down at him in the cramped space.

"Here." Madame Paget broke off a bit of flat bread from a bowl sitting on a shelf over the hearth, and the boy devoured it in three bites. I uncovered half of my basket and pulled off a small hunk of the venison roast for him.

He ate that just as quickly, then sucked his filthy fingers clean.

Jeanne and Romy came back with a bucket of water while Madame Paget was going through a trunk in the back room. She returned with a clean tunic made of sackcloth just as her daughters set the bucket on the hearth.

"Let's get you washed off, then we'll try this on you. It'll swallow you whole, but that's better than nothing, isn't it?"

The boy only blinked at her, and Jeanne giggled.

"Girls, in the loft or outside. It's getting a bit cramped in here."

The Paget girls grabbed their dolls and raced up the ladder to the loft, where they watched from overhead while their mother wet a rag and carefully cleaned the filthy child, who began to shiver from the cold water.

"There you are. Just look at your handsome face! It was very nearly hidden by all that dirt!" Madame Paget exclaimed, but the boy seemed unaffected by her praise. "Hands up, please." She raised her own in demonstration.

He lifted his arms, and she slid the tunic into place so that it settled around his calves like a nightshirt, the laces at the neckline hanging loose to his waist.

"That's better. Now, what's your name? Else, I'll have to call you 'Boy.'"

The child blinked again.

"You do have a name, don't you, child?" Madame Gosse demanded, in as amicable a voice as I'd ever heard from her.

The boy only shrugged.

"'Boy' it is, then." Madame Paget stood and wiped her hands on her apron. "Up the ladder with you and play with my girls, while we figure out what to do with you."

For a second, the child only stared at her. Then she gestured at the ladder, and he scampered up to the loft, before Madame Gosse could demand to know whether his legs were functional.

Madame Paget escorted us outside. "You will spread the word during your patrol, won't you, Grainger? Find out if anyone knows anything about a merchant wagon? We need to find out where he's from."

"Of course," he promised.

"I would accompany you," I said. "But I'm sure my mother will need my help with the Laurents' order for tonight." And she was probably at her wit's end, fearing that I'd perished in the dark wood.

Madame Paget turned back to Grainger. "If you see my husband, will you tell him what's happened? I believe he's still repairing the church roof."

"I certainly will. Adele, may I see you home?" Grainger asked, and I did not miss the smile the two ladies exchanged behind his back.

Grainger escorted me down the long side of the village square, but he didn't say a word until we got to my cottage door. "So, will I see you tonight at the ceremony?"

"You will. I'll be the one in the red cloak," I teased.

His gaze swept the full length of my body, setting my pulse racing, even though my cloak hid most of me—not to mention my new hatchet—from his sight. "It looks beautiful on you." He gave me a dazzling smile, as a lock of pale hair fell over his forehead. Then he turned and headed off through the village square.

I took a deep breath to slow my racing heart before I pushed open the door and stepped inside.

My mother let out a sob the moment she saw me. "Adele!" She dropped the knife she'd been using to slice an apple. "I was so worried—" Her jaw snapped shut as she glanced at my sister, who sat in front of our hearth darning a woolen stocking. "But you're okay? The delivery went . . . well?"

"It was a bit of an adventure," I admitted. "I broke the lantern. And I dropped my basket and ruined Gran's bread."

"Well, aren't you a clumsy clod?" Sofia declared, clearly delighted by the rare chance to tease me with a phrase I'd often used to describe her.

I stuck my tongue out at her as I set my basket on the table. "But Gran sent the venison back with me anyway. And she offered to trim my cloak in white fur if I'll replace her raisin bread next week."

My mother exhaled, obviously relieved. "I'm sure we can do that."

"Did you see any monsters?" Sofia had never been in the dark wood; Gran came to the village, occasionally, to see her. To spare her the risky trip.

"I felt more of them than I saw," I told her. Which was true. "But that's only the beginning."

My mother's brow rose as she picked up her knife. "Oh?"

"I found a child in the forest on my way home." I took off my cloak and hung it on a hook near the door; then I positioned my body to block Sofia's view as I hung my hatchet beneath it. "A little boy, alone and naked. He hasn't said a word. Madame

Paget has fed and dressed him, but we have no idea who he is or where he came from."

My mother laid her knife down again, her apple tart forgotten. "You found him in the woods?" Her voice sounded oddly high-pitched. "Where?"

"A bit off the path. But not too far from Oakvale," I added, before she could scold me for not following directions. "A merchant wagon had been attacked nearby. I think a monster got his parents," I added, pointedly holding her gaze. "A *wolf*, if I had to guess."

"*Mon dieu.* Is he all right? Was he scratched or bitten? Injured at all?" The reason for her concern was clear. If the child had been infected, he'd be as much a threat to the village as my father was.

Would my neighbors *truly* burn a little boy alive? The very thought sent a chill through my bones.

"No. We've examined him thoroughly, and other than some abrasions on his feet from walking barefoot in the woods, there isn't a mark on him," I assured her.

"A wolf killed his parents?" Sofia had clearly forgotten about the stocking she'd been repairing. "A *were*wolf?"

"Yes. Then, it seems, something even scarier got the wolf, while the child was hiding." And though I'd meant for my words to frighten her out of going near the woods, excitement glittered in my sister's bright green eyes.

"You *did* have an adventure!" Mama wiped floury hands

on her apron. "But now that you're back, I could use your help with this tart."

I grabbed my own apron and tied it on to cover my dress, though baking suddenly felt like a terribly dull task after my time in the forest. I was bursting with questions for my mother, but since they couldn't be asked in front of Sofia, they would have to wait. So I settled into the job at hand. "I'll finish the tart while you do the pies, then, tonight, I'll introduce you to a creature more astonishing than any monster roaming the dark wood: a child who doesn't talk your ear off!"

Sofia stuck her tongue out at me, and I laughed as I tugged on her braid.

"Worry not, dear sister. I believe we're stuck with you— wagging tongue and all!"

FIVE

W e spent the last bit of daylight finishing the Laurents' order, then as the sun set, I rebraided Sofia's hair and brushed the flour from her dress so she could help me deliver the meat pies to the village square. My mother would be coming shortly with the raisin bread and the tart.

"Elena!" I called as I stepped into the open, torch-lit space, one eye glued to my sister, who'd been entrusted with carrying one of the pies all on her own.

Elena's brown eyes widened with relief when she saw me. "Adele! I'm so glad you made it out of the woods safely! I can't believe you went out there alone!"

I wanted to tell her about the whitewulf, and the guardians, and the true meaning of my new red cloak. I wanted to tell her how scared I'd been, alone in the woods. That I'd almost been killed, but that I'd slayed a monster instead, and that it was likely only the first of many. I wanted to confide all the secrets and fear and excitement burning a hole in the end of my tongue and watch her eyes widen the way they had when I'd told her about the first time Grainger kissed me, and when I'd confessed, breathlessly, that I might *love* him. That I might soon be married to him, and that until then, I intended to sneak kisses every chance I got.

Most of all, I wanted to tell her how worried I was that this secret new responsibility would set me down a path I never knew existed. A path at odds with the simple life I'd planned with Grainger at my side and Elena in the cottage next door.

But I couldn't. So I told her the only truth I could. "I may have gone into the woods alone, but I came out with a new friend."

"I heard! The whole village is talking about that little boy and his poor parents."

"I think what they're talking about right now is your betrothal!"

Elena smiled as she relieved me of one of the pies, but I could tell from the stiff way she held herself that she was nervous. "Over here, please, Sofia. Thank you so much for the delivery!"

My sister beamed as she set her pie on the long table, near a whole roasted pig the butcher must have had over the fire all day. Then she scampered off to play with the other children, who were kicking around a leather-covered clay ball.

"So, how are you?" I grabbed Elena's hand and tugged her away from the crowd that was starting to gather. "Really?"

Elena scanned the square until her gaze found Simon

Laurent, standing next to his father, holding a wooden tankard likely full of ale. "I'm a mess. We're to wed as soon as the river thaws. This was an idea before, but now it all feels so . . ."

"Real?"

"Yes. And I do like him." Her cheeks flushed with the acknowledgment.

"What's not to like?" I teased her with a grin. "He's the second-best catch in the village."

She finally smiled. "He's wonderful. And I'm going to marry him, and you're going to marry Grainger, and someday Simon will inherit the sawmill and Grainger will be head of the village watch, and our children will be best friends. Everything's going to be just like you said it would be. Perfect."

"But . . ." I prompted when her smile began to fade.

"But . . . I don't know how to be a wife. Or a mother."

"Of course you do. You've been watching your brothers since they were little, and you help out with half the children in the village."

"Yes, but . . . I've never even been alone with Simon." She took my hand and squeezed it so hard I could hear the bones grind together. "What if it's different when we're alone together? What if we don't actually like each other, when there's no one else around? What if I'm bad at running a household? What if I can't give him children? What if I'm not . . . good enough?"

"Nonsense," I whispered, pulling her close. "Don't let your nerves get the better of you. You're going to be a great wife and mother, and with any luck, you'll only be ahead of me by a few weeks. All of our plans are going to work out, Elena. *All* of them."

Being a guardian wouldn't change that. I wouldn't let it.

"Starting right now." I glanced pointedly over her shoulder, where I could see both her parents and her betrothed headed our way.

"Everyone's looking at me." Elena's hand tightened around mine again, and I realized that she was just as nervous about taking this step into adulthood here in the village square as I'd been out in the dark wood, all alone.

We each had our own fears to face.

"Take a deep breath," I ordered softly. "Do you want to marry Simon Laurent?"

"I do." She snuck another peek at him, then she gave me a firm nod and a shy smile. "And he is *rather* attractive, isn't he?"

My own smile grew. "Yes, he is. And today is just a promise, right? A vow to make another vow later. You can do that. You can say the words," I assured her. "Then we can dance and eat all this food."

"Okay." Elena took a deep breath. Then she turned, just as her father called her name.

I watched Sofia play while the Laurents and the Rousseaus spoke in a private huddle. While the other villagers set out food and gossiped in small clusters. This moment was the beginning of everything I'd ever dreamed of for Elena, and everything I hoped to soon have for myself. Yet suddenly I felt . . . apart from it all.

I found my mind wandering back to the dark wood. To the feel of the wind in my fur and the earth beneath my paws. To that moment of triumph and relief, when I'd stepped out of the forest with a helpless little boy safe at my side.

How had my mother ever managed to keep a secret this big? Gran said that guardians were monsters, but surely we didn't *have* to be. Helping that little boy hadn't felt monstrous. Killing the whitewulf hadn't felt monstrous. It had felt . . . exhilarating.

How could baking bread, darning stockings, and chopping wood ever be satisfying work again, after the excitement of braving the dark wood? Of slaying a werewolf?

Grainger was the key. Domestic work *would* be satisfying, with him at my side. With our children crawling around at my feet. Mama was both a mother and a guardian, and I could be too—once I convinced my mother that Grainger and I belonged together.

After all, my destiny as a guardian aligned perfectly with his purpose as a member of the village watch. We both wanted to protect our friends and neighbors. Once he understood that, I had *no doubt* that he would accept my true nature and protect my secret.

Shortly after my mother arrived with the rest of the baked goods, Monsieur Laurent asked everyone to gather in front of the church, where Simon and Elena stood side by side before the beautifully carved front door, firelight flickering on their faces. Simon, standing straight and tall, vowed that he would soon take Elena in holy matrimony. Elena smiled bashfully as she repeated his words so softly that her mother had to motion for her to speak up, beaming brightly at her from the front of the congregation.

The ceremony was brief, but public, so that the entire village could stand witness to the fact that the Laurents and the Rousseaus had come to an agreement. That their children would be wed after the thaw, when the *marchet* could be paid to Baron Carre to secure his permission for the marriage.

After the ceremony, the potter brought out his lute and the feast began. Ale flowed. Villagers danced. There hadn't been an occasion to celebrate in Oakvale since the freeze, and most people cared less about why we were celebrating than about the fact that we *were* celebrating—much to Elena's relief. She did not relish attention.

Sofia and I each took a helping from one of the meat pies—a rare extravagance, even for a baker's child—and claimed spots around one of the fire pits in the square. Elena was busy accepting congratulations, along with her parents, but as soon as Sofia got up to play with the other children, Grainger sat next to me, still wearing his leather cloak, his sword hanging at an angle.

He looked dashing in the glow from the blaze, and as always, his attention made me feel conspicuous and special.

"The meat pie was delicious." He leaned in as he whispered,

and the warmth in my cheeks had nothing to do with the fire pit.

"My mother made those, but I baked the apple tart. Why don't you try some, so you can tell me how good it is?"

"I would, but I'm afraid of abandoning my seat to the competition."

"Competition?"

"Don't look now, but Lucas and Noah Thayer are watching you."

A chill washed over me. "They are not."

They were, of course. But their attention felt nothing like Grainger's.

A month before, on the way home from a delivery, I'd found myself drawn toward the dark wood—an impulse that now made more sense—where I'd found Lucas and Noah chopping down trees at the edge of the forest. While many of my neighbors whispered about the redheaded Duval women and their odd tendency to outlive their men, the Thayers had always been more open in their suspicion about my family. So I started to hurry past them. But then Noah stepped into my path, his ax propped on one broad shoulder. I could smell ale on his breath.

He pushed my hood back and grabbed a lock of my hair, then he looked right down into my eyes and said that red hair and freckles were surely a sign of beastly carnal desires.

Lucas dropped his ax, his eyes glazed from the ale, and said that maybe he and Noah should test my "proclivities" so they could expose me, afterward, as a harlot. To cleanse Oakvale of the stain I put upon it.

I slapped Noah's hand away and fled all the way into the village.

I'd heard similar, if subtler, opinions from a few others—half of Oakvale seemed to think that my father's fate meant my family was cursed by the devil—but Grainger didn't see me like that. He'd always made me feel cared for and protected.

"They *are* watching," he insisted with a glance across the fire pit at Lucas and Noah. "They're always watching you."

"How would you know that, unless you're always watching them?" I teased, doing my best to ignore the Thayer boys.

Grainger laughed. "I am very aware of my competition."

"They are *not* your competition. They're horrible, and they say vile things."

He dismissed my loathing with a quiet smile. "They're teasing the most beautiful woman in Oakvale to get her attention, but they'll give up, once we're wed." His smile faded, and I found just a hint of doubt in the line of his brow. "Did you speak to your mother?"

"I haven't had a chance, since she couldn't come with me this afternoon."

Grainger sighed. "Adele, you can't go out there alone again. It isn't safe."

I smiled at his concern, because he had no way of knowing

that I could see in the dark wood now. That soon I'd be able to take care of not just myself, but anyone else who had business in the forest.

"I'm only trying to protect you," he added, when I couldn't think of what to say. "I won't let anything happen to my bride-to-be. Assuming you'll have me." He frowned, his focus narrowing on me. "This delay . . . that *is* your mother's doing, isn't it? Because if you don't want—"

"No, I *do* want to marry you!" I grabbed his hand and squeezed it, and Grainger looked almost as surprised as I was by my boldness. "I do want to marry you." I said it softer that time, as I reluctantly slid my hand from his warm, calloused grip, before people could start to talk. "But all my mother has said on the subject so far is that the time isn't right. That we should wait for the thaw." Though now I understood that the timing wasn't her true objection. And that if I wanted to marry Grainger, I would have to convince her that we could trust him with our secret. That despite his position in the watch, he would *never* have us burned as witches.

"I've been making preparations," Grainger said. "I suppose I'm getting ahead of myself, since your mother has yet to agree to the union, but I can't seem to help it." His gaze captured mine, his blue eyes aglow with anticipation. "My thoughts are *consumed* with the day I can finally call you wife."

My heart thudded, deep in my chest. "What preparations?"

"My father has given me a parcel of land from what Baron Carre bestowed on him."

Monsieur Colbert had saved the local lord's ten-year-old son last winter, when he and a few other men from the village watch were escorting the baron and his family through the dark wood, on their way out of Oakvale for the season. Their wagon lost a wheel, and during the repair, the child had wandered from the path. When they heard him screaming, Monsieur Colbert ran off into the forest just in time to fight back a werewolf—a *whitewulf*, though he didn't know the term—with his sword and his lamp.

Knowing what I know now, I suspect my grandmother was working from the shadows, likely protecting the baron and his family from another monster they would never even know about. Yet Monsieur Colbert was the only one who could take credit for the effort.

In gratitude, the baron had granted Grainger's father a bit of land on the edge of the village.

"When the thaw comes, I will start building our cottage. It's a bit of a walk to the bakery, but—"

"I don't care about the distance." Nor did I care about the size of the cottage or the location of the land. I cared about Grainger's smile. About the way I had his whole focus when he met my gaze. "I'll talk to my mother again."

"What is her objection? I hope she has no reason to believe I wouldn't love you. That I couldn't take care of you. I—"

"That's not it. It isn't you she objects to, I swear it."

"Perhaps her objection is the institution of marriage itself." Grainger nodded toward the other side of the square, not far from my home, where my mother was attempting to preserve a proper distance between herself and Monsieur Martel, the blacksmith, who'd been trying to tempt her into matrimony since his wife had died in childbirth three summers before.

"It isn't marriage she objects to," I assured him, because as with my own potential betrothal, I suddenly understood her hesitance to remarry. She didn't want to keep her secret from a husband.

Yet according to Gran, my father had known. What about my grandfather? If my mother and grandmother had married and confided in their husbands, I should be able to as well. Shouldn't I?

"Were you able to find out anything about the boy from the woods?" I asked, reminded of him as a gaggle of children raced past, chasing a leather-wrapped ball. "Was the watch aware of a merchant headed toward Oakvale?"

Grainger blinked, caught off guard by my change of subject. "No, but in the morning we're sending some men to look for the wagon you saw. Hopefully some of the supplies can be salvaged and we'll be able to tell where the merchant hailed from, so we'll know where to send the boy, after the thaw."

"No one in the village recognizes him?"

"Not so far," he said, and that wasn't unexpected. Most of the villagers—myself included—had never left Oakvale. "Madame Laurent has family in Westmere, which she last visited right before the freeze, but she says she didn't see him there."

"He must be from Oldefort, then." I scanned the village square until I found a familiar blond head. The boy from the woods was sitting on the other side of the bonfire, between Jeanne and Romy Paget, while Madame Paget spoke with several of the other village women nearby. Romy and the boy each had a wooden bowl of vegetable stew, and Jeanne was poking at the fire with a stick.

"He'll be fine here until the thaw," I said, as Grainger followed my gaze. "The village won't let him starve."

The boy scraped up the last of his stew with a wooden spoon, then he let his bowl clatter to the ground, earning himself a startled look from several nearby villagers. He glanced around for a second, then his focus locked onto Romy Paget's still half-full bowl. His lips curled back from his teeth in a snarl I couldn't hear from halfway around the fire pit. Then he snatched Romy's bowl from her and held it up to his mouth, drinking from it like a cup.

"Hey!" Romy grabbed her bowl back. "That's mine!" She dipped her spoon into it, but before she could lift the bite to her mouth, the boy shoved her to the ground, where her bowl fell in the dirt.

Grainger and I were up in an instant, rounding the fire pit, but it was Jeanne Paget who hauled the boy off her little sister.

"Non!" she shouted, waving her index finger in his face. "We do not push people!"

Madame Paget picked little Romy up, and while she brushed dirt from her daughter's clothes, she patiently explained to the boy that there was a proper way to ask for more food, and that bad behavior would not be abided.

"Why don't I take him home with us tonight?" I said, while Grainger refilled the boy's bowl.

"Nonsense," Madame Paget insisted. "You don't have the room. And Romy's fine, aren't you, dear?"

Romy gave her mother a teary nod.

"Our little guest has been through something very difficult. He's lost his parents, and it stands to reason that he might have lost his manners for a bit, as well. But we're going to be patient with him, aren't we, girls?"

Romy and Jeanne both nodded dutifully, while the boy tore into his second bowl of food, oblivious to all the fuss.

"We're going to have to come up with something to call him, too," I said.

"We call him Tom," Jeanne said, smoothing down the front of her skirt after the little scuffle.

I glanced at her in surprise. "Has he spoken to you?"

"No," she admitted. "But he looks like a Tom, and he turns when you call him that."

"Really?" I glanced down at the boy, but he hadn't looked up from his bowl once since Grainger had handed it to him.

"Does he understand what you say to him?" I was starting to wonder if he spoke a different language.

"He seems to." Jeanne squatted in front of him, her hands folded in front of her skirt. "Tom, would you like a bit of apple tart? It's a special treat."

Finally, the child looked up. His gaze found Jeanne, and he nodded. Once. Then he went back to his bowl of vegetable stew.

Jeanne stood, beaming a proud smile at me. Then she frowned. "I suppose now I have to go get him a bit of your mother's tart." Grainger laughed, and Jeanne skipped off toward the banquet table with a good-natured smile on her face. She was every bit her mother's daughter.

"Madame Paget, I believe we may still have a couple of my brothers' old toys at home," Grainger said. "Would you like me to bring them over in the morning? For . . . Tom?"

"Yes, please," Romy answered, before her mother could even open her mouth. "I don't think Tom knows about sharing."

SIX

Sweat gathered on my brow, despite the frigid morning air, and I paused in my chore to wipe it with the back of my sleeve. My wood-splitting maul—the marriage of an axe and a hammer—was once my father's, and this morning, for the first time in my life, it didn't seem heavy and unwieldy in my hands.

Not unmanageable, anyway.

I swung the maul over my right shoulder, going up on my toes as my hand slid down the handle, just before impact. The maul landed in a preexisting crack in the log—a crack I'd aimed for—with a satisfying thunk, then slid into the wood, splitting it all the way down.

"Nicely done," Grainger said. "May I help?"

Startled, I whirled around, pushing hair back from my forehead with one hand. "I'm perfectly capable of splitting my own wood, thank you," I informed him with a good-natured smile.

And since my ascension the day before, the chore required less effort than ever.

I bent for the larger of the split pieces, positioning it on the stump.

"Well then, may I watch?" Grainger asked with one saucily arched brow.

"Don't you have chores of your own, Grainger Colbert?"

"Done as soon as the sun came up, Adele Duval," he teased.

"Well, you have three brothers to help," I pointed out as I adjusted my grip on the maul. "Here, it's just my mother and me." Sofia could gather eggs, darn stockings, and fetch water, but she was too small to help with anything like splitting logs.

"That's true. We're decidedly short on women, in the Colbert household. A problem I am trying my damnedest to remedy."

"How would your mother feel if she heard you say that?"

"Where do you think I first heard it?" Grainger's smile lit a fire in my belly. "She would love to have a daughter-in-law around to help out."

And yet I doubted I would be Madame Colbert's first choice. Though my grandfather had passed away in his sleep several years before, rumors persisted that, like my father, he'd been attacked in the dark wood, and despite the courteous smiles tossed our way around the village, there wasn't a mother in Oakvale who would want her son to marry into such a "cursed" family.

87

Fortunately, Grainger wanted me in spite of the rumors.

"Now the truth emerges." I swung my maul again and split the wood into two smaller, more manageable pieces. "You aren't looking for a bride. You're looking for another set of capable hands," I teased.

"Well, I *do* like your hands." Grainger dropped the sackcloth bundle he was holding and took the maul from my grip. He let it thunk into the stump, then he captured my hands in his. "Though I'd prefer to see them a little less calloused. Marry me, and you'll never have to split wood again."

"You think married women don't split wood?"

"My mother doesn't. She has a husband and four sons to keep firewood stacked against the walls of our cottage."

"I have no sons."

"I would give you sons." Grainger pulled me closer, his gaze burning into mine. "And daughters, if you insist," he added with a crooked smile.

I pulled free and smacked his shoulder as I wrenched my maul from the stump again. "And if we had only daughters?" Only redheaded daughters, saddled with a secret that could get us all burned at the stake?

"I would split wood for you all. I would split wood all day and all night, so my wife and daughters need not develop callouses from rough handles and cold climes."

I considered listing for him all the different ways a woman could develop callouses in her daily work, without ever touching a maul. Instead, I just smiled up at him. "If you spend all night chopping wood, I don't know how we'll ever get sons *or* daughters."

A giggle from behind the woodpile made my face flush. *Sofia.* She was supposed to be weaving nettlecloth. Not spying on me.

"Sofia! Inside!" I ordered, and as she danced out from behind the woodpile, I turned to Grainger with a smile. "Pray for sons."

He laughed. "Sofia. Tell your sister she should marry me."

"You should marry him, sister," Sofia said. "Before he stops asking."

"Grainger . . ." I scolded.

He picked up his sackcloth. "For now, I will accept your company. I'm on my way to the Pagets' with toys for Tom. Will you come with me?"

"I want to go!" Sofia spun away from the back door. "I want to play with Jeanne!"

There were only a handful of girls her age in the village, so she and the oldest of the Paget girls were frequent playmates. But that wasn't the real reason for her request.

"She wants to meet Tom," I told him. Madame Paget had taken the strange boy home last night after he'd pushed Romy, and he'd been the talk of the celebration, much to Madame Rousseau's chagrin. And Elena Rousseau's relief.

"*Everyone* wants to meet Tom," Sofia insisted. "Maybe I can make him talk."

"Get your cloak," I said with a sigh. "And tell Mama where we're going."

Sofia raced inside, but she was back a minute later with a gray cloak draped over one arm, clutching a cloth-wrapped bundle in both hands. My mother appeared behind her and pulled me aside while Grainger tried to get Sofia to actually put her cloak on.

"I gave your sister a rye loaf to take to Madame Paget, to help feed Tom," she said, crossing her arms over the front of her flour-splattered apron. Because even though the thatcher's family had taken him in, the community would come together to help support him. "I didn't get a chance to see the boy before they took him home last night, but, Adele, there's something really odd about a mute child found alone in the dark wood. You're *sure* he wasn't scratched or bitten?"

"I watched Madame Paget wash him, before she gave him a tunic. There wasn't a mark on him. But he just saw his parents slaughtered by a werewolf," I whispered. "That would torment any adult, much less a small child. Don't you think?"

She nodded, then her gaze flicked toward Sofia again. "Still, I want you to let me know immediately if you notice anything else odd about the boy."

"I will." Though so far everything about Tom could be described as odd.

"Come on then!" Grainger said, as my mother headed back

inside to begin the day's orders. He threw his sack over one shoulder and gestured for Sofia to head for the village square.

"Cloak!" I ordered as I plucked the loaf of rye from her hands.

"Where's your red one?" Grainger asked me, as Sofia finally tossed her own cloak over her shoulders, without bothering to tie the cord.

"It isn't really suited to chores." Though, evidently, it was perfectly suited to shielding my clothing from a splatter of blood.

"Mama said Gran made a red one for me too," Sofia told him. "But I can't have it until I'm older."

The very thought gave me chills. I didn't want my baby sister out in the dark wood. Not after what Gran had told me about her own sister's death. I couldn't lose Sofia. My *mother* couldn't lose Sofia.

"When am I going to be old enough?" Sofia asked, walking backward on the dirt path, in front of us.

"When you can split logs with a maul," Grainger told her.

"No," I insisted, a little harsher than I'd intended. "When Gran says you're old enough."

"Maybe she meant you to wear the red cloak at your wedding!" Sofia shouted, spinning in a circle with her arms out at her sides. Without missing a step. Her balance was certainly good. And she ran like the wind. I had to believe that by the time she was my age, she would be well prepared for her own trial.

"Yes," Grainger teased, bumping my shoulder with his. "Maybe that is what your *grand-mère* intended."

"Maybe so," I hedged.

"And she's going to line the hood with white fur!" Sofia added. "It would be beautiful at your wedding!"

"White fur?" Grainger's left brow rose. "Rabbit?"

I could only shrug.

"The watch went into the dark wood this morning to search for that wagon," Grainger whispered. "They found it and were able to salvage some of the supplies, though a lot of them had already been destroyed, and the food was long gone. But they weren't able to tell for sure where the merchants came from."

I sighed. That was no surprise.

"There he is!" Her gray cloak trailing behind her, Sofia took off across the square for the thatcher's cottage, where Tom sat on the front steps watching Jeanne tie a scrap of coarse nettle-cloth into something that resembled a doll. Next to her, Romy was playing with a doll made of the same material. "Tom! We brought you some toys!" The boy looked up as my sister raced toward him. "Isn't there something you want to *say*?"

"She means 'thank you,'" Romy supplied, when Tom only stared at Sofia with a blank look.

Grainger knelt to show the boy what was in his sack, and I stepped past Tom to knock on the frame of the front door. "Madame Paget, it's Adele. May I come in?"

"Please do!" she called.

"Will you watch her?" I asked Grainger.

He nodded, but Sofia huffed at me as I stepped into the cottage, where I gave Madame Paget the cloth-wrapped bread. "My mother sent this."

"Oh, do thank her for me." She set the loaf on a shelf.

"How is Tom? Has he said anything yet?"

"Not a word." Madame Paget returned to a half-sliced turnip at her table, where she picked up a knife and continued her work. "He grunts occasionally, which seems to be an affirmative answer to a question. And he shakes his head. But I've only seen him open his mouth in order to put food in it."

SEVEN

←————————➤

"Where's Sofia?" my mother asked as I stepped into our cottage. Despite the open front door, the heat from the oven was nearly overwhelming.

"She's kicking a leather ball in the square with the Martel boys." Despite the chores she was behind on, I had let her go play with the blacksmith's children after our visit with the thatcher's family because I wanted to talk to my mother in private. "Mrs. Paget thanks you for the bread."

"How is the boy? Is he speaking yet?"

"No, but he seems fine other than that. Grainger took him some toys. He likes children, you know."

She paused in her kneading to give me a look.

"Gran said Papa knew," I continued as I exchanged my cloak for an apron.

"Knew what?"

"About you. About guardians."

My mother sighed. "Of course he knew, *chère*. I don't know how one could hide a secret like this from her husband. But your papa's mother was a guardian, so he found out about all of this on the day of his sister's trial. By the time we met, he had no superstitious beliefs to hold against me." She stopped kneading, and the grief that passed over her features, even eight years after my father's death, gripped me like a fist tightening around my entire body. "As deeply as he cared for me—as perfectly as we fit together on a personal level—he was also uniquely suited to be the husband of a guardian." She turned back to her dough, but that old pain still echoed in her voice. "I miss him every single day. And I wish you could have had more time with him."

I wished that too. My memories of him seemed to fade more every day. "So, *both* of my grandmothers are guardians?" Which meant my father had an advantage as a suitor that Grainger would never have. He wasn't considered a threat to our family, because he came from a family like ours.

If I wanted my mother's blessing on my marriage, I'd have to convince her that Grainger wasn't a threat either.

"Yes, *chère*. This is in your blood." Her hands paused again, and pride echoed in her voice. "It's your legacy to uphold."

My father was from a town several days' ride by carriage to the west, but I'd never been there, and I hadn't heard much about his family. Including his mother.

"How many other guardians are there?"

"I don't have a number. I only know that there are guardians

95

nearly everywhere the dark wood stretches." My mother stepped back from the dough she was working and gestured for me to take over. "And the wood seems to stretch farther every year, infecting the landscape like a disease."

I turned the dough, pressing the heels of my palms into the warm, soft ball as I thought about that. There were forests in other places that were not like the dark wood. I knew that, but I found the idea difficult to truly understand. Woods where no monsters lived? Where normal daylight fell? Where travelers could move about in peace? Where people could hunt and forage? We'd never had such a luxury in Oakvale. Not in my lifetime, anyway.

As much wood as they cut, Monsieur Thayer and his sons never truly seemed to make a dent in the dense forest. And they certainly hadn't been able to prevent it from surrounding the village.

"Can the dark wood be stopped?" My stomach pitched at the thought that it might continue to devour the land, eventually overtaking little hamlets like Oakvale.

"If it can be, I do not know how," my mother admitted as she pulled a jar of raisins from the shelf. "What I do know is that we guardians are the only thing standing between the monsters in the dark wood and the people in our villages. And though I've been dreading your trial since the day you were born, I am relieved to have you at my side now, as all of Oakvale would be, if they understood. As your father would be, if he were still with us."

"Why did he go into the woods that day?" I'd asked that question many times before, but I'd never been satisfied with my mother's claim that she had no idea why he'd ventured into the forest alone. Maybe now that I knew the truth about her—about myself—she would finally tell me the truth about him.

"Adele." Her voice was little more than a whisper, yet it held a crushing weight. "This isn't the time, *chère.*"

"Mama. Please. Just tell me."

Her gaze found mine as she set the raisins on the table, and she sighed. "He was looking for a lost child."

I frowned, trying to read the truth in her eyes, but her expression was guarded. There was still more to it. "Why would you let him go out there alone, when he couldn't see in the dark wood? When you *could*?"

"Your sister was sick, and I was home with her. I didn't even know anything had happened until they brought him home, bleeding heavily and already raging with fever. He said he'd heard a child cry out from the dark wood."

"What child? Was it ever found?"

Her eyes fell closed for a second. "You were that child, Adele. Your father said he heard *you* call out to him from the dark wood. There is no other child he would have gone after on his own. He believed there wasn't time to gather a search party."

"But I wasn't in the wood. In my entire life, I never went into the wood alone, until my trial!"

"I know. We found you that afternoon, curled up asleep with

97

Elena Rousseau, in her loft."

Fresh pain sliced into me, reopening the old wound with a new and bitter depth. "The dark wood whispers lies in stolen voices. Everyone knows that. So why would he think I was really out there?"

My mother shrugged. "He knew that the forest called to you, even when you were a child. It seems to hold a particular, almost hypnotic appeal to a future guardian. Several times, we'd found you standing on the edge of the village, just staring into the darkness, and he was always worried that one day you would answer that call. Long before you were ready."

Guilt hit me like a blow to the gut. He wouldn't have believed the voice in the forest to be mine, if he hadn't often seen me staring into the dark wood. If he hadn't known I'd inherited a reason to walk into the shadows.

He'd died because of me.

My mother pulled me into a hug, heedless of the bits of dough drying on my hands. "No, Adele, it wasn't your fault." She took a firm grip on my arms and looked right into my eyes. "He knew you probably weren't really in the woods, but he couldn't take the risk that you were. That you needed him. He couldn't ignore your cries for help because he was your father, and he loved you, and he would have done *anything* to protect you."

"He told you that?"

"Yes. And in his position, even without the ability to see in the dark, I would have done the same thing. No parent can ignore her child's pleas. The dark wood knows just which fears to prey upon."

"I worried that's what I was hearing, when I found little Tom," I admitted in a whisper. "Everyone knows about the forest's deceptions. But when I heard him—"

"Don't *ever* do that again." My mother's voice was fierce, the flash in her eyes even more so. "You were very, very lucky to have found a child instead of a monster, but that isn't likely to ever be the case again. Do you understand?"

I nodded, and when she let me go, I turned back to the dough. But my thoughts would not stop racing. "How did you meet Papa?"

At first, I thought she wouldn't answer. That the memory I'd dredged up was too painful.

"I met him the day we were wed," she said at last. "I was not much older than you, though we were betrothed as small children, in secret."

I glanced at her in surprise. Childhood betrothals were common for royalty, and even for nobility, for whom marriage was often a way to form a political alliance or to merge fortunes. But for villagers like us who owned no land? And in secret? "Why?"

"Our parents came to an agreement to ensure that I would have a husband I could trust and that your father could contribute to the fight, even though, as a man, he could not become a guardian."

"That sounds like a business arrangement," I said.

She nodded. "Of sorts. Because it is very difficult for a guardian to be married to a man who does not—who *cannot*—know about her responsibilities. Who can't know where his wife goes at night sometimes, or what his daughters will become."

A sick feeling twisted in my stomach, and I poured my frustration into the dough beneath my hands, kneading it too hard. "Why can't Grainger know? His job is to protect people, and my job is to protect people. So why can't we work side by side?"

"Because he is the village watch, Adele, and no matter how it sounds, you and Grainger are not two sides of the same coin. He fights behind the shield of daylight. In the cocoon of firelight. He will never be able to understand that you need neither of those. Or *why* you need neither of those. He will never believe that a wolf can protect this village, instead of terrorizing it."

"You can't be certain of that," I insisted. "You don't know him."

"I *do* know him." She took a scoop of rye flour from the bin to start another batch of bread on the other side of the table. "He's a good man, but he won't understand that guardians aren't the same as a whitewulf. He will see teeth, and claws, and fur, and he will think *witch*. Then he will light a fire."

"No. Mama, he *loves* me. He would never do that to his own wife."

"Adele, he *will*." Pain echoed in the lines at the corners of my mother's mouth. "I watched my own husband burn. Because it was *necessary*. And that's exactly what Grainger will believe

100

about you. About your grandmother and about me. About your little sister, who knows nothing about any of this. He will watch us all burn, because his duty is to the village, and that's what he'll think he's doing. His duty." She sighed. "Your stars are crossed, *chère*. I hate having to tell you that, because I understand how you feel about him. How he feels about you. But it will never work. It can't—"

"It might."

She looked up from the table and her gaze intensified. "It *can't*. Because as I was, you have been betrothed to someone else since you were hardly old enough to walk."

"I . . . *what?*" My mind was suddenly empty as I grasped for the meaning of her unexpected announcement. "You *cannot* mean—"

"Do you think Grainger will show me how to make a ball?" Sofia practically yelled as she appeared in the doorway, her cheeks flushed from the cold, her eyes shining brightly.

"Out!" I shouted at her, desperate for just a few more minutes of privacy with my mother. "Go play, Sofia."

"Adele," my mother scolded. Then she turned to my sister. "Why do you need a ball?"

Sofia stuck her tongue out at me as she took off her cloak and hung it from a peg by the door, then she reached for her apron. "I'm faster than all the boys, and I can kick the ball farther, but I don't even have one of my own."

"Didn't your sister just help you make a new corn husk

doll?" my mother said, while I struggled to process both her announcement and the fact that I couldn't demand more details while Sofia was listening.

"Yes, but you can't kick a poppet down the street, Mama. Not very fast, anyway," she added on her way into the back room.

When the curtain fell behind my sister, my mother leaned across the table to whisper to me. "We'll discuss this more tonight."

"Tonight?"

"Yes." She glanced at the curtain. "It's time for your training to begin."

Before I could ask what, exactly, she had in mind, Sofia reappeared. She carried two shallow clay bowls of milk that had been sitting in the cooler back room since the day before, so cream could rise to the top. "I hate butter churning day," my sister mumbled as she set the bowls on the other table and began to skim off the cream.

"Yes, but you like fresh butter," Mama reminded her. "And she who churns the longest gets the first taste."

I rolled my eyes. I always churned the longest, and Sofia always got the first taste, because she was the youngest. That was the kind of white lie my mother justified by calling it "motivational."

How, exactly, would she justify failing to tell me that I'd been promised in marriage to a stranger when I was still just a small child?

EIGHT

"Sofia's asleep?" Mama asked as I snuck out of the back room, letting the curtain fall closed behind me.

"Like the dead."

She frowned. "I don't care for that expression."

That felt reasonable, considering. "She's sleeping like a baby," I amended, fighting the urge to start firing questions at her. Holding my tongue for the rest of the day had been almost as much work as churning butter and kneading dough, and now that we were finally alone, I felt like I was about to burst from my need for information.

Yet my mother was as calm and composed as ever, and I knew from experience that she would not talk until she was ready.

She wore a red cloak just like mine, except that white fur trim lined not only her hood, but the entire garment.

"You've had that since you were my age?" I asked, and she nodded.

Despite the combination of fear and relief I'd seen in her eyes when I'd returned from my trial intact, a rare gleam of pride shined in them now. It must have been difficult for her to maintain her secret for so long. "I only wear it at night, when I head into the dark wood."

"Why? It's beautiful."

She gave me a small smile. "I don't like to stand out."

"Should I save mine for our secret work?"

"No. Our neighbors have already seen your cloak and they'll find it strange if you stop wearing it."

"Did they see yours, when you headed into the woods for your trial?"

"No, because I was already in the woods. I grew up in the cabin, remember?"

Actually, I'd forgotten.

"How have you kept the trim so clean?" I asked, kneeling to examine the bottom hem of her cloak. Though the fur around her feet must have been brushing the ground for years, I could see no sign of use or discoloration in it.

"Whitewulf fur doesn't stain easily. Dirt seems to slide right off of it."

Come to think of it, the one I'd killed in the dark wood had looked pretty bright, despite presumably living in the forest.

"I always told your grandmother that we should use the fur for cleaning." My mother laughed softly. "But she said that would be disrespecting both the beast itself and the effort that went into slaying it."

"That does sound like Gran." I stood and took the leather belt my mother handed me. "You must have slain many of them, to have this much fur on your cloak."

My mother huffed. "I've dispatched many more than this fur represents. To say nothing of the other monsters."

The thought of how many must be out there sent a chill across my flesh.

"Are you ready?"

"Almost." I took my new hatchet from the shelf over the bread oven and dropped it into a loop on my belt, then I fastened my own cloak over my shoulders. "Should we take a lantern?"

"We can't sneak past the watchman on duty carrying a light, and we won't need one. You will see better in normal darkness too, now, not just in the dark wood." My mother hesitated at the door, turning to look at the curtain leading into the back room. "I've never left Sofia alone."

"She'll be fine. She sleeps like the— Um . . . babies," I said, and my mother's lips quirked up. "Did you ever have to leave me alone when I was little?"

"No. Your father was here to watch you when I had to venture into the dark wood. And you were old enough to take care of your sister in an emergency, by the time he died."

I'd been eight years old, the same age Sofia was now, but . . .

"I had no idea you ever left in the night."

"That's because I didn't linger in the front room talking," she chided with a smile. Then she pushed the door open quietly, and I followed her out into the cold night, relieved to note that she was right. My eyes made much better use of moonlight now.

We walked down the dark dirt path past the town square, headed toward the western edge of the village. Fear and anticipation buzzed beneath my skin at the thought of going back into the dark wood.

"What are we doing tonight, exactly?"

"Hunting. Patrolling. Learning. Testing your stamina and reflexes."

"By killing monsters?"

"Yes. Culling them from the population. That is the lion's share of our duty."

"When were you planning to tell me about my betrothal?" I asked as we quietly passed the potter's cottage.

"Let's try not to wake all of Oakvale," she scolded with a glance around at all the darkened homes. There wasn't so much as a candle lit in a single window. The only source of light, other than the moon and a sprinkling of stars, was the distant bob of a lantern to the east, carried by a watchman on patrol duty. And beyond that, the glow of the halo of torches defining the edge of the forest.

"I need to know," I insisted softly.

My mother sighed, then she glanced to the west, toward the

broad stretch of dark wood in the distance. She took my elbow and guided me somewhat insistently down the path until she could tug me behind a barn, to prevent the watchman on patrol from catching a glimpse of moonlight gleaming off her white fur trim.

"Mama, how could I be betrothed?" I snapped, having reached the end of my patience. "How could you not *tell* me I'm betrothed?"

"It wouldn't have made any sense to tell you before your ascension." Her jaw was set in a firm line, but her gaze looked worried. As if she weren't entirely confident in that decision. "Until you discovered what you are, you couldn't have understood the reason for the betrothal."

"And why couldn't you tell me what I am? Why wait until my sixteenth year, then lure me into the dark wood under false pretenses?"

My mother's sigh seemed to carry the weight of the world. "I'm sorry, Adele. That isn't how I wanted it. But the trial tests your instincts. Your reaction to danger, before you know what you're capable of. Spilling whitewulf blood triggers the first change into a redwulf."

"You couldn't have warned me? Or taught me how to kill a whitewulf?"

"It doesn't work that way. Guardians have tried that in the past, and the girls who knew what was coming failed to ascend. To transform. It seems that only those who act on true instinct are capable of claiming their guardian form. Which is why you can't tell Sofia any of this."

Her trial was eight years away, yet already I was terrified for my little sister. "This is *barbaric*."

"It certainly used to be," my mother agreed. "We used to have to send girls into the dark wood and just hope they ran into a whitewulf before something else killed them. That's how my aunt died. So your grandmother decided it would be safer to catch a wolf and release it directly into a potential guardian's path. Her innovation preserved the test of pure instinct, yet prevented me from running into something else in the woods before I'd spilled whitewulf blood. Before I'd claimed my destiny and my abilities. She likely saved my life *and* yours. And Sofia's. And by extension, she saved the lives of everyone we will protect over the coming years.

"Those people are why it is important for you to accept your calling. Your responsibility. And to marry a man who can give you daughters who will one day take up that same mantle."

My mother exhaled slowly, meeting my gaze in the moonlight. "Your betrothed is named Maxime Bernard, and he's a few years older than you. I believe he's seen nineteen summers."

"He's not Grainger," I said through clenched teeth.

"He lives in Ashborne, and he will—"

"Mama, are you going to *make* me marry him?" My voice sounded sharp with horror.

"Of course not. If you think you cannot learn to love him,

you may break off the betrothal. But you *will* at least hear me out. At least understand what your options are before you make your choice. And I certainly hope you know how very fortunate you are, to even *have* a choice."

I nodded, my jaw clenched hard enough to ache. I *did* know that.

"Max is a carpenter," my mother continued. "Having seen his father's work, I suspect he is a very *good* carpenter, and he's already built you a cottage on the southern edge of the village of Ashborne, a few days' journey to the north of here."

My gaze narrowed on her in the dark. "How do you know he's built a cottage?"

"Do you remember the merchant who came shortly before the freeze? He was from Ashborne. He brought me a message from Max's mother, assuring me that he is prepared for your union. That he has met his obligations, as negotiated by your father and me on your behalf when you were not yet two years old."

"He's prepared . . ." I closed my eyes, trying to think it through. "Which means he—this Maxime—must have known about our betrothal for some time?"

She nodded. "His mother assures me that he's eager to meet you. To begin your life together. To prove himself worthy of calling a guardian—of calling *you*—his wife."

"But I've never . . . Mama, I've never even seen him! He might hate me! I might hate him!" And even if I didn't, *he wasn't Grainger*!

109

And finally, the full impact of what I'd just heard hit me. "A cottage in Ashborne. I'm to live there? I'm to leave Oakvale? Leave you, and Gran, and Sofia?"

Sofia was only eight years old. If frequent visits couldn't be arranged, she would grow up with no better memory of me than I had of our father.

And . . .

"Mama, Elena and I are supposed to be neighbors! We're supposed to raise our children together."

"I know that's what you wanted, Adele, but a guardian has to put her duty before her personal interests. And this is what we agreed to in the negotiation." Pain flickered behind her eyes, and I realized that despite the arrangements she'd made, she dreaded the thought of my absence. Then her gaze went carefully blank. "All the other benefits of marriage aside, Maxime will provide you with a home, and in return, you will protect Ashborne from the dark wood."

"But . . . why? Why can't I stay here?" Assuming I accepted this union. Which I had no intention of doing. I intended to prove to her that Grainger would choose me over his duty to the village, if it came down to that. But how could I prove that without showing him what we were?

"Max's mother was only blessed with one daughter, and she died in infancy. The villagers of Ashborne need you. Whether they know it or not."

The field seemed to spin around me as I tried to make sense

of what I was hearing. "You're selling me in service to another village? To people I've never met? To a husband I've never even *seen*?"

"Adele, you are not the first couple to be betrothed as children. This is a common arrangement among guardians. Marriage is a contract with benefits to both parties, and your father and I made sure your needs were well-represented. You will be cared for. You will be *treasured*, which is much more than most new brides can expect. And you will be free to carry out your responsibility—to hunt monsters in the dark wood—in peace. Alongside a husband who will protect you from villagers likely to misunderstand."

"How will he do that?"

"He will explain away any necessary absences. He will answer any difficult questions. He will be your anchor to the community and your shield from suspicion. And he will be your confidant. As your father was for me." The longing and weariness in her voice spoke volumes about how much she still missed him.

"And Sofia?" I asked. "Have you sold her hand as well?"

My mother flinched, looking wounded by the accusation. "She will stay here, and in a few years, Max's younger brother, Alexandre, will come apprentice with Monsieur Girard." The local carpenter. "And when your sister is old enough, Alex and Sofia will be wed."

"If she agrees."

"Yes," my mother conceded. "And you could be instrumental in helping her see the wisdom of that."

"Assuming she survives her trial."

"Don't say such things," she snapped. "Sofia will be fine. She is already exceptionally fast and well-coordinated. As are you."

That was true. I'd beaten Grainger in every race we'd run since we were small children. Even now, when no one was watching, he would sometimes challenge me to a race around the northern village pasture, which inevitably ended with us collapsing into each other's arms and laughing like loons.

"I can't marry this Max, Mama. I don't even know him. And I love Grainger."

She stared at me for a long moment before answering, studying me as if she were assessing my sincerity. And finally she sighed, her breath a puffy white cloud against the dark night. "You will at least give Max a chance to win your heart. He'll be in Oakvale soon."

"He's coming here? Why?"

"To court you, of course. To get to know you in advance of your marriage. If you agree, you're to be wed . . . well, as soon as the next full moon."

Shock washed over me like an icy dip in the river. "That isn't possible. There's still the marchet. He'll have to—"

"That's all already taken care of. The Bernards are very eager to have you, Adele. He will treasure you. The entire village will love you."

My chest felt tight. I felt as if I were being carried along in the wake of my mother's plans for me, like a cart hauled behind a galloping horse.

How could everything have changed so quickly?

"You can't possibly be sure of any of that. Just because you and Papa were happy—"

"That wasn't always true for your father and me. It took some time, but though our marriage began as a strategic arrangement, it blossomed into a very special connection. We shared my secret from the beginning, and that became an iron-clad bond between us. We grew to love each other very much. And he loved you and Sofia even more. He wanted this safety and security for you, Adele. He traveled to Ashborne himself to negotiate the betrothal. He would want you to at least give Maxime a chance."

I groaned. That was the one statement she knew I would not argue with. I'd never gone against my father's wishes while he was alive, and I wasn't going to start now. At least, not without a reason that didn't sound like the whining of a spoiled girl over her own good fortune. Which meant I would have to meet this Max. I'd have to get to know him well enough to find a valid objection to the union.

"Fine."

"You will give him a chance to court you?"

I crossed my arms over the front of my cloak. "Do I have any choice?"

"Of course you have a choice. As I said, if you don't like

him—if you honestly can't imagine ever growing to like him—you do not have to marry him."

"But the people of Ashborne will suffer for my decision."

"Yes. I won't lie to you about that. Your betrothal is about more than the union itself. More than the children you will have. It is about protecting an entire village whose guardian will soon be too old to carry the mantle all on her own."

"That isn't fair, Mama."

"Life isn't fair, Adele. And without us, eventually places like Oakvale and Ashborne will be swallowed by the dark wood."

So many lives, all dependent upon my decisions. My discretion and my dedication to a mission I'd only just discovered.

The weight of such a responsibility threatened to crush me.

With a sigh, I turned away from my mother and marched quietly toward the edge of the village.

NINE

I held my tongue as we snuck through the dark, swallowing a series of objections to my arranged betrothal that I couldn't bring myself to voice, because they all boiled down to a single thought: This isn't fair.

That was the complaint of a child, and airing it would not earn my mother's respect or any further consideration of Grainger's proposal. So I decided to let everything I'd just learned truly sink in before I tried to argue further. I had no interest in meeting Maxime Bernard, but I could not contend with any of my mother's points, save one.

Grainger would *never* lead a mob against me. He loved me. We'd spent the past two years counting down the days until I would be old enough to wed, and we'd expected my mother to say yes immediately. Her hesitance had hit me like a tree crashing into the forest floor.

She wanted me to marry a shield. An anchor. A man beloved

enough by his own community and dedicated enough to my calling to protect me. And those were all things I wanted, too.

But I wanted them from Grainger.

As we stepped between two of the torches and into the forest, however, fear and excitement began to buzz within me, centering my thoughts on the challenge ahead. I'd been in the dark wood several times, but I'd never gone in *looking* for monsters.

I followed in my mother's silent footsteps, and light from the torches faded within a few feet as an unnatural chill washed over me. Then, a few minutes after we started walking, a violent screeching speared my brain like meat on a skewer. My hands flew to my ears, trying to block out the sharp, painful sound.

"You will get used to it, in time," my mother assured me as she flipped back one side of her cloak to expose her hatchet.

"What kind of creature makes such a horrible sound?"

"Most of the beasts of the dark wood have no proper name," she said. "That particular creature is a monstrous woman-like beast from the waist up, and a serpent from the waist down. And like most of the monsters we hunt, she feeds upon human flesh."

"A man-eating snake woman. Is she our target?"

"No, tonight, we're after goblins. There is a nest of them near here."

"Why are we after goblins, exactly?"

"Because they're plentiful and relatively easy to kill. That makes them good for skill-building early in a guardian's training." My mother suddenly swung her arm, and her hatchet thunked through a woody coil reaching for her foot. "Watch out for the vines."

I pulled my hatchet from my belt, on alert for anything slithering toward me from the darkness. "So, how do we find these goblins?"

"They'll find us."

"That's unsettling. What do they look like?"

She frowned at me from the shadows. "They look exactly like I described them in every bedtime story you heard as a child. So, you tell me. What does a goblin look like, Adele?"

Sudden understanding hit me like a frigid winter gust. *Of course* those weren't just stories.

"Um . . ." I fought the urge to close my eyes as I thought back over the tales she used to tell me. The tales she still told Sofia. "They're large, and their skin has a greenish cast. They have pointed ears, near the tops of their skulls, which gives them extraordinary hearing. And their eyes bulge a bit from their faces, though their sense of sight is not as well-developed as their hearing."

"Very good." She looked truly pleased with me for the first time since I'd returned alive from my trial.

"So it's their ears that will lead them to us?"

"It certainly will be, if you don't start whispering." But she smiled as she handed me her hatchet—virtually identical to my own—and when I took it, she untied the cord around her neck and shrugged out of her cloak.

"What are you doing?"

"Demonstrating." My mother's head turned sharply to the left, as a grunt echoed toward us from deeper in the forest, followed by a heavy thump and a chorus of twigs breaking. "They usually hunt alone, but I hear two heading for us right now. From the east."

I squinted into the dark, listening, but though I could hear the heavy footsteps, I couldn't distinguish two sets. Maybe that ability would come with experience?

She stepped out of her shoes as she reached back to untie the laces at the back of her bodice, then she tugged on the material to loosen it quite a bit. "One hatchet in each hand. It might take you a bit to get the hang of using one left-handed, but the skill will come with time."

"I— Mama, what are you doing?" I demanded in a fierce whisper as she knelt on the forest floor.

"Changing. I'll take the first one that appears. You take the second." And with that, she dropped onto her hands and knees, and before I could ask another question, her body began to . . . transform.

Her face elongated into the familiar shape of a muzzle, accompanied by a chorus of rapidly popping joints. Her arms thinned into muscular wolf legs, her palms plumping and fingers shortening as her hands became paws. Odd shapes rose and fell beneath the material of her bodice as her torso underwent an unseen transition, and finally, fur sprouted across her bare front legs in a reddish wave.

I could only stare as my mother crawled out of the confines of her dress and looked up at me from the forest floor. The entire process had taken only seconds. Would my own transition ever come so quickly?

Though she was only two-thirds the size of the whitewulf I'd killed the day before, she was still more than waist high on me, with a compact musculature that made me wonder what I'd looked like in my own redwulf form.

But before I could come to terms with the sight of my mother transforming into a wolf, another set of grunts echoed from the forest, and this time they sounded much closer.

My mother turned toward the sound, her entire frame tense. She began to growl.

My grip tightened on both hatchets, and as heavy footsteps thumped toward us, my pulse began to race with a potent combination of adrenaline and fear. Which was when I realized that I could *feel* the goblins coming. My heart seemed to beat in time with their steps. Energy buzzed across my skin, pulsing harder the closer they came. Yet when the first goblin finally lurched into sight from the distant shadows, I gasped with surprise.

It—no *he*; it was definitely a he—was huge!

Despite the weight of its footfalls and my mother's descriptions of a large greenish monster, I'd drastically underestimated the goblin's size in my imagination. This beast was easily one and a half times my height and at least three times my width. It was barrel-chested, its legs the size of small tree trunks, with arms like battering rams and fists nearly as big as my head.

Yet for all its obvious strength, the goblin was slow, and we redwulfs were *fast*.

Before I'd truly processed the monster's size, my mother leapt at it, snarling with her lips pulled back to reveal a muzzle full of sharp teeth. As her front paws slammed into the beast's chest, the goblin opened its mouth, and I got my first look at its most terrifying feature.

Saliva dripping from a triple-row of sharply pointed teeth, the goblin snapped powerful jaws at my mother's head. If he'd hit his mark, she would have lost an ear, but her momentum drove the beast backward. It stumbled a few steps, and as it fell to the forest floor, my mother clamped her muzzle around the monster's throat and ripped the flesh to shreds.

An instant later, the second goblin broke through the underbrush.

Stunned by what I'd just seen, I lost precious seconds while the goblin barreled toward me, breaking branches from trees with every lumbering swing of its arms. My mother yipped, startling me into awareness, and my hands tightened around the handles of both hatchets. And finally, I lurched into motion, my pulse pounding so hard that my head began to spin.

I swung with my right hand, aiming for the beast's head, but at the last second, I realized he was too tall. I'd never be able to reach. So I adjusted my aim. My blade thunked into the monster's thick left forearm, sinking in so deeply that I couldn't pull it out.

The goblin hissed at me, spittle flying from that triple-row of bared teeth, and when he jerked his arm up, I lost my grip on the hatchet, which remained lodged in his flesh.

The beast roared at me as he lunged, and I dove to miss a blow from his massive right fist. I landed in the underbrush and rolled over, dodging meaty feet as the monster tried to stomp on me like a bug. As I shoved myself upright, I transferred my remaining hatchet into my right hand, then I swung it as I spun, avoiding a blow that whooshed through the air where my head had been a second earlier.

This time my hatchet glanced off the goblin's other arm, so I swung again as I ducked another blow. My blade bit into the meat of his thigh, and he howled as I wrenched the weapon free. Blood poured from the wound, and I struck again and again, leaving gaping gashes in his pale green flesh. Dodging blows—until one landed on my shoulder.

The hit threw me sideways, the forest zooming past in a dark blur as I flailed in the air. My arm hit the trunk of a tree, and I crumpled to the ground. Air burst from my lungs, and I gasped, trying to refill them.

The earth shook as the goblin ran at me. He was slow, and I should have had plenty of time to get out of the way, but I *couldn't . . . breathe . . .*

The beast bellowed as he grabbed me by my left arm, drool hanging from his pointy chin, and lifted me two feet off the ground. He roared in my face, spraying me with more foul spittle as his rotten breath blew back my hood.

My mother yipped, but I didn't have time to process more than the simple imperative in that wordless command.

Do something, Adele!

I had no idea what to do. So I closed my eyes and swung my hatchet.

My blade thunked into thick flesh. The beast made a choking sound and lost his grip on my arm. I fell to the ground again, absorbing the impact on my right hip, and when I looked up, I was surprised to find my hatchet buried in the goblin's neck.

He blinked at me, giant hands hovering near the offending weapon for a second. Then he roared again as he pulled it loose and dropped it at my feet.

Blood sprayed the tree trunk at my back, over my head. The goblin gurgled for a moment, choking on his own blood. His hand slapped at the wound, trying to hold it closed, but to no avail.

A second later, he fell, his impact shaking the ground.

I picked up the bloody hatchet, and while I stood, breathing heavily from my effort to take down the beast, my mother threw her head back and howled.

The dark wood replied with a chorus of shrieks and howls from all directions, some obviously echoing from quite far away. They didn't seem to be celebrating with my mother—the vocalizations felt more aggressive than anything—but the sound sent a euphoric tingle sweeping through me.

My mother crouched near her dress, and while she changed

with a series of soft pops and creaks echoing from her joints, I rotated my left arm, trying to work the ache out of my shoulder. I could already feel a huge bruise forming on my other arm, from my impact with the tree.

"You did very well, Adele," my mother said as she sat up, in human form once again.

"I lost one of the hatchets."

She pulled her dress over her head, then brushed dirt from it and turned so I could help tighten the laces of her bodice. "You will soon be strong enough to wrench it free even if it hits bone. Why didn't you throw one at his head? You might have felled him without even having to get close."

"That felt like a big risk to take, considering that I've never done this before. I had no idea whether I could hit what I was aiming for."

When I'd secured her laces, she shook out her red cloak, then she bent to wrench the aforementioned hatchet from the dead goblin's arm. "I taught you to throw a hatchet when you were ten years old, and I don't think you've missed your target since."

"Yes, but that was for sport! For fun!" She'd challenged me to best her, using a target nailed to the side of our cowshed. "This was an entirely different situation!"

"*This*"—she gestured with one hand at the two dead goblins—"is exactly why I taught you to throw a hatchet, Adele."

Of *course* recreational hatchet throwing was really guardian training, just as her bedtime stories were actually instructional.

Did learning to knead dough, darn socks, and churn butter somehow also teach me to kill something?

"I'm sorry. Next time I'll throw the hatchet."

My mother took my chin in one hand and smiled at me. "You did a *great* job. It was your first goblin kill, and it was a complete success. Keep that in mind when you feel critical of your effort." She let me go and tucked a strand of hair behind my ear. "And your victory was unaided."

"Because you only stood there and watched. Please tell me you would have pitched in, if I'd needed it."

She threw her cloak over her shoulders with a dramatic swirling motion that seemed born of much practice. "Of course. My goal is to train you, not to get you killed. Though it would be in everyone's best interest if you were fairly self-sufficient in the dark wood before Madame Bernard takes over your training."

"Why would she do that? If I am to marry Maxime"—and I still had *no* intention of doing that—"why can't the wedding wait until I am fully trained?"

"Because that will likely take years, during which Ashborne will have only one guardian, while Oakvale has three. They need you, Adele." My mother bent to put on her shoes. "That's the entire reason you were betrothed."

"I am to be married to a man I've never met *entirely* because another village needs the protection of a woman they would burn as a witch, if they were privy to the details?"

"Precisely. It is a noble calling, not an easy one, Adele."

"Perhaps, if people are so eager to burn the women who would protect them, they do not deserve that protection."

She frowned as she slid her hatchet into its loop on her belt. "Grainger is among those people. As are Elena and Simon. Do they not deserve your protection?"

"Of course they do. But I cannot believe any of them would burn me for a witch, if they knew the truth. They are my *friends*." Though Grainger was much more than that.

"They *would* burn you, Adele. And the flip side of that coin is that if any of them were a threat to the village, you would take the necessary action, even if it broke your heart. *That is the mission*."

"They aren't a threat to the village."

"But someday they could become one. Just like your father did. And if that happens, you *will* do what needs to be done. As I did."

A sick feeling churned in my gut as the bitter reality of my new responsibility truly sank in. "I might be asked to kill *anyone*."

"That isn't likely. But it is certainly possible." My mother turned away, hiding her grief from me. "I know that better than anyone."

"So then, what am I supposed to do? Isolate myself, like you do? Reject friendship? Refuse love, because someday I may lose it?"

She turned to face me again, frowning. "I'm not—"

"You have no close friends, and you push Monsieur Martel away at every turn."

"Adele, I *had* love, and you will too." She sighed. "But what I had with your father would never be possible with Monsieur Martel. I cannot trust him like I trusted your papa."

"You don't know that."

Another sigh. "You don't have to isolate yourself, Adele. But you do have to be prepared to make hard choices. And to make them quickly, with the greater good in mind." With that, she took off through the forest, without waiting to be sure I would follow. Which, of course, I did.

For a while, we walked in silence, listening to the sounds from the woods. On alert for prey. Then she spoke again, softly. Without turning. "I understand how difficult it will be for you to give Maxime a chance."

"How can you possibly—"

She stopped and spun to face me so abruptly that I nearly collided with her. "Why do you think it is that Monsieur Martel pursues me so ardently?"

I shrugged. "Because the blacksmith has three children and no wife." And because my mother was beautiful enough to make him disregard rumors of a Duval curse. "He thinks that wedding you would solve all of his problems, as well as warm the empty side of his bed." The very thought of which angered me on my father's behalf, despite the fact that he'd been gone for so long

126

I could hardly remember the shape of his features, most days.

Despite the fact that I'd just criticized my mother for isolating herself.

"Adele!" My mother seemed more scandalized than a woman who'd stood naked in the forest minutes ago had any right to be. "Though I suppose that is part of it, the truth is that there are two other widows in the village as well as a handful of unmarried girls a year or two older than you who would fit the bill and be happy for a blacksmith's income. Monsieur Martel pursues me because we were quite fond of each other, in our youth."

"You . . . you had a lover, before Papa?" I frowned at her, feeling like I was meeting my own mother for the first time.

"Not a lover, really. But had he asked for my hand, I would have given it to him. Before I knew about my own betrothal."

"And did you accept Papa just like that? With no hesitance?"

"Of course not. I'm not asking you to do that either. I'm asking you to give him a chance. Give Ashborne a chance to earn your service, with Maxime as their emissary."

I exhaled slowly. "I've already said that I would."

"Good. He'll be coming soon with a merchant and will stay for a few weeks, to help with a carpentry project. During that time, I expect you to be true to your word." Excitement sparkled in her eyes again, heralding a change of subject. "And now that that's settled, it's time for you to call forth your wolf form." She reached forward and slid my hatchet free from its loop at my waist. "Before we patrol for the night, we're going to clear out that goblin nest, and this time you're going to be on four paws."

"How many are in a nest?" I asked as I reached back to loosen my own bodice.

"The most I've ever seen is eight."

Which meant we'd only killed a quarter of them so far.

My mother's smile gleamed in a beam of moonlight as I sank onto my knees in a drift of dry foliage. "It's going to be a long night, Adele. And I promise you're going to love every second of it!"

TEN

"I dreamed you were gone," Sofia said as a stream of milk hit the bucket clamped between my feet. She was supposed to be shoveling manure, but my sister had a way of delaying unpleasant chores for as long as I'd let her.

My hand stilled on the cow's warm udder. "You dreamed I died?"

"No, that you left in the middle of the night. With Mama. I dreamed I woke up, and I was all alone. But then I fell asleep again, and when I woke up, you were both there. And you overslept, you lazy bones!"

The tension in my arms eased, and I yawned as I continued milking. "You can't accuse me of oversleeping unless you actually *let* me sleep." Instead, she'd held my nose until I woke up gasping. And in the hour since, I'd built a fire in the bread oven, fetched water from the well, and begun the milking. "Keep shoveling, little goose," I scolded, and she stuck her tongue out at me. "And if you wake up alone again, rest assured that you are dreaming. Go back to sleep, and everything will be fine in the morning."

Sofia sank her pitchfork into the hay on the other side of our small cowshed, but instead of lifting her load, she squeaked, and the long wooden handle hit the ground. "What's that?" she asked, and I turned to see her pointing at something in the dark rear corner. "Adele, what's happened?"

I stood, taking the bucket with me so the cow couldn't kick it over, and squinted into the dim corner, where I found several stray feathers suspended in a thick, drying puddle of . . . blood. My hand clenched around the bucket handle and I gasped. "Sofia, go count the hens."

But she only stared at me with wide eyes.

"Go!"

She jumped, startled, then darted out of the small shed and across our narrow yard to the dome of mud and straw where our hens roosted, when they weren't pecking around in the dirt for bugs and dropped bits of grain. We were supposed to have four hens, at the moment, but—

"Two in the yard, and one in here," Sofia called out. "One's missing! The new fat one, from Monsieur Laurent!" She raced back into the cowshed, face flushed from the cold. "Is there another fox? Remember the one that ate the Girards' chicks last summer?"

"Yes, Grainger mentioned one had been spotted in town.

Here. Finish milking for me." I tried to hand Sofia the bucket, but she backed away from me.

"That's *your* chore!"

"Don't be a brat. I'll be right back." I shoved the bucket at her, and she took it because even at eight years old, she knew better than to spill milk.

I was on my way into the house to tell my mother about the dead hen when Grainger called my name. I looked up to see him headed across the village square toward me. "No patrol today?" I said in greeting.

He was wearing his everyday tunic and didn't have his sword.

"I'll be working at the sawmill today and tomorrow. I break for lunch at noon, in case you were wondering."

"As it happens, I *was* wondering!" I said with a smile. "I could bring bread and some vegetable stew, if you'd like to dine with me."

His smile warmed me from the inside. "I would be delighted."

"Though . . ." I frowned, feigning hesitation. "People might start to talk, Monsieur Colbert."

His smile widened and his gaze found my mouth, where it hung as if it were caught. "I certainly hope so."

Warmth gathered in my cheeks. What was I doing? I'd just promised my mother that I would give another boy a chance to win my heart. But did that mean I could no longer spend time with Grainger? What would I tell him about this Maxime, when he arrived?

"We have a fox," I blurted out, ruining the moment with my own nerves, as the complicated consequences of my promise to my mother suddenly became clear.

Grainger laughed. "An unusual pet. Whatever will you call it?"

"I'll call it the lining of my new shoes, if you'll be so kind as to dispense with it for me." Foxes rarely ventured into the village proper, because of the abundance of vegetation and rodents skittering through the fields on the edge of town, but they were the occasional nuisance. Though they usually stole eggs, this particular fox's offense was much more serious. "It ate our new hen overnight."

"Oh." His teasing smile faded. "I will keep an eye out. It's probably the same one Madame Girard spotted the other day."

"Thank you. I—"

"Sofia!" a young voice called, and I turned to see Jeanne Paget racing across the village square. She skidded for a moment on a frozen puddle, her hair flying out behind her. "There's a wagon!" she shouted in my direction as my sister came rushing through the alley from behind our cottage. "A merchant! It just emerged from the dark wood on the west side of the village," she added, stumbling to a stop next to my sister.

That was the second merchant in three days, and the fact that this one arrived intact likely meant that my grandmother had been protecting it.

Because my mother had told her to expect it.

My heart began to thump beneath my breastbone.

"Go and tell your mother," I said, and Jeanne nodded, then raced off toward the thatcher's cottage. "You too," I said with a glance at Sofia. "If we're lucky, he'll have honey." We were nearly out after making Monsieur Laurent's apple tart.

Sofia raced through the door of our cottage just as the rattle of wagon wheels drew my attention to the other end of the square. Grainger and I turned as the merchant rolled into view. His wagon was a simple, uncovered four-wheeled cart, piled high with barrels and baskets and pulled by an ox. The merchant himself walked alongside the beast of burden, guiding him around the frozen puddles and deep ruts in the dirt path.

"He must be from Oldefort," Grainger said, and that made sense, because Oldefort was the closest village to ours. "Maybe he came looking for Tom and his parents. Maybe he can tell us Tom's real name."

I shook my head. "It hasn't been long enough yet for them to be missed. For help to be sent."

The merchant stopped in the middle of the square, where he pulled something from his pocket to feed the ox, then he exhaled in obvious relief as he began blowing out the candles burning in the six lanterns hanging from all sides of his cart. The cause of his relief was obvious: he'd made it through the dark wood, armed only with firelight and—

A boy hopped off the back of the cart and tossed a large, oddly bulging leather rucksack over his shoulder. He blew out the last lamp for the merchant and patted the ox almost affectionately.

Then he turned, scanning what he could see of our little village. His focus lingered on my hair and his gaze met mine.

He smiled as if he knew me.

"Ashborne," I whispered, and Grainger turned to me with a confused look.

"What?"

"The merchant isn't from Oldefort. He's from Ashborne." As was the boy—the young man—who'd hitched a ride.

"How do you know?"

I looked up at Grainger, pointedly ignoring the new arrival. "Don't you have to get to the sawmill?"

"Yes. Of course. Though I hate to miss the excitement."

Based on the number of men and women already converging on the visiting merchant carrying bundles of wool and dishes of butter—one rolling a barrel of ale—the rest of the village shared his sentiment.

"I'm sure he'll stay overnight, at least," I assured Grainger.

"You're right. I'll see you at lunch." He squeezed my fingers for a moment, then he took off toward the Laurents' sawmill on the edge of town, where half of the village men would already be hard at work.

The young man holding the rucksack watched him go, his expression inscrutable, then his focus found me again.

I turned and headed toward my cottage, and I nearly ran right into my mother on her way out, carrying several fragrant bundles wrapped in clean nettlecloth. "*Chère*, will you please grab the cheese from the shelf? And that basket of dried figs."

"I . . ." I'd been planning to finish cleaning the cowshed for Sofia. Because I'd rather occupy myself with a pitchfork full of manure than go meet the boy who'd come all the way from Ashborne to ruin my life.

"Adele," my mother whispered fiercely. "You promised."

"What did she promise?" Sofia asked, coming out of the cottage with a wooden crock of butter in her arms.

Mama gave me a look. "To help carry our wares."

"This is the last of our cheese," I pointed out as I reluctantly headed inside and pulled it from the shelf.

"We can make more," she insisted. "Assuming the merchant is even in the market for cheese." But even if he wasn't, he would buy ours. Mama made the best cheese in Oakvale.

I hooked my arm beneath the handle of the fig basket and followed my mother and sister into the village square, where we joined the crowd already gathered around the merchant's cart—a mid-winter surprise, unexpected by everyone but us.

"I'll take that." Mama shifted her burden into one arm and took the cheese from me. "And you can set the basket down."

Before I could ask why she suddenly no longer needed my help, I became aware of a presence behind me. "Madame Duval?" a deep voice said, and I whirled around, so startled I almost kicked over the fig basket.

My mother turned a brilliant smile on the dark-haired boy with the bulging rucksack. "You must be Maxime Bernard."

"Max," he insisted, while I stared at the mud beneath my feet, trying to cool the flames burning in my cheeks. Trying to deny a surprising urge to lift my head and take a good look at the man my parents intended for me to marry. To see if he was as handsome up close as he'd appeared from across the square.

Not that that would sway me one single bit . . .

"It is a pleasure to meet you, Madame," he continued. "You are exactly as my mother described you. Though I wasn't expecting *this* delightful little dove." He reached out and ruffled my sister's hair, and she beamed up at him as if he were her new best friend.

"This is Sofia," my mother said. "And this"—her gaze landed on me with an expectant weight—"is my oldest daughter. Adele."

"Adele." The boy held his hand out for mine, and when I didn't take it, he only gave me a crooked smile, which triggered the appearance of a single dimple in his right cheek. "It is my *greatest* pleasure to make your acquaintance."

Well, that felt like a bit much.

"Monsieur Bernard," I said with a noncommittal nod, and to his credit, his smile didn't falter at my less than enthusiastic greeting.

From the gathered crowd, Elena lifted one eyebrow at me over the basket full of folded linen she held, waiting for her turn to haggle with the merchant. I could only give her a shrug in reply, well aware that half the village was watching my interaction with the newcomer.

"I'm Max," he said, as if he hadn't just introduced himself to my mother. "I've come from Ashborne to aid your carpenter with a project."

Yes, *that* was why he'd come.

"Well then, I suppose you'll want to go meet Monsieur Girard. He's just down that path, to the right." I pointed, in order to be hospitable and helpful. And to hurry him along.

"Oh, I don't think he'll be expecting me just yet." Max winked at me. He actually winked! Then his voice dropped into a faux conspiratorial whisper. "He likely doesn't even know I'm in town yet."

"In that case, Adele, why don't you show Max around the village?" My mother's voice flowed thick and sweet like honey, and I scowled at her, begging her silently not to throw me at him *quite* so obviously.

"Don't you need my help here?"

"I think your sister can manage the figs. Can't you, *ma chérie*?"

"Of course!" Sofia, that little traitor, looked thrilled by the idea of so much responsibility.

"Well, I . . ." I could feel half the crowd watching me, and I knew Grainger would hear about this within the hour.

"I promise not to keep you long." Max extended his arm, bent at the elbow. "If you would do me the honor."

"Of course." But only because there was no polite way to

get out of such a request. Yet I did *not* take his arm. "That's our cottage, over there." I pointed across the square as I led him away from the crowd. "My mother is the village baker, so it's always quite warm inside."

"And I would imagine it smells nice."

"Like rye bread, mostly. But she also makes sweet breads and tarts, and the occasional meat pie."

"That all sounds amazing, after three days of eating stale flatbread and dried squirrel."

"It took you three days to get here from Ashborne?"

Maxime nodded, and a lock of dark hair fell over his forehead, shading his bright hazel eyes. "About half of that spent in the dark wood. We can't go very fast in the forest, of course." Because neither he nor the merchant could see beyond the fall of their lamplight. And the path to the north meandered quite a bit, according to Gran.

"Monsieur Girard lives down that way, where you can see sawdust spilling out onto the path. And just down there, on the edge of the village, is the sawmill." I pointed at the water wheel, where we could see two men with pickaxes breaking up ice in the race, which diverted water from the river to power the mill. On the edge of town, more men would be punching through the river ice to expose the current beneath—back-breaking labor the village depended upon. "I suspect you'll see quite a bit of both the carpenter and the sawmill."

"Should we head that way, then?" Maxime started down the

path, but I grabbed his arm and pulled him to a halt. Grainger would hear about the newcomer soon enough. I'd rather not have him see me escorting another boy around the village.

"Later. Down this way we have Monsieur Paget, the thatcher, and Monsieur Martel, the blacksmith."

"I feel like your entire village is staring at us," Maxime said as I led him out of the square and down the path, toward the smithy.

"They are. We don't get many strangers in Oakvale, and a winter visitor is especially rare because of the danger of the dark wood."

"It's much the same in Ashborne," he replied. "And my friends will no doubt stare even harder when they see such a beautiful woman on my arm."

I stopped, heedless of the slushy mud sliding beneath my shoes, and turned to glare up at him. "You're making quite a few assumptions, Monsieur Bernard."

Finally, his crooked grin faded. "I apologize, Adele. Mademoiselle Duval. I—" His mouth snapped shut while he studied my expression, evidently reassessing his approach. "I'd assumed your mother had explained why I'm here."

"To apprentice with Monsieur Girard." I tilted my head and stared up at him with my most innocent expression. If he'd truly come here to court me, he could at least declare his intentions properly. "Is there no carpenter of sufficient skill in Ashborne?"

Max flinched as if I'd slapped him, and guilt settled into the pit of my stomach. "My father is an excellent carpenter. As am I. I am here to *assist* Monsieur Girard, not to apprentice with him. But that's not . . . I mean, again, I'd assumed your mother had explained . . ."

"Pardon me. I shouldn't have teased you." I pasted on a smile, trying to pass off my jab as a joke while guilt continued to eat at me. I hadn't intended to insult his father. "I know why you're here, and I promised my mother that I would give you a chance. But you should know that someone has already asked for my hand. Here, in Oakvale. So, I'm really only doing this for my mother. Because I promised."

Max blinked, and a flicker of uncertainty passed over his expression. "Well, I am glad to hear that you're a woman of your word," he said at last.

A second wave of guilt washed over me at the irony of his sentiment; whatever I had promised my mother, I couldn't believe that anyone but Grainger would have a place in my heart.

I cleared my throat and started forward on the path again. "Two of our most skilled alewives live down this way. Of them, Madame Gosse, the potter's wife, makes the best brew." I lowered my voice to a whisper. "And after a mugful, you can *almost* abide her company."

Maxime's laugh brought out that dimple again. His hazel eyes sparked with a mischief that said he wasn't going to let me change the subject. "Adele. I didn't realize I was coming to Oakvale to compete for your hand, but I relish the opportunity."

He leaned closer and whispered, "I am burdened with a bit of a competitive streak."

"Wonderful," I said, and he chuckled at my lack of enthusiasm. "But this really isn't a competition. I promised to give you a chance, but I never said it would be a *good* chance."

A somber determination took over his features. "I must admit, I'd hoped you'd be as eager to meet me as I was—as I am—to meet you."

"I am sorry to disappoint you, but as I understand it, you've had a bit longer than I have to get used to the idea of our . . . betrothal." The word still felt strange on my tongue.

"Oh, I see." He took another long look around the village before turning back to me. "When, exactly, did your mother explain all this to you?"

"Last night," I admitted, and somehow the sympathy that took over his features irked me even more than his overconfidence had.

"Well, that is unfortunate, but I think I understand. From your perspective, this other man's interest in you predates mine."

It wasn't only an issue of timing, but . . . "And from your perspective?" I was honestly curious.

"I've looked forward to making your acquaintance for three years." He captured my gaze with an intensity that made his hazel eyes look more green than brown. "I learned about my mother's mission when I was sixteen, just like you did, and that's when she began preparing me to meet you. To start our lives together and move forward with our destiny."

Our destiny?

"And?" I found myself oddly captivated by the earnest note in his voice. "Now that you've met me, what do you think?" I spread my arms, inviting him to truly look at me for the first time. "How do I measure up with . . . whatever you imagined?"

"You are beautiful. And fiercely outspoken," he added, without taking his focus from my eyes.

"And that disappoints you?" Of course it would disappoint him. What man would want a woman with a tongue sharper than her bread knife? Wasn't that why I was taking him to task so adamantly, even having just met him? To foster his disinterest?

"Not in the least." Max smiled. "I expected your tongue to be as sharp as your hatchet, your will as strong as your . . . fighting form. I haven't seen you in action yet, but—"

"You want to see me fight?" Surprise thickened my voice, and I started walking again, drawing us farther from the square full of my friends and neighbors.

"Of course. I understand you've only just had your trial, but I look forward to seeing what you bring to our union. Our *potential* union," he amended.

And for a moment, I could only stare at him.

"What I bring to this potential union . . ." I mused, repeating his words as I started us down the path again. "What I bring to your entire village, I suppose."

"That is our hope."

"But it's my understanding that your village doesn't know it needs my help. As my own doesn't know."

"That's true. But *I* know. My family knows. So I suppose you're *our* hope. Though I didn't realize our arrangement was in such doubt."

I let a moment pass in silence. "And what is it *you* bring to this potential union?"

"Whatever you need." He said it without hesitation. And with a crooked smile that could only be called charming. "An ally. A partner. A confidant. I've built us a cottage in Ashborne. It's small, but it is quite well made, if I do say so myself, and there's room to build on, should you need more than I've accounted for."

I considered that in silence. A cottage was no small thing. Most newly married couples had to stay with family until arrangements could be made for a home of their own, which often took years.

"And children," Maxime added at last. "I will give you children. Daughters, hopefully. But I wouldn't mind a son, as well. If you're willing."

"Monsieur Bernard, I'm afraid we take what we're given, in that regard."

He laughed loudly enough to draw more stares our way, from the square now in the distance. "I meant, if you're willing to give me children," he said. "I don't want to make any more assumptions."

Again, I responded with silence. But this time my pause felt . . . thoughtful. He wasn't horrible, this Maxime. A little too sure of himself, but definitely not horrible. Maybe he and I could still be friends, after Grainger and I wed.

ELEVEN

By the time we made it back to the village square, my mother and sister were near the front of the line at the merchant's cart. When we joined them, Mama began introducing Max to our neighbors as the son of a childhood friend she hadn't seen in years, and everyone seemed eager to talk to him. After he'd shaken hands with half the village, she insisted that I show him the bakery and give him something to eat, promising that she and Sofia would join us shortly.

I waited for him to politely decline, but instead, he thanked my mother for her hospitality. Leaving me with no choice but to show him my home.

"This hinge is loose," he noted as I pushed the front door open. "I could fix it for you."

"I'm sure Mama would appreciate that," I said as I gestured for him to take a seat at the table. He sat, eagerly studying the room around him while I served him a hunk of bread and a bowl of last night's vegetable stew, which had been kept warm over the banked fire all night.

"Did you bake this?" Max asked around a bite of bread. He'd bitten off a huge chunk, without bothering to soften it in his stew like any normal person.

"Yes. Several days ago. Careful, or you'll break a tooth."

"Nonsense. It's wonderful," he insisted.

I laughed. "You're a terrible liar, Maxime Bernard."

"Okay, it's a little stale, but that has nothing to do with the skill of the baker and everything to do with the passage of time. And anyway, I was practically raised on stale bread and pottage—"

As was I, and everyone else in our little village.

"—so I find this quite a comforting meal."

"I'm glad, because dinner will look about the same." There was rarely much else to eat in the winter.

Max's grin grew. "Are you inviting me for dinner?"

"No, I—" My face flushed. "I assume you'll be with the Girards by then. I just meant . . . I was trying to be polite."

"Monsieur Girard did offer me housing for the length of my stay, but I've already accepted another invitation." Max carefully watched for my reaction. And suddenly I understood.

"You're staying here? With us?"

"In the cowshed," he said, still watching me. "At your mother's insistence."

Of course my mother had invited him. Which explained

why she'd been so eager to introduce him to our neighbors as a proper acquaintance.

I poured myself a bowl of stew, hoping that a full mouth might prevent my tongue from lashing out in exasperation.

"I should introduce myself to Monsieur Girard this afternoon," Max said, dipping his bread into his bowl. "But I would like to go into the wood with you soon, if you're amenable."

"To watch me hunt?" Why did that thought suddenly make me nervous? I didn't want Maxime. I wanted Grainger, no matter how kind and accepting Max was of my destiny. Yet suddenly the thought that I might be a disappointment to him felt like a paralyzing weight on my chest.

It was one thing for me not to want him. But it would be another thing entirely—an embarrassing, shameful thing—for me to prove myself unworthy of protecting the village of Ashborne.

"Yes," he admitted with a shrug. "And to meet your grandmother. Is it true she lives in the dark wood?"

"What do you know about my grandmother?"

Max blinked at me. "Madame Emelina Chastain is a legend. At least among her fellow guardians."

"Around here, she's considered more . . . eccentric." Mad, actually. I'd once heard Grainger's father say that Gran was too damn stubborn to die, even living surrounded by monsters.

At the time, I'd thought he was right.

"So, she truly lives in the dark wood?" Maxime prodded.

"She truly does," I said with a soft smile as I scooped another bite from my bowl. "I'm going to see her next week. She has a cabin in a clearing, about half an hour's walk from the edge of the forest. Which she evidently beats back with a hatchet, chopping seedlings the moment they take root. I only learned the other day that her cottage wasn't in the wood at all, when it was built. Evidently *her* parents—"

"Adele?"

I spun on my stool to find Grainger standing in the open doorway, his brows arched in disappointment to find me in the company of a strange man. Which was when I remembered that I'd offered to bring him the very lunch I was now eating with Maxime.

"Grainger! Oh, I'm so sorry! I completely forgot about lunch." Though the spoon in my hand seemed to be making a liar out of me. I dropped it in my bowl and stood, then I found that I had nothing to do with my hands.

"And you would be?" Grainger stepped into the room, his wary gaze trained on Max.

"Maxime Bernard." Max stood and offered Grainger his hand.

Grainger shook it without even glancing at me. "You're one of the merchants from Ashborne?"

"Actually, I'm a carpenter, here to assist Monsieur Girard with some woodwork. I only hitched a ride with the merchant. You're a friend of Adele's?"

"I'm sorry." I forced my hands to stop twisting together

before I broke my own fingers. "Max, this is Grainger Colbert. He's a member of the village watch, and he works at the sawmill when they need him."

"The watch." Max glanced at me in surprise, an almost imperceptible wariness in the arch of his brows. The very same sentiment shined in Granger's eyes as the two studied each other.

"Yes, the watch." Grainger's focused shifted to me, then back to Max. "How do you two know each other?"

"My mother and Madame Duval are well acquainted from childhood," Max said, his lunch evidently forgotten. "Which makes me a friend of the family."

"And yet I've never heard your name."

"Adele hasn't mentioned you either," Max returned. And suddenly I felt like I was choking on silent aggression, thick as smoke from a bonfire, as the two of them seemed intent on staring each other down.

"Actually, Maxime, I *did* tell you about him. Just not by name." My words felt so sharp they threatened to cut my tongue on their way out. "Grainger, would you care for some stew?"

"Thank you, I—"

"Well, hello!" My mother pushed past Grainger to enter her own home, which suddenly seemed terribly crowded. "Grainger, I see you've met Maxime?"

"I have." He stepped closer to me to make room for Sofia, who came in carrying a clay pot of honey, our empty fig basket hanging from her arm.

"Let me take that." Max relieved my mother of the sack of salt she carried, leaving her with only a folded stack of nettle-cloth. The merchant had obviously approved of the cheese that had been wrapped in it.

"Thank you. Just put that on the shelf over the oven, if you don't mind." She set her cloth on the larger table usually used for baking, then turned to survey the room with both hands propped on her hips. If she weren't my own mother, I probably wouldn't have noticed the subtle tension in the line of her jaw. "Well, aren't we a crowd today?"

"I'm not staying," Grainger grumbled. "I have to get back to the sawmill. Adele, will you walk with me?"

"I . . . Of course. Won't you take some stew on the way?" I handed him my own bowl without waiting for his reply, then I added a hunk of bread to it.

"Thank you."

"I'll be right back," I said, and as I followed Grainger out the door, my mother drizzled honey onto a large hunk of bread and handed it to my sister, who eagerly dove into a treat that was probably intended to keep her tongue too busy to wag.

"So, Maxime is a friend of your family's?" Grainger said, scooping a spoonful of stew from his bowl as we headed down the muddy path.

"Yes. Though I only met him this morning."

"Your mother likes him," he said around another bite.

150

"She likes you as well," I insisted, nerves buzzing around my insides like a hive of agitated bees.

"Do *you* like him?"

I shrugged, clasping my hands at my back. Wishing I'd grabbed my cloak. "I hardly know him."

"That isn't an answer." He tore a hunk of softened bread off with his teeth.

I couldn't really blame him for feeling threatened, considering the reason that Max had come to Oakvale. "He seems nice enough. In fact, he'll probably make a fine husband—for someone *else*." I smiled up at him as I took his arm.

Grainger's scowl slowly faded as he dipped his bread into the stew. "When you didn't come by the sawmill at noon, I worried that something was wrong. I didn't expect to find you having lunch with another man."

"The morning didn't go how I expected either. I'm sorry that our lunch slipped my mind, but it would have been rude of me not to offer him something to eat, while he was a guest in my home."

"You're right, of course. It's just that he looked so comfortable in your company."

"As I said, I've only just met him, but I suspect Maxime Bernard would look comfortable hopping on one foot, buck naked in a snowstorm." The lie sat heavy in my gut.

But Grainger smiled, evidently appeased. "Well, thank you

for the stew." He sopped up the last of the broth with his bread, then he handed me the empty bowl and spoon. "Will I see you tonight?"

"If you like."

"Oh, wait, I'm on patrol tonight."

"Tomorrow, then," I assured him, and Grainger nodded.

"Tomorrow." He leaned forward to kiss me on the cheek, and his warm lips lingered longer than usual on my skin. Then he turned and headed for the sawmill while I made my way home.

I found my mother alone in our cabin. "Max has gone to meet Monsieur Girard," she said as she ladled stew into a bowl for me from the pot still hanging over the fire. "And Sofia is playing with Jeanne Paget." She set the bowl on the table and poured me a small cup of ale.

"So, what do you think of him? Of Max?"

"He's a bit arrogant." I sat at the table and picked up my spoon. "But also knowledgeable."

"And handsome. Surely you've noticed that he's handsome?"

"Well, I do have eyes." I took a bite and chewed slowly, enjoying my mother's exasperation. "Yes, he's handsome," I finally admitted. And if the stares he'd gotten from the village square were any indication, every woman in Oakvale agreed with my assessment. "But so is Grainger."

"But you can't confide in him the way you can in Max. And that's only going to get worse, as more and more of your life becomes about being a guardian." The wariness in her voice spoke of long hours and exhaustion beyond anything I'd understood before.

She wasn't wrong. But she also wasn't being fair to Grainger. "Mama, I want to take him into the dark wood with me."

"Max?" Her eyes lit up. "I think that's a great—"

"No. Grainger."

That light died. "What? Adele, what do you—?"

"I want to take him with me to see Gran. He's already offered to accompany me any time you can't. So we'll head down the path, and if he happens to notice that I can see better than he can in the dark—"

"No. That's too dangerous."

"I'm not suggesting we tell him anything or let him see me as a wolf. But I think he can be trusted." And I *had* to prove that. "What better way to know for sure than to *ease* him into an understanding of my abilities and see how he reacts?"

"No."

"We'll go slow. I'll point out something just beyond the fall of our lamplight—a flower, or a tree with an interesting shape— and when he raises the lamp to see it better, he'll understand that I have very sharp eyes. And—"

"No."

"And that'll be it for now. I'll just start getting him used to the idea that I can see a *little* better than he can in the dark wood, without giving myself away. And when he accepts that—" My

153

mouth snapped shut. No need to mention the next steps, before I had her on board with the first. "Well, we'll go slowly, is what I'm saying. Just sort of testing the waters."

"And what happens when you're in the dark wood with Grainger and you see a monster? Or someone who needs protection, like that unexpected merchant wagon? Are you going to turn your back on your duty to keep our secret? Because that's what it would come down to. You would have to decide whether to reveal yourself and save a life, or protect our family and let someone die. And if Grainger rushes into the fray, that someone could be *him*. What would you choose, Adele?"

"I—" I stared down into my stew, trying to come up with the right answer to an impossible question. "I don't know," I said at last. "What is the right thing to do, in that situation?"

"There is no right thing to do." My mother pulled out the stool next to mine and sank onto it. "The life of a guardian is full of impossible choices, and the best you can do is avoid putting yourself between a rock and a hard place to begin with. Which means you should *never* be alone in the dark wood with a member of the village watch."

I exhaled, my lips pressed together, because arguing with her would do no good. "I understand."

"Do you? If you show Grainger what you are and he reacts badly, it will be too late. And the truth is that you'd be putting many other guardian families at risk. If word about us gets out, people will start seeing monsters in every shadow. Guardians will be hunted by the very villagers they're trying to protect, and along the way, innocent women suspected of being one of us will be hurt. You have to keep all of that in mind when you decide whom to marry."

"I know," I mumbled, staring hopelessly down into my bowl. But knowing was one thing. Accepting was quite another.

A couple of hours after sundown, a knock echoed from the front door, and I looked up from the apron I was sewing. "Come in!" my mother called out, using a paddle to remove a loaf of bread from the oven.

The front door creaked open, letting in a brisk gust to combat the heat from both ovens, and Max appeared in the doorway. My sister jumped up to greet him, clutching her rag doll to her chest.

"Sofia! How lovely to see you again. I've brought you something." Max knelt and pulled a small object from his pocket. When she squealed with excitement, I saw that he held a little horse, carved from a scrap of wood.

"Just for me?"

He handed the horse to her. "*Especially* for you."

"Well!" Mama beamed at him. "You've certainly managed to charm my youngest daughter!"

"Last week, she was charmed by a bug in the garden," I reminded her, and Max laughed, his hazel eyes lighting up at my jest, and I had to begrudgingly admire his good humor.

My mother brushed flour from her hands and pulled out a

stool for him at the table. "How did you find Monsieur Girard and his workshop?"

"Very well indeed. He has somewhat of a sour expression most of the time, but he smiles out in the workshop—at the very scent of fresh wood, in fact—and he is well-equipped for the work. My father would approve."

"Madame Gosse says he's sour-faced so often because his wife's voice is the very pitch of a rooster's crowing," my sister announced with a giggle.

"Sofia!" my mother scolded. "How would you like people to discuss your voice in such terms?"

"That would be impossible, Madame Duval. Both of your daughters have such lovely speaking voices," Max insisted, and Sofia beamed up at him.

"I've changed my mind." She looked boldly at me with her new toy clutched in one hand. "I think you should marry Maxime."

"Yesterday you said I should marry Grainger. If I left all my choices up to you, I'd never get a thing accomplished."

"You should marry them both!" Sofia declared with another giggle.

"For heaven's sake, child," my mother chided. "Busy your troublesome tongue with some stew, and then off to bed with you."

"I must apologize for my sister," I told Max with a pointed glance at her as she ladled some stew into a bowl for herself. "She doesn't know when to hold her tongue."

"She speaks her mind. There's a certain charm in that."

"Let's hope someone agrees with you, when she's old enough to marry."

"I'm quite certain my little brother would agree."

My hand froze mid-stitch as his declaration hit me like a blow to the gut. I'd forgotten about Max's brother. About my mother's arrangement for Sofia with Alexandre Bernard. Would she find out as suddenly as I had, only after her trial? Was there any real reason she couldn't be told earlier? Would it hurt for her to be better prepared, at least for her betrothal?

With one look at my expression, Max cleared his throat and raised his voice, signaling a change of subject. "Sofia, would you like to see something else I made?"

"Yes!" she shouted around a mouthful of food. "Is it another horse?"

Instead of answering, he sank onto the stool next to hers at the table and bent to pull a small book, bound in soft leather from his satchel.

"What's that?" I asked as I set a bowl in front of him.

"This"—he laid the book on the table, evidently inviting me to examine it—"is the most valuable thing I own. Go ahead."

I picked up the book and untied the thin strips of leather holding it closed, then I folded back the soft front flap. "Where did you get this?" The only books I'd ever seen belonged to the church.

"My mother gave it to me. She spent more than she should have, when a merchant offered it to her. What do you think?"

I flipped through the book, only to discover that most of the pages were blank. Puzzled, I frowned at Max, and he laughed. "It's actually a ledger, intended for bookkeeping, but I use it for another purpose. Start at the beginning."

So I turned to the first page, where I found a drawing of a beautiful woman with round, wide-set eyes and a dimple in her right cheek. She looked a lot like Max. "Your mother?" I guessed.

"Yes."

"You drew this?" I stared at the drawing, stunned. "You're very talented."

"Thank you," he said as he tore a bite from his hunk of bread, avoiding my gaze as if he suddenly felt modest.

My mother clearly wanted a peek at the book, but the hopeful way she was watching us told me she that she wouldn't interrupt our conversation for anything.

Captivated, I turned the page and found a beautiful drawing of a charming little cottage I'd never seen before. The one he'd built for us in his village?

It was small, but pretty—everything he'd promised. This page was an image from the life that was waiting for me in Ashborne, should I choose it, and staring at it suddenly made that alternate path feel *tangible*, where before, it had felt like a . . . like a passing thought, insubstantial as a puff of smoke on the breeze. Something I could just wave away and forget about once Max went home.

Would Ashborne be harder to forget, now that I'd had a glimpse of it?

I turned another page and found an adorable little boy a few years older than Sofia staring out at me. Behind him, looking over his shoulder, stood a man who looked so much like the boy he could only be his father. Around the edges of the page were a series of less detailed sketches of that same man and boy, from various angles, as if Max had been practicing capturing their features.

"Is this your brother?"

"Yes. Alexandre. He's twelve," Max said. "And that's our father, behind him. Alex is training to be a carpenter as well."

Sofia rose from her stool and peered over my shoulder. "He looks a lot like you."

Max smiled. "That's what people tell us. But he's a bit quieter than I am. A little shy. My mother thinks he'll grow out of it."

I certainly hoped so, if he truly intended to court Sofia, some day.

The next page held a drawing of a building I'd know anywhere.

"This is our church!" I turned to Max, astonished. "You drew this since you got here?"

"I had some spare time while Monsieur Girard and his wife were . . . arguing. So I went out to the square to sketch. It's a beautiful building."

"The pride of the village," I told him. "The community came together to build it when I was Sofia's age."

"I'd like to see the inside soon."

"Of course. How long have you been drawing?" I asked as my mother put wooden cups of ale on the table for Max and me. Drawing was not a common hobby in villages such as ours, where paper was scarce. "How did you learn?"

"A couple of years ago, a monk got stuck in Ashborne when the river froze over, so he decided to remain until the thaw, rather than braving a trek through the woods. He stayed in the church, and the village fed him in exchange for his sermons. The first time I delivered food from my mother, I saw him working on something. He explained that he was an illustrator, and he had in his possession several unfinished manuscripts, which he was working on to pass the time.

"I asked if I could watch. Then I asked if he would teach me. And he agreed."

"He taught you to draw people?" Sofia asked.

"No." Max smiled at the memory. "He was mostly working on illuminated letters. Have you seen any?"

My sister shook her head.

"They're highly detailed and colorful letters drawn in a manuscript. The first letter of a book or of a chapter, usually. They can take weeks—sometimes months—to complete. But he showed me how to draw some simpler things, on scraps of paper. And I really enjoyed it."

"You're very good at it," Sofia said.

"Thank you. I find it very relaxing."

"You should draw *monsters!*" she declared, her eyes suddenly aglow with the possibility.

I huffed. "That doesn't sound very relaxing."

"Actually, I think that would be a very interesting challenge," Max said. "Unfortunately, I can't see in the dark wood, so any monsters I draw would have to come from my own imagination."

Sofia shrugged. "Mama makes up stories about them. You could make up drawings."

"Or . . ." I shrugged. "Maybe someday someone who's actually seen the monsters will describe them for you in detail."

Max's smile seemed to light up the whole room. "I cannot imagine a more generous gift."

At once, I understood my mistake. As impressed as I was by his talent and his desire to help the guardians, I hadn't intended to volunteer my own eyes for his art project.

His mother seemed much more suited to that role.

TWELVE

I stepped out of the cottage with a full basket hanging from my arm, my gray cloak draped over my shoulders, bracing myself for a cruel gust of frigid wind. My sister darted around me, a pitchfork in one hand, our empty milk pail in the other, her long red hair flying out behind her as she raced across the patch of dirt behind our home, headed for the cowshed.

"Sofia!" Romy Paget appeared in the mouth of the alley, carrying a leather ball. An instant later, her sister, Jeanne, and little Tom raced to a stop behind her, winded, their cheeks rosy from exercise and from the cold. "Come play with us!"

"Yes, come!" Jeanne called. "We're going to race Tom to the barn, and you're the only one who can beat him."

In the week since I'd found him in the woods, little Tom had yet to say a single word that I knew of. However, he had formed an oddly sweet sort of friendship with the Paget girls, who treated him like a little brother.

162

Sofia dropped the pitchfork and set the pail in the dirt, but I clamped one hand on her shoulder before she could run off with her friends. "She may, after she's done her chores."

"*Please*, will you milk the cow for me?" my sister begged, staring up at me with big green eyes.

"I have deliveries, Sofia. I—"

"Hey, give that back!" Romy shouted, and I turned to see Tom holding the leather ball. Romy tried to take it from him, since he'd clearly just plucked it from her grip, and when she reached for the ball, he bit her.

Romy screamed, clutching her arm, where blood welled from the wound.

"*Non!*" Jeanne snatched the ball from Tom, her little brows furrowed. "We do *not* bite! You go back home right now." She pointed in the direction of her cottage, and little Tom hung his head as he sulked off toward the Pagets' home, looking more confused than contrite.

"Let me see." I knelt next to Romy, reaching for her arm, but she brushed away her tears and swiped one hand over the bite, smearing a few small drops of blood across her skin.

"It's fine." She sniffled. "He just doesn't know any better."

"So I see." I stood and ruffled her hair. "Why don't you go home and let your mother put a poultice on that? When Sofia finishes her work, she can come over. But maybe you three could play poppets today, and leave Tom alone to think about his behavior?"

"Okay." Pouting, Romy waved to my sister, then she and Jeanne headed in the direction of their cottage.

"Milk and muck." I pointed at the bucket and the pitchfork. *"Then* you may go play."

"Fine." Sofia picked up the bucket, and I smiled at her dramatic pout as I headed down the alley.

"Elena!" I called as I rounded the front of our cottage, pleased to find her sitting in the village square. "You've saved me a trip!" I headed across the square toward a bench made of a split log, where she and Simon were seated.

The flush in her cheeks said I was interrupting a private conversation, and his smile told me it had been going very well. In the days since their betrothal, many of Elena's fears had been allayed through nothing more than the charm of Simon's company.

"I have your mother's order. Two loaves of rye, as well as a little raisin tart, in thanks for your help with the churning yesterday."

"Thank you," she said as I pulled the cloth-wrapped bundle from my basket. "Sit with us."

I had a few moments to spare, so I sat next to Elena, then leaned around her so I could see Simon. "What were the two of you discussing?"

"Children," he admitted with a smile. "And how many we might like to have."

"And did you come to a consensus?"

"Yes." Elena laughed. "We've decided on 'just enough,' rather than 'far too many,' as Simon suggested at first."

"How very specific and well-thought-out. I hope—"

"Adele!"

I spun on the bench at the sound of Grainger's voice and found him jogging toward us, his sword swinging in its scabbard. Something rust-colored dangled from his fist, and as he came to a breathless stop, I realized he was holding a fox by its tail.

"You've caught it!" I stood, and a drop of blood dripped onto my shoe from the poor dead animal. "This very moment, evidently."

"Yes. And you shall have its pelt as lining for your shoes, just as you requested."

"*Merci*, Monsieur Colbert." I ran my hand over the fox's fur, admiring it. "My toes thank you for your generosity."

He pulled me close, careful to keep the dripping fox at arm's length. "I'd rather have thanks from your lips."

"My lips? Shall I sing your praises, then, from the center of the village square?" I teased, smiling up at him.

Simon laughed. "Oh, give the poor man a kiss, Adele. He's earned it. Come, Elena." He took her bread delivery and tugged her up by one hand. "Let's give them a moment alone."

"So?" Grainger whispered, as Simon escorted my best friend toward her family's cottage. "Have I earned a kiss?"

"Maybe *one* kiss. On the cheek." We were, after all, standing in the middle of the village square.

"I will take what I can get," he said.

I stood up on my toes and pressed my lips to his cheek, where I let them linger for a moment against the rough stubble, while I inhaled his scent.

"If I bring a rabbit for your gloves, will I have earned another kiss?" he murmured as I sank onto my heels again, still staring up at him.

"Of course."

His brows arched. "And if I deliver that rabbit in a more private location, might your kiss land on my lips instead of my cheek?"

"That is a good possibility, yes," I assured him with a smile.

"Mademoiselle Duval, you've just ensured that Oakvale will stay pest-free for the duration of winter."

I laughed as I tugged him onto the bench with me. "Well then, I feel as if I've done the village a service." I set my basket down and linked my arm through his, determined to take advantage of this semi-private moment, because while Maxime had used the week since he'd arrived to charm my mother and sister and find out everything he could about me, I hadn't yet found a way to prove that Grainger could be trusted with our secret.

"Grainger, what's the most frightening thing you've ever seen in the dark wood?"

He frowned, caught off guard by my change of subject. "I can't see anything in the dark wood. I saw a dead ogre once, when my father dragged it into the torchlight from off the path,

166

but other than that, I've seen very little. Though we hear plenty from the forest."

"Did your father kill the ogre?"

"No, he just found it. It appeared to have been killed by another beast. Likely a wolf. A good thing, too, because it was not far from the village."

Was that my mother, protecting villagers who scorned her? Or maybe my grandmother?

"But wouldn't it be great if you *could* see out there? Or if *someone* could? Wouldn't it help to be able to see what you're up against?" If he acknowledged that, then surely he would eventually understand how useful the rest of my abilities were.

"No one can see in the dark wood, Adele."

"But what if someone could?"

"That person would likely come under a great deal of suspicion over the source of such an unnatural gift."

Witchcraft. People would think the ability to see in the dark wood was witchcraft.

"But what about you?" I only needed *him* to be willing to keep my secret. "What would *you* think?"

"What is this about, Adele? Why are you asking about monsters no one will ever see and live to talk about?"

I shrugged. "Curiosity. I hear a lot of strange things from the forest on the way to my grandmother's house."

"Well, that is a dangerous curiosity indeed. You'd be better served putting those monsters out of mind entirely and

accepting an armed escort when you must go into the woods."
He leaned in until his lips grazed my ear. "I know a certain
good-looking young watchman who would gladly accompany
you any time."

"I will take you up on that the next time I have no escort.
But do you *really* think curiosity is dangerous?"

"I think indulging it is dangerous. Fear of the dark wood is
natural and healthy, and it keeps people safe."

An uneasiness settled into the pit of my stomach. "So then,
you think curiosity is what? Unnatural and unhealthy?"

"Unusual, at the very least. Most people don't want to know
what's out there. They trust the watch to keep them safe, as they
should. I worry that your curiosity could be misconstrued as a
fixation. Especially considering—"

His jaw snapped shut, his brows furrowing as he studied
my stricken expression. "I'm sorry. I didn't mean that the way
it sounded."

"Especially considering what?" My red hair and wanton
nature? Grainger didn't believe any of that.

He took my hand and squeezed it. "I just meant that with
your grandmother living all alone out there, and your father
wandering into the forest alone and unarmed . . ." He shrugged.
"Most of the village already thinks your family is strangely . . .
receptive to the dark wood, and if you display an interest in
unnatural abilities and strange beasts, I'm worried they'll start
to believe that of you as well."

"That I'm receptive to monsters." I wasn't even sure what that meant, yet it felt like a slap to the face.

"And to . . . the lure of evil."

"People have been saying things like that about my family for as long as I can remember, Grainger." And if I truly *were* a monster, I might be tempted to let those people get eaten. "But I didn't think you believed any of it."

"I don't," he insisted, his gaze holding mine. "You know I don't."

"But it bothers you." How could I not have seen that? Grainger liked me in spite of the rumors, and he consistently brushed them off as harmless gossip. But *of course* they bothered him.

His hand tightened around mine. "It bothers me for your sake. Because I love you, and I don't want to see you injured by idle tongues. Which is why I think you should avoid asking so many questions about the dark wood. Try not to seem so interested in whatever is bumping around out there in the forest. No good can come of that."

I studied his gaze, searching for some faint ray of hope. "You think there's *nothing* good out there? Truly?"

"Adele, I don't know what's out there. But I do know that nothing good can survive for long in the dark."

"Romy can't play tomorrow," Sofia announced around a bite of stew-soaked bread. "She's got a fever. So Tom and Jeanne and

I are going to tell her stories, while she rests. Only Tom doesn't talk, so he'll probably just listen."

"A valuable skill, indeed," I teased, and my sister stuck her tongue out at me.

"Is Romy's stomach upset?" my mother asked from the chair where she sat weaving nettlecloth.

Sofia shook her head. "Her mama says it's just a fever and fatigue."

"Well, I'm sure she'll be fine in a few days."

"Thank you, Adele," Maxime said as he sopped up the last of the broth from his bowl. "That stew was delicious."

"You said that last night."

He grinned, hazel eyes sparkling in the glow from the hearth. "And it was just as true then."

"That's because it's the very same stew we eat most nights."

"Adele," my mother admonished. "You would do well to learn to accept a compliment with grace."

"Of course, you're right," I acknowledged through clenched teeth. "Thank you, Max."

The problem wasn't this one compliment; the problem was that Maxime Bernard was *made* of compliments. Everything I said, he found amusing. Every chore I performed, he declared flawless. His pursuit of me was a sugar-coated endeavor, as if I were a fly to be drawn with honey.

As if he thought of nothing else, all day long. Which made

170

me conscious of every move I made and skeptical of every word he said.

"I helped with dinner," Sofia announced, her head held high as she dipped a spoon made of antler into her bowl.

"No wonder it was so good!" Maxime said as he stood from the table, and she beamed up at him. "Are you ready, Adele?"

"Ready for what?" Sofia asked, as he plucked my red cloak from a hook by the door. "Are you going for a walk, this late?"

"Adele promised to show me the village."

"You've already seen the village," Sofia said, her stew forgotten. "It isn't that big, you know."

Max laughed. "You caught me. I'd just like a chance to make a good impression on your sister."

"Then you should bring *her* a present." She held up her little wooden horse as a demonstration.

He gave her a wink and a grin. "Now, why didn't I think of that?"

I rolled my eyes at him. "The two of you are incorrigible."

My sister frowned up at me. "What does that mean?"

"It was a compliment," Max assured her.

"It most certainly was not." I tried to snatch my cloak from him, but he pulled it out of my reach with a smile. Then he draped the garment over my shoulders, without taking his focus from my eyes, and his fingers brushed my chin as he tied it closed.

"Good night, Sofia," he said as he pulled the front door open, letting in another frigid breeze. She waved, then when she bent for a bite, he took my hatchet from the high shelf and motioned for me to grab my leather belt on the way out into the dark night.

"He's *rather* handsome," Sofia utterly failed to whisper, and Max laughed as he pulled the door closed behind us.

"Don't let that go to your head," I warned as I buckled my belt beneath my cloak. "She also finds charm in a snake's slither through the dirt."

Max handed me my hatchet, and I dropped it into its loop. "So you don't agree with her assessment?" He picked up the lantern my mother had prepared for us.

I turned to look up at him, and I was almost irritated at how brightly his hazel eyes shined in the moonlight. "Maxime, are you fishing for a compliment?"

"In fact, I am."

"Well, I'm afraid you're going to need better bait." I turned and headed toward the east end of the village.

"Mademoiselle, you injure me." He jogged to catch up with me, one hand over his heart, clutching at a phantom wound.

I huffed and walked faster, hoping he didn't see well enough in the dark to avoid pits in the path. Or to notice my faint smile.

Ahead, the flash of a lantern caught my eye, and I pulled Max into the shadow of the lean-to on the side of the sawmill, hiding our own light from sight.

"If you wanted to be alone with me, all you had to do was ask," he teased. But when I didn't smile, his grin faded. "Monsieur Colbert is on patrol tonight, isn't he? And you don't want him to see us together."

I peeked around the corner of the building and exhaled. The lantern was gone. "Yes," I admitted. "But not because we're doing anything wrong. We aren't."

My mother and me being seen out at night, carrying weapons, would have added to the perception that the Duval women were unnaturally independent. That might even have spawned rumors that we were practicing witchcraft in the dark wood. But being seen out alone with Max was an entirely different kind of danger.

Anyone who saw us would assume the Thayer brothers were right about my wanton nature. And I couldn't do anything to spawn further rumors about myself. Not now that I knew they bothered Grainger.

"It would just be too difficult to explain to him that . . ." I shrugged.

"That you're taking me into the dark wood in the middle of the night to introduce me to your grandmother and possibly to fight monsters? Yes, that's a bit complicated."

I stepped back onto the path, and Max followed. In silence. I'd only known him for a few days, but I already understood that silence was not his natural state. "Aren't you going to try to convince me that if I marry Grainger, my life will be a series of lies and secrets, and I'll never be able to confide in him?" An opinion he surely shared with my mother and grandmother, considering his personal stake in the matter.

"That's your business, Adele. I don't want to win your hand based on what he can't be for you. I want to win based on what I *can* be for you. What we could be for each other."

His quiet confidence was a pleasant change from outright arrogance, but it was his unwillingness to criticize Grainger to gain the advantage that truly caught me by surprise, and I found myself studying him in the dark. Reassessing.

"How do you know what we could be for each other? We only met a week ago."

"I didn't know, at first. I have a duty here, just like you do, but I didn't know what to expect from you. I wasn't even sure we'd get along. Then I met you." He turned to give me a moonlit grin. "I knew you'd be fast and strong, by virtue of your destiny, but you also turned out to be smart, and funny, and beautiful. You are more than I could have expected, in every possible way, so while I am wooing a guardian on behalf of the entire village of Ashborne, as selfish as it might sound, I am thrilled to be competing for your heart on my *own* behalf."

"Stop." I gave in to a frustrated sigh. "Just stop. Please."

Max frowned. "Stop what?"

"The more praise you throw at me, the less impact it has. We both know I'm not perfect, but according to you, I can do no wrong."

"I never said—"

"I haven't exactly welcomed you here, yet you insist that my stale bread is 'crusty and delicious.' My crooked stitches are 'endearing.' And you think I'm beautiful when I have manure smeared across my forehead and hay in my hair."

His eyes narrowed. "And you'd rather I find you unappealing?"

"I'd rather you were sincere. I want you to stop looking at me like I'm some kind of angel sent to save your village and understand that I'm only a girl."

"You are *not* only a—"

"I am. I just found out I'm a guardian, but I've been sewing crooked stitches and making a mess out of mucking the cowshed my entire life. I love my sister, but sometimes I want her to go away. I hate churning butter, but I would fight you for the last smear of it from the bottom of the crock, when I'm feeling selfish. I am *just* a *girl*, and you can't keep thinking of me as some faultless savior, because you are setting yourself up for severe disappointment."

Max blinked at me in the moonlight. His shoulders slumped a little as he exhaled, and his gaze felt heavy with the weight of whatever he was about to say. Whatever he'd been holding back. "I know you're not perfect, Adele. I just . . . I've never tried to woo a girl before, and I didn't expect you to be in love with someone else before you even met me. And the truth is that I'm *not* thrilled to be competing for your hand. I wish you were

175

as excited to get to know me as I am to get to know you, and since you aren't, I just . . . . I wanted you to know that I really like you."

"Do you, though? Isn't it possible that you only think you like me because you believe we're supposed to be together? Because your family—your entire village—needs me?"

"No." He gave me an earnest little smile as he reached out to tuck a stray strand of hair into my hood. "I like you. Crooked stitches and all. I especially like how willing you are to speak your mind, because that means I always know where I stand. Even if I'm not yet where I want to be, in your eyes."

I stared at him for a moment, as what he was saying sank in. "Okay then. Thank you for telling me the truth." It was good to know that his arrogance came from feigned confidence in his ability to win me over. But as disappointed as he was to be competing for my hand, at least he *knew* he was competing. Grainger had no idea, and that didn't seem fair.

We walked on in silence, and this time that was my doing. I felt like I understood him a little better now, yet I had no idea what to say.

At the edge of the village, Max stopped on the path, eyeing the point where it disappeared into the dark wood. We stood side by side in front of the halo, studying the great, dark expanse in solemn silence. The first few feet of trees were easily visible, thanks to the ring of torches, but beyond that, the dark wood was an unnatural ocean of gloom, so murky that from where I stood, I could only make out the general suggestion of trunks and branches.

Max probably couldn't see a thing.

"Does the dark wood completely enclose Ashborne?"

"Since before I was born," he confirmed. "My mother says it has spread with a frightening speed for the past twenty years or more. If we aren't able to beat it back, the monsters will eventually occupy more territory than humanity does." He turned to me then, and his fingers twitched, as if he wanted to take my hand.

Instead, he reached for the hem of his dark wool tunic and begin to lift it, along with the lighter linen garment beneath.

"What are you doing?" Alarm fired through me and I glanced around to make sure no one had followed us, even though it was the dead of night.

"Showing you what's at stake for us, in Ashborne." He raised the material, and before I could object again, my gaze caught on a thick line of gnarled pink scar tissue beginning just above his right hip, easily visible in the glow from the torches.

"Oh!" I gasped, my horror growing as he continued to lift his tunic, exposing more and more of the gruesome scar angling toward his left shoulder. "What happened?"

"I've been going into the dark wood with my mother for three years, to help her as best I can. Last spring, she fell sick, and I went into the forest on my own to watch out for a small caravan. But despite years of experience and training, I cannot do what comes naturally to you, Adele. What you were *born* to do.

"I never saw the creature that attacked me," he continued. "If the caravan hadn't heard my scream—if they hadn't come running with torches, frightening off the monster before it got more than a shallow swipe at me—I wouldn't have made it out of the forest alive."

How brave must he be—how deeply must he care for his village—to have left the path in the woods without a guardian's ability to see in the unnatural darkness?

As fascinated as I was horrified, I reached for the thick line traversing his flesh, my fingers skimming the smooth, shiny scar. "I can't believe you survived this."

"I very nearly didn't. If this wound were four claw marks instead of one—if there'd been any chance I was attacked by a wolf—they wouldn't have *let* me survive." Max took a deep breath, and I snatched my hand back, embarrassed to realize I was still touching him. Suddenly aware that beneath the healed wound, his flesh was . . . very well formed.

He let his tunic fall back into place, a spark of amusement shining in his eyes before his somber expression returned. "I know it isn't fair of me to heap our burden upon you, Adele, but if you won't come with me—if you won't build a family with me in Ashborne—when my mother dies, our village will be completely defenseless against the wood."

THIRTEEN

My mother's instructions were for me to take Max straight to Gran's cottage, and not to veer from the path. For the past week, she and I had been patrolling the forest every night, enforcing a well-established, largely uninhabited buffer zone just inside the woods. Because according to my mother, the deeper one went into the dark wood, the more numerous the threats became, and while the occasional beast came near Oakvale before backing away from the halo of light, the only creatures that regularly encroached upon the village—and the only ones willing to venture past the torches, on a very rare occasion—were whitewulf.

But seven days' experience did not qualify me to go hunting without her, even with Maxime at my side. So we were only to visit my grandmother tonight.

"Adele," Max said as we stepped through the tree line and into the woods. "I have a gift for you."

I rolled my eyes. "My sister is putting ideas in your head."

He laughed. "No, I brought this with me from Ashborne. And to be clear, it comes with no obligation. I'd like for you to keep it even if you choose not to marry me."

He stopped just inside the forest, where moonlight and torch-light still penetrated, and hung our lantern on the branch of a tree. Then he swung his leather rucksack onto the ground. It was large and still oddly bulging, and when he opened it, I saw why.

"What is that?" I asked as he pulled out a strange device made of wood and metal. There were aspects of it that looked familiar: a thick, taut string and a frame similar to that of a bow.

"It's called a crossbow. Have you ever seen one?"

I shook my head, and when he offered me the device, I took it, eager to examine it. I was surprised by its weight.

The weapon had a bow-shaped frame, attached to a wooden stock that ran perpendicular to the string. On top of the bow was an iron lever with two hooks that caught the string. Fascinated, I pulled back on the lever, grunting with the effort, and that placed tension on the hefty string like an archer pulling back the string of a longbow. Only this device, for all its heft, was shorter and more compact.

"Well, that didn't take you long to figure out." Max's voice held a satisfaction that warmed my belly, deep inside.

I shoved that feeling aside before I could be forced to truly study it, choosing to focus on the new weapon instead. "This is . . . *wondrous*! Are there arrows?"

"Bolts. I can only fire a couple of them in a minute, but with your strength, you'll probably be much faster, once you get the hang of it."

"If I'm set upon by multiple monsters, there won't be time to reload, but a single shot from this—if my aim were true—could take down one enemy so I could use my hatchet on another." I finally looked up from the crossbow to see Max holding a length of wood about as big around as my finger. Its end was sharply pointed, and I could see several more of these "bolts" sticking up from his bag. "Where did you get this?"

"I made it," he announced, with no small amount of pride. "With a little help from the Ashborne blacksmith, for the metal parts."

"*You* made this?"

"Your skepticism feels like a bolt to the chest, Adele."

"I'm sorry. I just . . . this is amazing! How did you explain this to your friend, the blacksmith?"

"We'd seen soldiers carrying them, and I thought we could fashion one of our own. He was up to the challenge, as long as I paid him for the work. My mother liked it so well that she asked me to make another for her. With any luck, the blacksmith will be done with his part by the time I get back. He thinks I'm using this first one to hunt, while I'm away."

"Well, that could be true, I suppose. If this thing will take down a troll, it'll probably take down a deer or a boar."

"Yes, in a normal forest. But it would be dangerous for me

to fire a crossbow in the dark wood, considering that I can't see two feet beyond the glow of my lantern. Here. Let me show you how to load a bolt."

"I think I understand it." I took the bolt he held out and laid it in the groove carved down the center of the wooden stock. Then I folded back the lever to pull the bow string. "This is the trigger?" My finger brushed a wooden protrusion on the under-side of the device.

"Yes, but don't pull that until you're ready to—"

"I know." The machine felt natural in my hands. Delight-fully heavy and sturdy. It *made sense*, not just mechanically, but almost . . . spiritually. As if it were a part of me, like my own arm. "This is amazing. Thank you so much! I can't wait to try it!"

Max's smile seemed to be blooming from deep inside him. "Well, I know we're supposed to stick to the path tonight, but I'm sure that tomorrow you'll get that chance. With your mother." He seemed disappointed that he wouldn't be there.

"You deserve to see your creation in action. I promise I'll come out here with you again," I told him. "But for now, just . . . stick close to me, okay? For your own good."

"Of course." And for once, there was no sparkle in his eye. No crooked grin on his face. He was completely serious. "I don't have your abilities, but my ears are pretty good, and I'm happy to lend them to the cause. To help you in any way I can, for as long as you'll let me."

I blinked up at him, puzzled by that thought. "You're happy with that arrangement? With the idea of spending your life assisting a woman?" That wasn't typically how marriage worked.

Max frowned. "Perhaps I haven't been *entirely* clear about that. I don't want to be your assistant, Adele. I want to be your partner. I may not have your extraordinary gifts, but I *can* contribute to this fight. And I look forward to the chance to prove myself."

"*You* want to prove yourself to *me*?" Surprise echoed thick in my voice.

"Of course. The fate of an entire village depends upon me convincing you to come home with me. I won't lie; that's a lot of pressure. But I'm ready for the challenge." His grin returned, an echo of the confidence he'd been emanating since the moment he'd arrived in Oakvale. But now I understood the source: Max was as dedicated to protecting his village as I was to protecting mine, and he seemed determined to attack that task with enthusiasm and a smile.

"Okay," I said at last. "Let's go, before the watch shows up again and sees our light."

Max closed his rucksack and swung it over his shoulder, then he plucked our lantern from the branch he'd hung it on. I sucked in a deep breath and lifted the crossbow in both hands. Then, together, we headed down the path.

Despite my mother's directive, I found myself fighting an

urge to leave the path and venture deeper into the woods, as if the forest itself were tugging on a string tied to something deep inside me. The dark wood seemed determined to convince me that I was finally where I belonged. That I was . . . home.

That was a trick, of course. A chilling illusion intended to lure me to my death. So I swallowed the irrational urge. Max and I walked on in silence, ensconced in our bubble of light, a shield that had never felt so fragile to me before I'd seen for myself what dangers the forest had to offer. Fortunately, though the dark wood was a chorus of strange and unidentifiable sounds, most of those sounds seemed to be coming from a distance.

"I look forward to meeting your grandmother," Max said softly, just when the silence was becoming too much. "She truly is a legend, at least to my family. Choosing to live alone in the dark wood, among the beasts."

"She's definitely . . . unforgettable. She—"

A sharp hiss echoed from my right. I spun toward the sound, my pulse roaring in my ears, my new crossbow aimed and ready.

"Can you see it?" Max lifted the lantern to his right side, squinting in the direction the hiss had come from, but his gaze was unfocused. He couldn't see past the light.

"Not yet. It's probably just a snake."

"It's much bigger than an ordinary snake," he whispered. "It only sounds small because it isn't very close yet."

"How do you know?"

"I can tell from the echo. You're right about it being a

184

serpent, though. There's another noise along with the hiss. Sort of . . . beneath it. Do you hear that?"

I closed my eyes and stopped walking, in order to concentrate. "I hear a . . . slithering. Could that be vines? The vines out here have minds of their own."

Max shook his head. "Can you hear how that slithering is . . . heavier? Thicker-sounding than the vines?"

"Yes." Now that he'd mentioned it.

I opened my eyes to frown at him in the glow from the lantern. "How are you doing that? How can you hear such specific details?"

His grin radiated satisfaction, his face shadowed in every dip and crevice from the low angle of the light. "I've had a lot of practice."

But there was clearly more to it than that. "You're being modest."

He chuckled softly. "I'm not often accused of that. But yes. I've spent the past three years focusing on my hearing to compensate for the crippling darkness."

I frowned up at him, trying to understand. "You *listen*, in the dark wood? For what?"

Max shrugged. "Footsteps. Exhalations distinctive enough to be identified. Slithering. Growling. Huffing. Sometimes even an eerie silence. I've trained myself to identify many of the monsters that live in the dark wood by the sounds they make. As I said, I wouldn't fire a crossbow into the dark, but I *can* help you. I can tell you what's coming and from which direction. And how many of them there are."

"And that's what you were doing, when you were injured?"

The light of pride dimmed in his eyes. "Yes. My ears can be a help to you, but they aren't enough on their own. I can't do for Ashborne what you can."

Yet, as reluctant as I was to admit it, he was better equipped to be out here than anyone from the village watch. And his skill was the result of years of practice and dedication, even though he'd been under no obligation to take such risks.

"So, it's a very big snake?" I said, when I couldn't think of how else to respond.

"Yes." That glint in his eye was back. "It's huge, with a row of spikes that lie flat along its spine until it's threatened. I've only seen glimpses of it, because they don't come into the light intentionally. But my mother has described it in detail."

"And it's little threat, as long as we have the lantern?" I whispered as I took another step, bowing to the demands from my legs to keep moving.

He nodded. "I only know of one creature that isn't thwarted by firelight."

"Whitewulf?"

"No. They aren't bothered by daylight, which is why they're the biggest threat to any village. And they'll occasionally sneak through the halo, but they won't go near someone carrying a flame. I only know of one beast that will."

186

"What beast is that?" I suddenly felt embarrassed by my own ignorance—despite the fact that I'd only been a guardian for a week—and envious of his three years of experience in the dark wood, even if he couldn't see the creatures he'd been learning about.

Was Max jealous of my vision? My speed and strength? I couldn't help wondering how he really felt about the fact that even if he trained for a lifetime, he would never be able to see the monsters he fought.

"Fear liath," he replied. "My mother says they come from far north of here, but the rampant spread of the dark wood across the landscape has let creatures from many different places mingle in the cursed forest."

"What is this *fear liath*?" I whispered as the light from the lantern bobbed around us, casting harsh shadows behind every tree branch.

"They never come close enough for me to see more than a human like silhouette, but they're one and a half times the height of a man. They bring on an uncontrollable feeling of dread. Of panic. The closer they come, the more hopeless your task begins to feel. The more inevitable your death. The first time I saw one, my fear became so overwhelming that, had my mother not been there to steady me, I might have run screaming into the woods, my lantern abandoned and forgotten, just to escape that feeling. To reclaim some hope."

"You would have run off alone into the dark wood? Without

your light?" My voice sounded thick with skepticism, but Max only nodded. "Wouldn't that just put you at the mercy of whichever beast finds you first?"

"It certainly would. I know it makes no sense if you've never felt it, but that's how strong the *fear laith*'s influence is. Hasn't anyone from Oakvale ever just . . . disappeared? Have you ever lost an entire party in the dark wood, with no explanation?"

I nodded slowly. Twice, in my lifetime, we'd lost an entire merchant party when the village grew desperate enough, in the depths of winter, to brave a journey through the dark wood for supplies from a neighboring village. We hadn't found so much as a single body.

"Chances are good that when people abandon the path and leave behind their light, it's because they've panicked under the influence of the *fear liath*."

We continued down the path for another couple of minutes in silence, while I considered the threat this *fear liath* represented. Did it have less influence on a guardian, or was it just Max's mother's experience that let her keep her head when he would have panicked?

Finally, I spotted the fork in the path that would lead to my grandmother's clearing. "Do you still hear the snake creature?" I could discern the occasional slithering sounds, but they were faint, and I couldn't be certain I wasn't hearing vines.

Max nodded. "It's following at a distance."

"Gran's cabin is only a few minutes from here. Soon, we'll

see the light from the torches she keeps lit."

He stopped at my side, his eyes glowing with excitement in the flickering light from the lantern he held. "You want to hunt the serpent, don't you?"

I lifted my gift. "I *am* eager to try this out," I admitted. And not just out of a sense of duty to protect my village. It was exhilarating to think of the power I'd be wielding with such a weapon. "But we're not supposed to leave the path, which means we'd have to lure the beast to us. And if we're going to do that, this is the best place." Because if I were unable to kill it, we could flee toward the safety of my grandmother's clearing.

His grin swelled into a true smile. "I'm ready whenever you are."

"Is there anything else you can tell me about this serpent?"

He thought for a moment, his hazel-eyed gaze holding mine in the lamplight. "It'll be fast. Faster than one would expect from a creature so large. Stay in motion so it can't strike at you. Aim for its head. After you've fired one shot, if it isn't dead, hand me the crossbow, and I'll load another bolt for you." Max set the lantern in the center of the dirt path, then he swung his rucksack onto the ground next to it and pulled out a second bolt. "Ready?"

"Yes." *No.*

Fighting monsters was my destiny. My obligation to the world. Yet intentionally attracting a beast from the dark wood without my mother by my side still seemed foolish, even if

189

Gran's cabin *were* close enough to run to in an emergency.

"Okay. Here goes." Max lifted the lantern toward his face, and his gaze held mine for a second, as if he were giving me a chance to change my mind. When I didn't, he winked at me. Then he blew out the flame.

"Listen." Max's eyes were closed. His knuckles creaked as his hand tightened around the bolt in his fist. And all at once, it occurred to me what incredible—what *unreasonable*—trust he was putting in me.

"Why?" I whispered, as we waited in the dark.

"Why what?" His breathing was deep and even. There was no sign he was the least bit worried.

"Why would you assume I can do this? Why would you trust me with your *life*, when you hardly know me?"

Silence settled between us, and I realized his eyes were open, as if he were trying to look at me. "You are Emelina Chastain's granddaughter. Celeste Duval's daughter. This is in your blood, and you passed the trial. Beyond that, your mother has spoken about how capable you are," he said at last. "And, Adele, I'm not just trusting you with my life. I'm hoping to trust you with the lives of every man, woman, and child in my village. And there isn't a doubt in my mind that you're up to the challenge."

My eyes narrowed as I scanned the darkened landscape, determined not to let him down.

Suddenly the slithering grew noticeably louder, and it was punctuated by a hiss. I spun toward the sound just as a huge, shadowy shape wriggled out of the darkness, traveling in a side-ways S-shaped motion, just like an ordinary snake would. It slithered rapidly toward me, dead leaves crunching beneath its weight, an arrangement of thin, spiky quills cascading over the top of its head to lie flat along the length of its spine. Even with most of the serpent's body on the ground, its head was as high as my waist.

My heart pounding, I raised the crossbow and aimed it at the serpent's wide, triangular skull. The beast rose until it towered over me, hissing, its mouth open to reveal a set of massive, sharply pointed fangs, as well as several rows of sharp teeth and a long, forked tongue.

I pulled the trigger.

The force of the bolt firing echoed up my arm and into my shoulder, as if I'd slammed into the broad side of a barn. The serpent hissed as the bolt bit deeply into the flesh just below its jaw.

"Reload!" I shouted as I shoved the crossbow at Max, and to my amazement, he had his eyes closed again as he loaded it, feeling for the groove in the stock with the fingers of one hand. He'd clearly had a lot of practice.

While he wrenched the lever back to pull the string taut, I jerked my hatchet from my belt and gripped the handle as I lifted my arm over my head. The snake was too big and much too dangerous, with those massive fangs, to be fought up close. So I took a risk and threw the hatchet with all the force I could muster. It sailed end over end to thunk into the serpent's neck, imbedded in the beast's scaly flesh.

The monster hissed again, and its movements slowed.

"Where was the hit?" Max asked as he held the loaded crossbow out to me.

"Its neck. Along with the first bolt." The serpent hissed again, its tongue snaking out at me. Then it began to move to the side, and for just a second, I thought it might retreat. Then—

"Move!" Max shouted, and when I didn't process his direction quickly enough, he threw himself at me, knocking us both off the dirt path just as the serpent's massive tail whipped toward us. I landed in the underbrush with my face in the dirt, Max's arm across my back, but he was on his feet in an instant. I sprang up a second later and snatched the crossbow from the ground.

If he hadn't gotten us off the path, the beast's tail would have hit us both, crushing us as it tossed our broken bodies deep into the dark wood.

"It's hurt." Max spun, clearly tracking the slithering sound as it moved around us, though his eyes were closed. "But they have thick scales, and even thicker muscle. You're going to have to hit the head."

"Okay," I said as I took aim, following the beast as it circled us. "But if I miss, we run. Follow the sound of my footsteps."

"Got it," Max said as the beast bore down on us again, its scaly body twisting along the ground much faster than should have been possible—he was right about that. "Kill it, Adele."

I sucked in a deep breath to steady my aim. Then I tilted the bow up a little, to compensate for the downward pull of the trigger. The snake lunged at us again, hissing, a little off-kilter from its injuries.

I pulled the trigger.

The bolt pierced the serpent's skull, right between its eyes, with a sickening thunk-squish. The beast let loose a brain-scrambling screech—a sound that didn't seem like it could have come from a snake. Then its forked tongue fell limp, and the monster slammed into the ground with enough force to shake the earth beneath our feet.

For a moment, I could only gape at the massive serpentine corpse. "Well done!" Max clearly knew exactly what the thud had meant.

"I can't believe it," I murmured, stunned.

"Believe it." He stepped closer, his eyes open and aimed at my face, though he couldn't possibly see me. "Believe in yourself, Adele."

"You had as much to do with that as I did," I insisted, my heart racing with our victory.

"Then believe in *us*. We could be an incredible team. What you do is important and dangerous. We cannot afford to forget that. But victory is a thrill, *every single time*, and you'll need someone to share that with." He reached out, and his hand found my cheek in the dark. His thumb stroked over my lower lip. "Someone who can understand the race of your pulse, keeping you up at night. The dizzying euphoria that follows success in battle. Someone who can celebrate with you. Someone who will celebrate *you*."

My head spun. I felt like I was falling. As if I'd just leapt from a cliff, cold air rushing past me, with the ground far below.

As if I might never touch the earth again.

And Max, I understood, was now inextricably tied to this feeling of triumph. His touch was a part of this moment and no matter what happened next, it always would be.

I wasn't sure how to feel about that.

Had he done it on purpose? Had he intentionally insinuated himself into the euphoria of victory to give himself an edge in the battle for my heart? For my hand?

Was that clever of him, or manipulative? Or was it simply an instinct, brought on by the rush of his own pulse?

The truth was that I didn't know him well enough to be sure.

I stepped back, and his hand fell from my cheek.

"Let's get your weapons." He didn't try to touch me again, but I could hear that his breathing had quickened. I could tell that his pulse was racing too, from the exhilaration of this moment.

I led him away from the path into the impenetrable gloom of the dark wood. When I stopped beside the massive felled beast, he swung his rucksack onto the ground again and held out one hand. "The bolts?"

I settled the strap of the crossbow over my shoulder, then I had to plant one foot on the serpent's thick scales in order to pull the bolts one at a time from its flesh. They'd bit in deeply, and if not for the beast's massive size, the first might have been fatal. But the snake was thickly muscled, and its scales were a bit like armor plating.

Max pulled a cloth from his bag and wiped the bolts off, then he stored them while I used my foot to brace myself again, so I could pull my hatchet free. I accepted the cloth he offered and cleaned the blade, then I used its sharp edge to pry loose several of the basilisk's thick scales.

I couldn't tell, in the dark, what color they were.

"We've attracted attention," he whispered as I led him back to the trail. "Can you hear it?"

I could, though there were so many sounds closing in on us now that I couldn't make sense of any one in particular. "It's okay," I said, despite the urgent pounding of my heart. "We're almost to the clearing."

"You were great," Max whispered, squeezing my arm gently. "I knew you would be."

But all I could think, as I guided him to the right at the fork in the path, was how relieved I was not to have let him down. To have gotten us both killed. "Your crossbow and your ears were much appreciated," I said at last.

"I wish I weren't blinded by the dark wood." His sigh carried the first true frustration I'd heard from him, and it felt like another peek behind his charming smile. A glimpse at his true thoughts. "Though, rest assured that should any of the monsters venture out of the dark wood and into sight, I would not hesitate to fight at your side. If you'd have me."

I huffed. "And now you've cleverly circled back to the subject of our union."

Max chuckled softly, his eyes unfocused in the dark. "We never strayed from that subject, Adele." He cleared his throat. "So, since you know what I hope for, in a marriage . . . what do *you* want?"

I exhaled slowly, still walking as footsteps and odd snorts closed in on us. "I know you and your village need a guardian. But as selfish as this may sound, what *I* need is someone who wants me not for what I can do for him—and his village—but for *who I am*. And you don't really know me yet. You can't possibly."

"I know enough to know that I want to know more." He couldn't see me. Yet again, he was looking right at me, as if his gaze were pulled toward my face through some force independent of sight. And with his words echoing in my head and the ghost of his touch still haunting my cheek, a warmth began to coil up from the pit of my stomach. Pulling me toward him, not just there, on that path in the dark wood, but in my head. In my—

"Come along, you two, before that ogre sneaking up behind you rips you each in half."

I looked up to see my grandmother standing on the path

ahead, the light from her cabin backlighting her silhouette. "Gran—"

"Move!" she snapped, and I tugged Max toward her so suddenly that he stumbled on the dirt path.

"Why didn't you bring a light?" I asked, as my grandmother ushered us toward the clearing.

"Because I didn't come from home."

"What? Where did you come from?" I exhaled as we broke through the dense forest into the lit clearing surrounding her cabin, and when Gran didn't answer, I turned to frown at her. "You were in the woods, weren't you? You were following us?"

"I was protecting you, as I'd protect anyone who wandered into the dark wood unprepared."

"We weren't unprepared!"

"No need to sound offended. But you've only just passed your trial, child. Fortunately, you have quite an accomplice here." Her gaze rose to take in Max, and my face flamed when I realized what she'd witnessed, between us. "And you must be Maxime Bernard. I am—"

"Madame Emelina Chastain," he said. *Enchanté.*

A smile spread slowly over my grandmother's face as she offered him her hand, and I could see that Max had charmed yet another member of my family.

"I assumed Adele would bring you to meet me, sooner or later, and I'm very pleased it was sooner."

She'd known I would bring him. Which meant she knew exactly why he had come to Oakvale. As I'd suspected, my mother and grandmother were in on this together.

"Your good name precedes you, Gran," I told her. "He was dying to meet you."

"Well, the dying part is completely unnecessary, boy. But I am pleased to meet you as well. You're Michele Marchand's boy, *non*? The firstborn?"

"Yes. Though she's Michele Bernard now." Max's eyes widened as he looked around the clearing. "This is incredible. Is it . . . safe?"

"Well, you shouldn't walk too close to the tree line. But as long as I keep the torches lit and chop down any seedlings that gain purchase, it seems to be."

"Amazing . . ." Max breathed.

"Wait, you know his mother?" I said, as we followed my grandmother across the clearing toward her cabin.

"Not well, but we've met. Remarkable woman. Strong and smart."

"That she is," Max agreed. "And she's eager to meet Adele."

Gran glanced back just in time to see my frown. "What's the matter, child? You don't want to live in Ashborne? If memory serves, it's a nice town. On the river, just like Oakvale."

Though that comparison meant very little. Most villages formed on the bank of a river, for access to clean water, as well as for the ease of travel.

"It's complicated," I told her as she opened the door to her cabin and ushered us into the warm interior. "There's a lot to think about."

"Yes, I suppose there is." She glanced at Max, who shrugged.

"I am not the only man vying for her hand."

"So I've heard." Gran's brow furrowed as she turned back to me. "Why don't you serve our guest some stew?"

I took a bowl from the shelf.

"Oh, really, there's no need," Max said. "We just had dinner."

I laughed, knowing Gran would insist.

"Nonsense," she said, right on cue.

I directed Max to a chair in front of the fireplace, then I ladled stew into his bowl from the pot hanging over the fire. "It's usually venison," I said as I handed him the bowl.

"Well, tonight it's rabbit," Gran informed me as she opened the chest at the end of her bed and pulled out a bundle of bright white fur.

"I stand corrected." I left Max by the fire, my own food forgotten as I crossed the room. "Is that . . . ?"

"Yes. It's for your hood. There's enough to trim your entire cloak, of course, but a guardian can't display that much white-wulf fur until she's gained some more experience. So if you'd like to take some of it home, you're welcome to line warm clothing with it. Or make gloves for Sofia."

"It's so soft . . ." I ran my hand over one thick length of the fur, marveling at the fine texture. The spotless color.

"It does make wonderful gloves," Max said, around a bite of stew. "My mother gave me a pair at Christmas last year."

"Speaking of gifts, I see you've acquired one." Gran nodded at the crossbow I'd propped against the wall next to her front door.

"Did you get to see it in action?" Max asked, with a glance toward the far wall, as if he could see through it into the dark wood, where we'd battled the snake.

"I did!" Gran beamed at him. "It's a fearsome piece of craftsmanship."

His intense gaze caught mine, and when he spoke, my face began to burn like banked coals. "A weapon is only as fierce as the warrior who wields it."

FOURTEEN

"Adele! Good morning!" Grainger called, jogging down the muddy alley between the bakery and the cottage next door. "I was hoping to catch you on my way to the sawmill."

"Good morning," I said as he stepped into the small yard at the back of our cottage.

"Morning, Grainger!" Sofia swung the empty milk pail at her side, and in her free hand, she clutched the horse Max had carved for her. A few weeks ago, she'd woken to find it standing on the table at her place, showing off a brand-new mane made of snow-white fur.

Whitewulf fur, snipped from the bundle Gran had sent back with us.

Sofia had hardly let go of the horse since.

"Is everything okay?" Grainger frowned, studying my face. "You look a little pale, and you've seemed tired lately. In fact, yesterday you almost fell asleep in your lunch."

"Monsieur Colbert, your concern is unnecessary—but very sweet." I smiled up at him. The truth was that I felt like I'd hardly seen him all month, though I'd made a point to have lunch with him nearly every day. Between my training and Max's increased attention, the structure of my days had changed, and I would *not* let my relationship with Grainger suffer because of the new demands on my time. "Everything's fine," I assured him. "I've just been very busy."

"She's making clothes for Tom!" Sofia piped up. "I'm helping!"

"Elena and I volunteered to see that the boy has what he needs," I explained. "The basics, anyway."

But the real cause of my pale and somewhat haggard countenance was the fact that I'd spent the first half of every night for the past month in the dark wood hunting beasts and perfecting my aim with the crossbow.

Mama was a thorough instructor, teaching me about dozens of different dark-wood monsters while she drilled me on the fundamentals of fighting in both my redwulf and human forms. But as fascinating as all the beasts and their histories were, the most remarkable creature in the dark wood was, without a doubt, my own mother. She'd always been determined and independent—she'd run the bakery and raised two daughters all on her own since my father's death—but in the forest she seemed to truly come alive. And she was *fearsome*! Fast and strong, with shocking reflexes and a phenomenal coordination that made me

202

wonder if I would *ever* attain such skills.

Yet, a couple of weeks ago, she'd claimed that she was tired and asked Max to start accompanying me.

I believed she was tired; I certainly was. But I also believed that was a convenient excuse to send me into the dark wood with Max, so he could prove how very useful a part of my life he could be. Even though she would never have sent me off alone in the middle of the night with any other boy.

Subtlety was not my mother's strong suit. Yet her gamble was a clever one. I'd improved significantly with the crossbow, and Max and I had fallen into a comfortable rhythm, wherein he could reload the weapon in seconds while I fought with my hatchet, effectively doubling the number of blows I was able to deal. All while he listened for approaching beasts.

And though I'd kept my distance from Max in the village during the day, after every kill in the dark wood, I'd found myself drawn to him physically, breathless from our victory. I had come to anticipate the brush of his fingers against mine as we passed the crossbow back and forth. The feel of his arm beneath my hand, as I guided him through the dark.

We didn't talk about those little touches. About how I'd come to associate them—to associate *him*—with the exhilaration of the hunt. And as guilty as I felt during the day about those stolen moments, my adventures in the forest with Max almost seemed to take place in some other world, removed from my life in Oakvale. In a domain of our own, where expectations and rumors from the village didn't matter. Where they didn't even exist.

I'd lived in two worlds over the past couple of weeks, with Grainger lighting my life like the sun during the day, and Max shining bright at night like the charming glow from the moon. That dual existence couldn't last. I *knew* it couldn't last. Yet I had no idea how to realign both halves of my life without losing something important.

A gust of wind blew down the alley, drawing me out of my thoughts, and I shivered from the cold. Grainger pulled me close, and the familiar feel of his hands at my waist sent a welcome thrill through me. Lunches hadn't been enough. I'd *missed* him. So I rose onto my toes and pressed a kiss against his lips.

"Mademoiselle Duval, people will talk," he teased as I settled onto my heels again, and I laughed.

"People are always talking about something. At least we'll be keeping the village entertained, during the long winter months."

"Speaking of people talking, did you hear that Madame Gosse is missing a hen?" he asked as he let me go.

"I hadn't heard. There's another fox in the village?"

"It hasn't been spotted yet, but I'm on patrol tonight, and I will keep an eye out." His focus dropped to the steaming bowl of porridge in my left hand. "Breaking your fast outside today?"

"That's for Max," Sofia informed him, and I clenched my jaw to hold back a groan. "He didn't come in for breakfast, so Mama said to take it to the cowshed."

204

"To the . . . ?" Grainger turned a questioning look on me. "He's staying here? I'd assumed he was with the Girards."

"In the cowshed," I clarified. In case he'd missed that detail. "He's sleeping in the cowshed. My mother invited him. She's a friend of his mother's."

"So I've heard." His frown deepened. "I'll come with you and say hello. I've seen Maxime's work on the church, and it's very good. I was considering asking him to help with a little project I'm about to start," he added with a knowing wink in my direction.

Startled, I nearly choked on air. Grainger was going to ask Max to help him build a cottage on his father's land. *Our* cottage. Where he planned to live as my husband.

Suddenly I felt as if night and day were about to collide and crush me between them.

"I don't think he's up yet—" I began, but that assumption died when a single high, clear note rang from the cowshed, then fell into a familiar melody.

Max was whistling the little tune he always seemed to be humming beneath his breath as we crossed the village toward the dark wood.

"Come on, then." Grainger took off toward the shed, and I hurried through the slushy, half-frozen mud after him, while my sister rushed ahead.

"Max!" Sofia threw open the cowshed door. "We brought you breakfast!"

Surprised by our entrance, Maxime spun around, holding a disk made of braided straw coiled around itself.

"Breakfast," Sofia repeated, pointing at the bowl I held. "What's that?" Her gaze narrowed on the straw disk.

"It's an archery target," Grainger told her.

"That's right." Max looked uncomfortable for the first time since I'd met him. He'd been working on the target for several days, intending to take it to my grandmother's clearing, where I could practice with my crossbow, safe from both beasts in the dark wood and prying eyes from the village.

But obviously no one else in Oakvale was supposed to see his latest gift to me.

"Are you an archer?" Grainger stepped forward to inspect the target, from which a short tail of straw rope still hung unsecured.

"Not by trade. Though most men in Ashborne know how to handle a bow."

"A fletcher, then?" Grainger frowned, obviously trying to figure out why a fletcher would be assisting the village carpenter. And staying in our cowshed.

"No. I was just . . . trying to keep busy."

"Here." I held the bowl out to him, and Max set the target down so he could accept it, obviously eager for the change of subject.

"Thank you."

"Well, I guess I'd best be off to the sawmill," Grainger said, having evidently forgotten he was going to request Max's help. "Adele, will you walk with me?"

"I would, but I'm afraid the cow won't wait. Unless my lovely little sister would be willing to milk her for me."

"I'm only lovely when she wants something from me," Sofia stage-whispered to Max, who gave her a sympathetic smile. "If I milk the cow, will you let me help with Monsieur Beaumont's gingerbread?"

She would be willing to do one of my chores, in exchange for helping with another of my chores?

I shrugged and heaved an exaggerated sigh, much to Grainger's amusement. "Well, I suppose—"

"Romy!" a familiar, high-pitched voice called out from a few cottages down. "Tom!" It was Jeanne Paget. "Romy! Where are you?"

Sofia took off down the alley, the empty milk bucket swinging at her side, and I turned to follow her with both boys at my heels. We rounded our cottage to see the older Paget girl headed toward us, scanning the village square and the alleys between cottages as she shouted out for the two younger children.

"Jeanne!" I called. "What's wrong?"

She scurried down the dirt path toward us. "Romy and Tom weren't in the loft when I woke up this morning, and Papa told me to find them."

"How is Romy? Is she feeling better?" I asked.

Jeanne shrugged. "She's still running a fever during the day, but at night she feels better. Mama says her illness is 'lingering,' but I think she's feigning sick because she'd rather play than sleep."

"Maybe Romy and Tom are playing hide-and-seek." Sofia shoved the milk bucket at me. "I'll help you find them!"

"Fine. Go help Jeanne. But don't go near the dark wood!" I shouted after them as the girls scampered down the dirt path, suddenly worried that, like me, Sofia could feel the eerie call of the forest. "Come back as soon as you've found them!"

"Well, I should go, too," Grainger said.

"As should I." Max handed me his empty bowl. "Monsieur Girard likes an early start to the day."

And with that, they each headed off in opposite directions, Max toward the carpenter's and Grainger toward the sawmill, leaving me standing alone on the path between them, holding an empty bowl and a milk bucket.

I spent the morning baking with my mother, sweltering in the heat from the oven, even with the front door standing open to provide relief. Max came back for lunch, and Sofia followed him through the door less than a minute later.

"They've just disappeared," she said as my mother set a hunk of stale bread and a piece of salt-cured herring in front of her. "You don't suppose, do you, that Tom might have gone back into the dark wood? To try to get home to Oldefort, to the rest of his family? That he might have taken Romy with him? The Pagets are very worried."

My mother's frown said that the Pagets were not alone in their concern.

"I'm sure they're fine," Max assured her around his first bite of fish. "Few people would wander into the dark wood without a very good reason."

"Isn't going home a good reason?" she asked. When Max had no answer for her, he tweaked her nose and told her to eat.

She obeyed without a single smart word in return.

"Adele," my mother said, as she went back to her dough. "I think I might send you to your grandmother's this afternoon, with a fresh batch of bread." She seemed to think about that for a moment. "Or maybe I'll take it myself, if you can finish up here." But, of course, what she would really be doing was searching the dark wood around the village for any sign that Romy and Tom actually had wandered into the forest.

"I want to go!" Sofia announced through a mouthful of herring.

My mother's kneading hands went still. "No."

"But I want to see Gran's cabin. To see *monsters*." She shrugged. "Then I want to go see Ashborne. Max says it's lovely, and while the river's frozen, I can't get there without going through the dark wood." My sister frowned as she amended her thought. "I can't get *anywhere*, without going through the dark wood. And I want to go . . . somewhere."

"Why on earth would you want that?" I demanded, more sharply than I'd intended. Her willingness to put herself in danger terrified me.

"*You* may be scared to leave Oakvale, but I want to *see* things!" Sofia declared, her eyes shining with the prospect.

"I'm not scared," I snapped at her. I'd been out in the woods for weeks, fighting monsters. Not that I could tell her that. "It's just that this is home, and I don't need anything else. I have friends here. I'm happy here."

"No, you aren't." Sofia rolled her eyes at me. "You have one friend. And Elena's not going to have time for you soon, because she's marrying Simon—"

"Simon's my friend too," I insisted.

"—and she's going to have babies."

"That's not—"

"And people talk about you. About us. I hear them, and—"

"You've heard people talking about us?" Horror trickled like ice-cold water down my spine. I'd assumed my little sister was unaffected by the whispers about us, but considering her love of eavesdropping, I should have known better. "You shouldn't listen to unfounded gossip."

"What do they say?" Max glanced from me to Sofia, then back.

"That we're witches. That Adele is immodest and lustful." My little sister's eyes narrowed, while my cheeks burned. She turned to our mother, whose kneading had begun to look aggressive. "What's lustful?"

"It's complete nonsense," I told her. "Just cruel people talking about things they know nothing about."

"Well, I don't know why you'd want to stay here with all these cruel people, when you could live anywhere you want."

"This village may not be perfect, but it's home," I told her. And I felt even more anchored to Oakvale now that I truly understood my ability—my duty—to protect it.

"Well, I'm going to travel and see some things when I'm older. But I'm already old enough to go see Gran, aren't I, Mama?"

"No," our mother said again, through clenched teeth. "Absolutely not."

"You are a silly moppet," Max declared with a smile and another tweak of her nose. Then he gave me a reassuring look over her head. "The dark wood is no place for a child. But fear not, Sofia. Adventure awaits you, someday. I feel that in my bones."

I could only hope she'd be willing to wait for "someday."

Reluctantly, my sister turned back to her lunch, and a few minutes later, Max met my gaze. "Is that true?" His good-natured smile had faded into a look of deep disappointment. "You don't ever want to leave Oakvale?"

An ache swelled in my chest. "Max . . ."

I was very conscious of Sofia listening, as she picked at her food, and though my mother didn't pause in her work, I knew she was listening as well.

I wasn't sure what to say. I'd been honest with Max from the beginning about Grainger. About the plans I'd had for my own future, before my mother ever told me about *her* plans for me. Yet after the time we'd spent together in the woods—after the connection we'd formed—I suddenly felt like staying loyal to Oakvale would mean hurting him.

And as inconvenient as his arrival had been, I did *not* want to hurt him.

Yet in allowing myself to bond with Max, I'd already hurt Grainger, even if he didn't know it.

There would be no way to make everyone happy. To meet all of my obligations. To keep all of my relationships intact. And part of me wished I could just freeze us all in this moment, while I still had both Max and Grainger. Before I had to decide whether to abandon my neighbors or forsake the citizens of Ashborne.

I exhaled slowly, fighting a terrible pressure building inside me. A dreadful guilt.

"It's okay," he said at last, watching my silent struggle. "I understand." Yet he ate the rest of his meal in silence, while my mother aimed disappointed looks at me from the table where she was now rolling dough into little balls.

I kept my mouth full of food, so I wouldn't be expected to say anything else.

After lunch, I loaded my basket with several large scraps of linen I'd been working on in the evenings. "You aren't delivering pastries this afternoon?" Max asked as he fastened his work belt at his hips.

"Not today. Elena is minding Monsieur Martel's children, and I promised to keep her company. We're going to sew a new tunic for little Tom."

We'd already made him a pair of long woolen socks and a cloak—labor that had passed quickly, because as usual, we'd chatted the hours away while we worked. Yet for the first time in our lives, the conversation felt one-sided. Elena told me all about the preparations for her wedding, and as excited as I was for her, the details felt bittersweet, both because I hadn't had time to help her with them and because every word she spoke reminded me that I hadn't been able to give Grainger an answer yet on the subject of our own betrothal.

As happy as I was to hear how close she and Simon were growing, especially since I'd hardly seen her in the past few weeks, I ached to be able to share with her in return. To tell her about the new divide in my life and ask her advice on how to knit the pieces of myself back together. But I didn't have the right to divulge my family's secrets without their knowledge or permission, yet hiding things from Elena made me feel like I was losing her. Like we were drifting apart.

Fortunately, it seemed she might not truly notice that distance. At least not until after the excitement of her wedding had passed.

"May I walk with you as far as the carpenter's workshop?" Max asked, drawing my thoughts back to the task at hand.

I hesitated, reluctant to encourage more rumors by taking another stroll through town with him. But it was just one walk through the village with a family friend—hardly a scandal, no matter how it felt.

"Of course."

He took my everyday cloak down from its hook and draped it over my shoulders.

My mother and Sofia walked a few steps behind us, on their way to check on Madame Paget and see if the absent children had reappeared, before my mother headed into the forest.

"So, are you ready to try out the target tonight?" Max leaned closer to whisper over my sister's prattling.

"Yes." Over the past few weeks, I'd practiced with my new weapon on several beasts from the dark wood, but as much as my aim had improved, I was hoping the straw target would give me a chance to become truly comfortable with the weapon without the pressure of a life-or-death situation. "I really appreciate—"

A scream froze me mid-step, and I looked up just as Elena backed into the dirt path from the blacksmith's yard, heedless of her skirt dragging in the mud. She had one hand clasped over her mouth, the other clinging tightly to the arm of the youngest of the Martel boys while she stared into the sizable barn to the side of Monsieur Martel's open-air workshop.

My mother and I raced to Elena's side with Sofia and Max

on our heels, just as Madame Gosse burst from her cottage down the path, having heard the scream. Monsieur Martel dropped his hammer and rushed from his workshop with his oldest son in tow. His forehead was creased with worry until he laid eyes on his youngest two children and could see that they were unhurt.

"Elena, what's wrong?" I asked.

Elena finally uncovered her mouth, and her hand began to tremble as she pointed at the barn. "I've found Romy Paget and little Tom. In the barn." Her entire arm was shaking now. "Margot, come away from there!" Elena darted forward and grabbed the five-year-old Martel's arm before she could venture into the shadowy depths of her own barn.

"Elena?" Monsieur Martel frowned at her. "What's happening?"

"Romy and little Tom are in your barn, Monsieur," she said. "Both covered in blood."

A chill skittered up my spine, and Sofia grasped at my hand, her eyes wide and scared.

"Mon dieu!" Madame Gosse gasped, as Monsieur Martel pulled his young daughter close. "I'll go get Madame Paget."

"Elena, keep the children with you," my mother said, and I recognized her commanding tone from our training sessions in the forest. "Everyone else, wait here." Then she raced toward the barn, her cloak billowing out in her wake.

I shoved my basket at Sofia and took off after my mother, my pulse roaring in my ears almost loud enough to drown out the sound of Max's footsteps pounding the earth behind me.

It took a second for my eyes to adjust to the darkness of the barn, but the scents of manure and livestock both felt normal. "There," my mother whispered, and I followed her to the right, where we could hear the rustle of hay from the open stall at the back.

"Mon dieu," my mother breathed as she stared into the stall. I peeked around her arm to find little Tom standing in a bed of hay, completely naked, smeared in blood from head to toe. Behind him, Romy Paget lay unmoving. Also naked and covered in blood.

I choked on a shocked cry, and Max gasped from behind me.

"Maxime, please help Adele keep everyone back. Especially Madam Paget. She shouldn't have to see this."

Tom blinked up at us, mute and unmoved by our horror.

"Wait," my mother said, as Max turned to do as she'd asked. "May I have your tunic?"

"Of course." Max set his leather rucksack on the ground and pulled his shirt over his head.

I stared into the blood-splattered horse stall, transfixed by my own horror, until—

Romy moved.

But surely I'd imagined that.

"Mama." I stepped past her into the stall and knelt at the little girl's side, uncomfortably aware of Tom blinking mutely at me from a foot away. And sure enough, Romy inhaled again, her tiny chest rising, just barely. "She's alive. In fact, I can't find . . ." I frowned, studying her closer. "There are no wounds. This isn't her blood."

"What?" My mother pushed past Tom to kneel next to me, where she inhaled deeply, as something pale caught my eye. A feather. And once I'd seen the first one, all the others seemed to jump out at me from the shadows.

"It's a hen," I said, just as my mother breathed the word "chicken" on a relieved exhalation. "Likely the one Madam Gosse was missing this morning."

"Madame Duval?" Max said, and I looked up to find him staring down at us, his tunic hanging from one fist, his scarred chest exposed.

"They're fine. Romy's asleep, and she still feels warm." My mother pressed one hand to the child's forehead, then jerked it back, shocked. "Yes, she's still quite sick. Will you carry her please, Max?"

"Of course."

I backed out of the stall to give him room, and Max handed me his tunic as he knelt to pick little Romy up, cradling her in both arms. As he carried her into the center of the barn, I draped his tunic over the little girl.

"Adele, will you bring Tom?"

"Of course," I said, and as my mother bent to pick up Max's leather sack, I knelt next to the naked child, to put myself on his eye level. "Tom, what happened to Romy? To the hen?" Its head lay on the ground, inches from the mound of hay where she'd lain. "Did you kill the chicken?" I whispered. "Did you *eat* it?" As unthinkable as that idea seemed, the child was covered in blood, and there was nothing left of the bird save for its head, some feathers, and what I now realized were a few bloody, sinewy bones. "Tom. Did you eat the bird? Did Romy?"

The child said nothing. I couldn't even tell for sure that he understood my question.

"Adele," my mother called.

I stood and took Tom's hand, trying to ignore the sticky feel of the blood dried to his palm and fingers.

Gasps went up from the small crowd gathering as we emerged from the barn with the two children. "It's fine. They're okay," my mother announced. "The fox has struck again, and it seems the children found the remains of Madame Gosse's hen."

That was a loose interpretation of what we'd found, indeed, but neither Max nor I argued with it.

"They were playing with the corpse?" Madame Rousseau breathed, one hand pressed to her chest. Murmurs from the crowd echoed her shock.

"Romy was likely delirious from her fever," my mother said. "I doubt she knew what she was doing."

"And the boy?" Grainger's mother demanded from the edge of the gathered crowd.

Before my mother could reply, Madame Paget pushed her way to the front of the small gathering, Jeanne's hand clasped in

218

hers. "Celeste!" she cried. "What's happened?"

"Romy's still sick." My mother's determined stride cut a path through the crowd as she led Madame Paget away from the barn, and Max and I followed in their wake. "Let's get her cleaned up and back in bed."

The crowd dispersed as we took the children back to the thatcher's cottage, whispered questions and suppositions following in our wake.

Madame Paget led Max and my mother to the back room of her home, where she asked Max to lay Romy on the low straw mattress. While Madame Paget began washing the sick child with rags and water from a bucket, my mother sent Jeanne and Sofia to play at our cottage, then she pulled Max and me aside.

"Adele, take Tom outside and get him cleaned up," she whispered. "He's no danger to you, but don't let anyone else near him. Especially his mouth. Do you understand?"

"No!" I shook my head with a glance at Romy, through the open curtain into the back room. "I don't understand any of this."

"I'll explain once I've seen to Romy," she insisted as she motioned us toward the door. "Just keep him out back and away from everyone else, including Max. I mean it, Adele. Don't let anyone else *near* that boy!"

FIFTEEN

I took Tom behind the thatcher's cottage and Max drew a bucket of water from the rain barrel for me. But as my mother had instructed, he stayed several feet away from the child, whom he'd begun to watch warily.

"You don't think he found the dead hen and just . . . played with it. Do you?" I whispered as I wiped blood from Tom's chubby little cheeks. I didn't fully understand what was happening, but my mother's strange and unsettling instructions told me that though she'd blamed Romy's fevered delirium, my mother believed Tom was really the source of all the trouble.

"I can't imagine why he'd do that." Max stood back, studying the child's face as I uncovered it with my rag, bit by bloody bit. "You really found him in the dark wood?"

I nodded. I couldn't remember telling him that, but Tom was a frequent topic of speculation in the village. "Naked and alone, near his parents' wagon. They were killed by a whitewulf, but there wasn't a scratch on the boy. Yet my mother's treating him as if he's dangerous to more than just chickens." Tom blinked up at me as I wiped his forehead clean, but despite the fact that we were talking about him—about his parents' deaths—he made no attempt to communicate. "What am I missing?" I asked Max as I rinsed my cloth in the bucket.

"I'm not sure, yet. He doesn't speak?"

"Not so far. I found him shortly before before you arrived, and I don't think he's said a word since then, though he nods on occasion."

"So he understands, then?"

"He seems to." I rinsed my rag, and as I began on the child's shoulder, I looked right into his eyes. "Tom? Do you understand what we're saying? Did you eat that chicken raw?"

But he only blinked at me.

Max frowned at the child but maintained his distance. "Open your mouth, please."

To my surprise, the boy obeyed, evidently more willing to follow directions than answer questions.

"Is that . . . ?" I squinted into his mouth. "There's a feather wedged between two of his teeth." And I decided to leave it there, considering his history of biting. "Why would you eat a raw chicken? I *know* Madame Paget feeds you."

But, of course, Tom gave me no reply.

"Sofia and I found blood and feathers in our cowshed a while back," I told Max as I stood. "We'd assumed a fox ate our

221

missing hen." But now we had bizarre and gruesome evidence to the contrary. Romy and Tom, it seemed, had had the run of the village overnight, unbeknownst to either the watch or to Max and me.

"What's wrong with the little girl?" Max asked. "Her name is Romy?"

I nodded. "She has some kind of fever. It began as swelling and warmth where Tom bit her, but it's spread and lingered."

"He bit her?" Max's frown deepened. Then he pulled me gently but insistently away from little Tom, who still stared at me mutely. "Does your mother know about the bite?"

"I'm not sure. Why? What does this mean?"

"I don't want to jump to conclusions," he hedged. But those conclusions were suddenly crystal clear.

"No." I shook my head. "That isn't possible. Tom wasn't scratched or bitten. He never developed a fever. He can't have been infected."

And yet . . .

"Mama!" I called from the back door to the Pagets' cottage. Over her shoulder, I could see that Romy had been washed and dressed in a clean tunic, and that her mother was applying a wet cloth to her forehead. The child's cheeks glowed scarlet with fever in the dim light.

My mother stood and looked past me into the yard, where Tom still stood near the barrel, Max several feet from him. Then she followed me out the door, pushing it closed on the way.

"What's wrong?" she whispered.

"That's what I want to know. What's going on?" I stopped her in the middle of the yard with one hand on her arm. "You know there was no fox, don't you? You know they ate Madame Gosse's hen? And probably ours?"

She sighed. "I am aware. But if I'd said that, the village would have come after the boy with a pitchfork." Because small boys didn't generally slaughter hens with their bare hands and eat the flesh raw. Naked. "They might have come for Romy too."

"You knew it was chicken blood, didn't you? Before you even saw what was left of the bird?" I asked. My mother nodded. "How?"

"I could smell it. Take a good whiff of the blood on your rag," she suggested. "And remember that scent the next time you cut yourself, slicing bread. The next time you slaughter a chicken. Blood from different sources has different scents. You should be able to tell that now." Now that I had ascended. "If you pay attention."

My mind spun with that knowledge as I followed my mother the rest of the way across the yard.

"What is happening?" I whispered as she studied Tom, still splattered in grisly blood from the neck down. "Did you know he'd bitten Romy?"

"I figured that out when I realized the children were the ones hunting our chickens, and Madame Paget just confirmed my suspicion. Though I should have realized it earlier. I should have come to see Tom the day you found him." Guilt twisted her features. "I was just so distracted by your trial and Elena's betrothal ceremony, and I assumed that since he had no bite marks or scratches, he was no danger to the village. But if I'd made time to see him that day, or any day since, I would have known. I could have prevented all of this."

"Should we be discussing this in front of Tom?"

My mother gave me an odd look. "He already knows everything we're saying, Adele."

"And what exactly *are* we saying?"

"Should I assume . . . ?" Max left the rest of his question unspoken as his gaze fell pointedly onto Tom.

"Considering that Adele found him in the woods? That he doesn't seem to speak, he *does* bite, and he evidently can catch and eat a raw chicken, in the middle of the night? I'm afraid so."

"You're saying he's a wolf? But there wasn't a scratch on him when I found him, and as a little boy, he can't be a redwulf. So how is that possible?" I demanded.

She knelt and pressed her nose into the boy's hair, as if she were kissing the top of his head the way she kissed Sofia several times a day. But her deep inhalation gave away her intent.

She cursed softly again as she stood. "Smell him."

I knelt and sniffed the child's head, surprised that he still seemed content to simply stand there. He smelled faintly of sweat—clean, pre-pubescent sweat—and not-so-faintly of blood.

But beneath that, there was something else. Something oddly distinctive, and . . . wrong. Different, anyway. Yet familiar.

"He smells like a whitewulf," I whispered, staring at my mother with my brow knit low in confusion. "But how, if he wasn't bitten?"

"There's more to it. Close your eyes," my mother whispered. "Inhale his scent again, and let it roll through your mind. Let it sink in."

Again, I did as she asked, and sudden understanding crashed over me with the force of a frigid northern wind stealing my breath. Shocking my senses. "Tom wasn't infected by a whitewulf," I whispered. "He was *already* a whitewulf."

"Yes." My mother tugged me several feet away from the boy, and Max followed, while Tom sank into the dirt to draw with his finger.

"So, he isn't the son of the merchants killed in the dark wood?"

Mama shook her head slowly and lowered her voice to little more than a whisper. "I suspect he's the son of the wolf who killed them. The wolf *you* killed during your trial."

I sucked in a deep breath as I thought that through, watching the boy trace shapes in the dirt. He looked so young. And oddly innocent, despite the fact that he was covered in blood.

Chicken blood. Not human blood.

"Okay. So, he's a werewolf," I said at last. Then I lowered my voice even further. "But he's also just a kid. Yes, he's snuck out and killed a couple of hens, but if that's the worst of it—"

"That's not the worst of it." Max's grim declaration matched the somber look in his hazel eyes.

"And I know he seems to prefer to be out at night, but he's perfectly fine in the daylight," I continued. "So maybe he's different than the other whitewulfs. Maybe he's more like us . . ."

"Adele, he's no different from the others of his species," my mother said. "That's why we keep torches lit. Because unlike the other monsters in the forest, it isn't light that drives off a whitewulf—it's fire. And they are *not* like us. In fact, their species is the inverse of ours."

"What does that mean?"

"Whitewulfs are wolves able to take on human form, but even then, they never stop thinking like a wolf. Redwulfs are people able to take on a wolf's form, but even then, we never stop thinking like a human. Which means that, despite our similarities—despite the fact that we're both *loup garou*, our differences are *profound*. Whitewulfs devour human flesh. That's why they can't live in human villages, like we can. They would quickly be discovered and killed. Though not without taking half the village with them."

"Mon dieu," I whispered, as the distinction she was drawing began to sink in. "And now I've brought a little whitewulf into the village? To prey on our chickens, and"—my gaze found the back door of the Pagets' cottage—"on our *children*? Will he try

226

to *eat* Romy? Was that why he bit her?"

My mother exchanged another look with Max, and in one devastating instant, I finally understood what I'd unleashed upon the village. "He bit her." And she had a fever, just like my papa had, when they'd pulled him from the dark wood. "She's *infected*?"

Mama gave me a grave nod. "Yes. If she survives the fever, little Romy Paget will become a whitewulf, and a terrible danger to all of Oakvale."

Despite the questions rolling around like marbles in my head, my mother insisted that we continue our discussion from the privacy of our own cottage. After the state in which we'd found the children, it wasn't difficult to talk Madame Paget into letting us bring Tom with us, so Max and I walked him back to the bakery while my mother stayed to help with Romy.

While we waited for her, I finished washing chicken blood off of Tom, then I lent the boy my spare tunic and sat him at the table with a hunk of bread and a bit of pickled herring. But before I could start questioning Max about what he knew about whitewulfs, someone knocked on the front door frame.

I looked up to find Grainger standing in the open doorway. His gaze hardened when he saw Max sitting at the table.

"Adele. I heard you've had some excitement. Is everything okay?"

"Yes." I took a deep breath, struggling to hide my frustration with the interruption. He had no way of knowing that his kind impulse to check on me was standing in the way of information I desperately needed. Or that his jealousy was compounding an anxiety that already seemed to be squeezing the air from my lungs. "Elena found Romy Paget and little Tom, here, in Monsieur Martel's barn, covered in the blood of Madame Gosse's missing hen. Evidently they found the remains."

"And *played* with it? That's an odd choice of toy."

"We're not entirely sure what happened, but Max was kind enough to help me get Tom cleaned up and fed." Though it was clear from the way the boy was picking at his food that his belly was still plenty full of raw chicken.

"How is Romy?" Grainger turned back to me without a word for Max. "Still feverish?"

"It doesn't look good, I'm afraid," Max said.

Grainger's gaze snapped back to him. "You are acquainted with the Pagets?"

"We've met in passing."

"Here a month, and the entire village loves him," Grainger muttered, clearly waiting for me to insist that I was the exception to that statement.

I frowned at him. My feelings for Grainger hadn't changed, but I *did* like Max. I wasn't sure yet what that "like" meant, or how deeply rooted it was, but I *was* sure that I didn't like Grainger's newfound willingness to openly take jabs at Max. Even if I understood why he felt provoked.

Before I could figure out how to reply, my mother stepped into the cottage.

"Good afternoon, Madame Duval," Grainger said. "Adele tells me Romy Paget is still ill?"

"Yes, unfortunately her fever has proved quite persistent."

"I'm sorry to hear that. I should be getting back. Adele, will you walk with me?"

I swallowed my frustration—an odd feeling, when I'd never been less than excited to spend time with Grainger before—and summoned some manners, even though I really wanted to speak to my mother and Max. "Of course. Part of the way, at least."

"Monsieur Bernard has made himself at home with your family," Grainger said, as we started down the muddy path.

"He's—"

"I know. He's a friend of the family."

"Yes. And he was helping me with Tom," I said, with a glance back at the bakery, which made Grainger frown. But as conflicted as I still was about my nights in the dark wood with Max and the effect they were having on my relationship with Grainger, the whitewulf pup revelation had put things into a stark new perspective.

My personal dilemma felt much less important, now that I knew the entire town was at risk from a threat I had brought into our midst. I found I suddenly had little patience for Grainger's jealousy, even though he had no way of knowing about the larger issue.

"You have care of the boy now?"

"For the moment, at least. Madame Paget has her hands full. And I should get back. I have a lot of baking to do, and we're trying to figure out why, exactly, two small children were playing with a dead chicken. Which won't be easy, with Romy passed out from her fever and Tom not speaking."

I was babbling, evidently trying to compensate for what I couldn't tell Grainger with an outpouring of everything I could. And as frustrated as I was in that moment, keeping secrets from him still felt . . . *wrong*.

"The boy still hasn't said anything?"

"Not one word."

"That *is* odd." Grainger exhaled heavily. "Fine, then. I'll let you get back. But I do hope to see you tomorrow?"

"Of course," I said, fighting impatience as he leaned down to kiss my cheek.

The feel of his lips lingered, a warm reminder of our connection that made me feel guilty and conflicted as I rushed back down the path and into my home.

Inside, I found Tom curled up on the floor, fast asleep, as far as he could get from the fire. I closed the front door, in spite of the heat from the oven, to keep us from being overheard.

"Okay, will someone please explain to me what's happening to Romy Paget? She's had a fever for weeks—how much longer will it last?"

"I don't know," my mother admitted. "If she were an adult,

she'd have already succumbed to the fever or become a white-wulf, but I have no experience with infected children. In fact, this is a tragedy I'd hoped never to be faced with."

"Would this happen if I were to bite someone? If Sofia were?" She was old enough to know better now, of course, but most small children bite, especially when they're teething. Were redwulf children a danger to humans?

"No." My mother used a rag to wipe off her work surface, then she pulled her largest bowl from a shelf and scooped flour into it. "A redwulf can only be born, and she can only be female. That's not the case with whitewulfs. Their nature passes through infection—in the womb or through a bite, like Romy's. And whitewulfs can be men or women."

"Or boys and girls. Tiny, innocent little boys and girls . . ." I murmured with a glance at Tom, who still lay asleep on the floor.

"Unfortunately," my mother began, and I looked up to find both her and Max watching me. "They may be even more dangerous to this community than an infected adult would be, because they pose no obvious threat. If a grown man or woman were found covered in the blood of a slaughtered hen, our neighbors would assume him or her to be mad, at best, a practitioner of some dark art, at worst. But Madame Paget will not hesitate to care for her sick child. And she has no idea that anything that upsets Romy—hunger, pain, the fever itself—could cause her to lash out from an instinct she can't possibly understand or control."

231

"You think she would bite her own mother?"

Max shrugged. "That's how a wolf pup defends itself."

And suddenly it occurred to me how easily Tom could have bitten Grainger, when he'd carried the boy into the village, the day I'd found him. Or—

"Sofia!" My sister's name burst from my tongue. "She played with Tom and Jeanne earlier this week."

"He's no more threat to your sister than he is to you, because women of our bloodline cannot be infected by a whitewulf." My mother leaned into her work, kneading the dough from her shoulders. "However, if either Tom or Romy bites anyone else, the snowball that is this fledgling epidemic will begin to roll downhill, picking up speed and size as it flattens this entire village."

"Epidemic?"

"Normally when a whitewulf bites, it kills and consumes, unless it's driven away before its victim dies, as was the case with your father." My mother wiped a smear of flour from her chin with the back of one forearm. "But we're talking about children. While they're young, I suspect they're far more likely to scratch or bite to defend themselves than to kill. Which means that, should they feel threatened or cornered, or even just confused, they could lash out and infect people who have no idea what's happened to them. Who could then infect others. And so on."

Though I was already suffering from vivid mental images of Tom and Romy growing into bloodthirsty little monsters, it hadn't yet occurred to me that they could unleash a plague of whitewulf infections upon Oakvale.

Guilt hit me like a burst of cold wind, stealing my breath. I sank onto a stool at the table. "This is because of me. I brought him here." I glanced at Tom again, and when I found him watching us, still curled up on the floor, another chill traveled down my spine.

Could he understand us? Beyond that, even if he knew the words we were saying, did he truly comprehend what we were talking about?

"But what else was I supposed to do with him? I had no idea he was a whitewulf. I couldn't just leave a child alone to die in the dark wood. That's what would have happened to him, right?"

"Without his mother?" Mama shrugged. "Quite possibly."

I lowered my voice even further, hoping Tom wouldn't hear. "Do you think Gran knew about him when she caught his mother?" The beast whose blood was intended to trigger my own transformation.

"I can't imagine she did," my mother said. "She wouldn't have left him out there alone."

But I couldn't tell, from her phrasing, what the alternative might have been.

Gran would understand that any whitewulf pup she left alive would only grow into another threat to be dispatched, before it could snatch a terrified villager from the path and eat him. Would she really have chosen a different whitewulf for me to kill, if she'd known about the pup? Or was my mother saying Gran would have killed little Tom when she captured his mother?

As horrifying as that thought was—wulf or not, he was still just a child—the truth was that if I'd left Tom to his fate in the dark wood, little Romy wouldn't have been bitten.

I turned to Tom again and was relieved to see that he'd gone back to sleep. "So, what are we going to do about Romy?"

"As harsh as it sounds," Max said, staring into an untouched tankard of ale, "what's best for everyone is if she succumbs to the fever."

"That does sound harsh," I breathed. "Especially considering that Madame Paget has already lost two children." Most mothers had, of course. We'd lost my baby brother at just two weeks old, several years before Sofia was born.

"Losing her to the fever would be a mercy, considering the alternative," my mother insisted as she added pungent starter from a clay pot left to grow yeast from flour and water. "You know what will happen to them both, if anyone figures out what they are."

Flames crackled in my memory, accompanied by the phantom scent of burning flesh. "But they're just *children*." So far, they'd only proven a danger to the village chickens.

She worked the starter into her flour, taking out her frustration on the dough in stiff, harsh motions. "And yet, they will grow into vicious monsters that crave violence and feed on human flesh."

"Is that certain?" I asked, devastated by the prospect.

"Unfortunately," my mother said through clenched teeth.

An overwhelming wave of hopelessness crashed over me, sucking the air from my lungs. "So then, her fate is much the same, regardless. Either she dies of the fire raging beneath her skin, or of the one the village will light around her."

"No." My mother abandoned her dough and wiped her hands on her apron. "It is our duty to make sure she suffers neither of those fates."

Dread settled into my soul like smoke, too thick to breathe through. "You want to *kill* her?" I demanded softly. "No." Romy was just a child. My mother and I were there when she was born!

"I don't think we can afford to wait and see if she recovers," Max said, and little hairs stood up all over my arms. "The safest thing to do, for the entire village, is—"

"*No,*" I repeated. "There has to be some alternative to killing a child."

"Adele, I know this is difficult." My mother rounded her work surface to lean against the end of it closest to me. "But we have a responsibility to the village. This is part of a guardian's duty."

"Isolation," I said, determined to find some way to save her. "We can isolate her, so that no one else will be infected, while we wait out the fever."

Max leaned back in his chair. "How will you explain that to her family?"

"And afterward, what then?" my mother asked gently. "If she survives, what will we do with her?" She glanced at Tom. "With them both?"

"I don't know! Release them into the dark wood, and hope some whitewulf mother takes them in? Or let nature take its course? Either way, that's better than us killing a five-year-old," I whispered, my voice so soft I could hardy hear myself. "I can't believe we're even talking about this."

"We have *no choice* but to talk about this," my mother snapped softly, and I looked up, surprised to find her bright green eyes shining with frustration. "Our job is to protect our neighbors from the threat of the dark wood, even when that threat ventures into the village itself. Even when that threat looks like a harmless child. You must be prepared to make difficult decisions, and in this case, that involves weighing the survival of an entire village against the lives of two—"

The front door flew open, cutting my mother off in mid-sentence, and Sofia burst into the room on a gust of icy wind. Her eyes were wide, her red waves a wild, tangled mess flying around cheeks flushed from the cold. "Madame Paget sent me, and I ran all the way!"

"What is it?" my mother asked, visibly recomposing herself as she pushed the door closed. "Is it Romy? Is the fever worsening?"

"No, it's broken! She's awake, and she's asking for Tom," Sofia said, and I followed her gaze to see that the boy had been startled awake by her arrival. "Can I take him to her?"

"No!" I shouted, and Sofia jumped, shocked by my response.

"Why not?" She glanced around the room in confusion, as the obvious tension seemed to sink in. "What's wrong?"

"Nothing. I'll take Tom." My mother took off her apron and hung it on a hook by the door, leaving her fresh dough to rise on her work surface.

I started to suggest that maybe Tom should stay at our house, but then I came to a conclusion my mother had obviously already reached—that the Pagets were at risk with Romy in their house anyway, and that indulging Romy's request might keep her calm, which could keep her from biting or scratching anyone.

"Tom?" Mama held one hand out to the child on the floor, and he stood to take it.

"Can I come?" Sofia asked.

My mother hesitated. "Yes, but let Tom keep Romy company. You and Jeanne can go play in the square." A plan no doubt intended to keep Jeanne away from the two little whitewulfs.

"Well, so much for my isolation idea," I said, when the door had closed behind them.

"It was kindhearted," Max said, yet I could tell from his tone that he thought it was also impractical. "But now we have to deal with the reality in front of us. There are two whitewulf pups in Oakvale, and if we don't do something, they're eventually going to bite someone. Someone *else*, in Tom's case."

"And, presumably at some point Romy's going to change into a little wolf puppy, as Tom has evidently been doing at night. Do you have any idea when that will be?"

Max shook his head. "No. But when she does, the village will assume the entire Paget family has come under some evil influence."

A chill crawled over my flesh. Could he be right? Would my neighbors believe that the Pagets were . . . receptive to the dark wood?

"Does she have pox?" Sofia poked at the hunk of venison roast in her bowl.

"No, it isn't pox." My mother set a second bowl of venison and broth in front of Jeanne Paget, along with a hunk of stale bread.

"Is it the plague?" Jeanne asked, as she dipped her bread into her broth.

"No, it's just a fever," I told her. "And your sister's recovering already."

My mother had convinced Madame Paget to let Jeanne stay the night with Sofia, so she could focus on caring for Romy, who still felt weak. But we'd had no luck trying to save Madame and Monsieur Paget from the risk of a bite, because we couldn't tell them that their daughter was a whitewulf.

238

Which meant all we could do was hope that even with her strange new lupine instincts, Romy wouldn't bite her own parents, and that they knew enough about Tom's tendency to bite to stay away from his mouth. Because Romy would not be separated from him.

And because bringing him back with us would only have put Jeanne at the same risk of a bite that her parents were in from Romy. At least this way, the threat was contained to one cottage.

While the girls ate, my mother gestured for me to follow her into the back room. "You should have seen them," she whispered as she sat on the edge of her straw mattress and resumed braiding the candle wick she'd begun the day before. "As soon as he saw her, Tom climbed into the bed with Romy, and they curled up together to sleep, like pups born of the same litter."

I sighed as I sank onto the bed next to her. "In a way, I suppose they were."

"There isn't going to be a pleasant solution to this, Adele. I need to know that you understand that."

"I do." I picked at the edge of the blanket. "Do you . . . ? Do you still think we'll have to kill the children?" I whispered.

"I don't see that we have any choice but to give them an easy, humane end. Quickly. I'll offer to watch them both tonight, so Madame Paget can get some sleep, and I'll take care of it then. I think I can manage it so that her parents believe Romy's fever came back in the night, and she succumbed to it. But Tom . . .

Well, what Sofia thought when he was missing makes sense. He has a history of sneaking out at night, now, and who's to say he didn't wander into the woods, trying to make his way home?"

"You don't think it'll seem like a coincidence if Tom runs away the same night Romy dies?"

"I don't think we have a choice. And I think people will be willing to believe that once Tom lost his best friend in the village, he wanted to go home. He's been through a lot, even if our neighbors don't have an accurate understanding of the tragedy."

"And you can do that? You can live with yourself, after you've taken another woman's child from her, right under her own roof?"

Her hands went still, her knuckles white in their grip on the wick she was weaving. "I don't really have any choice."

"Like you didn't have a choice, when you let Papa die?"

My mother flinched. "Yes," she said at last. "Sometimes a guardian has no choice. Even more often, she has no *good* choice."

"Who found him?"

"You don't remember?" she asked, and I shook my head. My memories of that day were of my papa. Of the horror of his mauled leg and his fever-glazed eyes.

"Grainger's father. Monsieur Colbert was on patrol, and he saw your papa go into the woods. He lit a torch and went in after him, and within minutes, he heard your father cry out. He followed the screams and drove the whitewulf off with his torch and his sword, then he dragged your father from the woods. But it was far too late to save him."

"So you let them burn him."

My mother's exhalation seemed to deflate her. "There was *no way* to let him live, *chère*. None. He was infected. He would have become a whitewulf, and they are not like us. He understood what was happening, and he did not want to unleash a beast like that upon the village."

"How . . . ?" Grief swelled within me, fresh and throbbing. "How could you *bear* it? How could you just stand there and—" My voice broke beneath the agony of the memory.

"That was the worst day of my life, Adele. The hardest thing I've ever had to do was nothing at all." She gripped the edge of the mattress with hands white from the strain. "I had to stand there and do *nothing* while they tied your father to the post and piled wood around him. I had to do nothing when they lit the kindling. While he screamed, devoured by the flames. Because he *would not hear* of me objecting. I tried to talk him into it anyway, while I was laying poultices over his legs. While the priest, and the baron, and Monsieur Colbert were conferring over his fate, in our front room. Because how could I not try to spare him such a horrible death? But pleading for the life of a beast that consumes human flesh would have cast suspicion of witchcraft upon our family, and he wouldn't let me endanger myself or you girls. He believed that submitting to his fate was his duty. That finally he would be protecting me—protecting *us*—from a monster."

From himself. She didn't have to say that part aloud for me to hear it. To finally grasp his sacrifice.

I'd been there. I'd seen my father in the bed and I'd heard my parents whispering. I'd seen Papa tied to the post and I'd smelled his burning flesh. How could I possibly have understood so little of what was actually happening?

"I had no choice, yet I've never forgiven myself," my mother said. "And I won't blame you if you can't forgive me either, now that you know."

What would I be forgiving her for, if he made his own choice? For not finding the opportunity to kill my father herself? To give him a less painful end?

That was exactly what she was trying to do for Tom and Romy. But this wasn't the same. My father made his own decision, but the children wouldn't get that opportunity.

"There has to be another way, Mama. Let me take them into the woods. I could lead them far enough that they can't find their way back, and they could just . . . live there. Maybe some other whitewulfs will find them and take them in."

She shook her head slowly. "They'll only grow up to be two more threats to this village. We'll have to hunt them eventually anyway."

"At least then we won't be killing helpless, innocent *children*. We're supposed to be *guardians*. But how are we any different from the monsters in the dark wood, if we're willing to do that?"

She sighed again. "We are a different kind of monster, Adele. The beasts in the forest do horrific things to people. We do horrific things to *protect* people. And that is rarely easy. It's rarely neat, or clean, or pretty. Yet it still must be done. Even when that makes us monsters."

But I couldn't live with that. With being a monster.

Slaying beasts? Yes.

Hiding part of myself from all of my friends? If I must.

Killing small children in their sleep? *No.* I couldn't accept that as a part of my destiny.

"Let's ask Gran." I took my mother's hand and squeezed it, holding her gaze just as fiercely by candlelight. "She doesn't know about any of this yet, and maybe she'll have a better idea." Or maybe she'll like my plan better than my mother's.

"We need to act quickly—"

"A couple of hours. I'm only asking for a couple of hours, Mama. Max and I can go talk to her right now to fill her in. Get her advice. All I'm asking is that you stay here with Sofia and Jeanne until we get back. Just . . . don't do anything until we know her thoughts. Okay?"

Finally, she nodded. "But *only* a couple of hours. We need to do whatever we're going to do before the sun comes up, Adele. We can't let this risk continue for even one more day."

SIXTEEN

I pulled my cloak closed, glad for its warmth, but in spite of the frigid temperature, I couldn't make myself raise the hood because every time I did, I saw bright white fur around the edges of my vision. Gran had sewn the trim onto my hood weeks ago, but now, every time I saw it, I remembered that it had come from Tom's mother's corpse.

"Adele, are you okay?" Max asked. If we weren't still in the dark wood, on our way home, he would stop walking and look straight into my eyes, trying to assess the problem. He did that a lot, and most of the time, lately, he got it right.

"No, I'm not okay." Despite my hope that she would agree with me, Gran's grim advice had come as no real surprise. "I understand that the only way to protect Oakvale is to remove Romy and Tom from the village, one way or another. I also understand that we'll be cleaning up a mess I made."

"You didn't know—"

"It doesn't *matter* that I didn't know he was a whitewulf. It doesn't matter why this happened. What matters is that I put us in this situation, and now I have to fix it. What matters is that those children, as dangerous as they may be, aren't malicious and haven't done anything wrong. They haven't hurt anyone. But they're the ones who're going to suffer for my mistake."

"Tom bit Romy," Max pointed out, and though he was probably trying to help me feel better about what had to be done, I kind of wanted to punch the calm logic right out of him.

I didn't *want* to feel better about this.

"Tom wasn't trying to infect her. He was just arguing over a toy, the way puppies nip each other over a prized bone. Because he was raised as an animal in the woods, and that's what they do." I sighed, and my steps began to slow on the path. "I understand that they can't stay in the village, but I think that the best thing for everyone is to take them both into the dark wood and—"

"No. Adele." Max's tone was gentle, but he sounded . . . frustrated. "The best thing for everyone would be to eliminate the threat, rather than leave it to grow large enough to eat a human being. Just like both your mother and grandmother said."

"You *actually* think we should kill them?" My temper snapped, and I turned to him on the path. "What if it were your child? What if it were *our* child?"

My question caught him so off guard that he stumbled, and the swinging lantern cast wild swaying shadows all around us. "Ours?"

"Hypothetically speaking." The words rushed out as warmth gathered in my cheeks. "Could you abandon our child in the dark wood to let nature 'take its course'? Or could you 'eliminate the threat' presented by your own flesh and blood? A child you taught to walk and talk?" A child I'd carried?

"Adele, we wouldn't have any choice. The fact that the child was ours wouldn't give us the right to let it threaten children belonging to the rest of the village."

"I know. I just . . ." I exhaled again. Then I forced the confession over my tongue. "I want this to be as hard for you as it is for me. I need to know that it isn't easy for you to sentence two small children to death, Max. Otherwise . . ." Otherwise there was no point in even *pretending* to consider him as a suitor, because I couldn't spend the rest of my life with someone who could make such a horrible decision so easily.

"Mon dieu," he whispered, as understanding seemed to wash over his features in the light from his lantern. Then he grabbed my hand and held it. *"Of course* this is hard for me. I'm horrified by what this means for those children, but I've tried to keep my personal feelings to myself, because they don't change anything. And because I didn't want to make this harder for you. I was trying to help you by not muddying the waters."

"Truly?"

"Yes. God, Adele, this isn't what I want." His gaze held mine with a blistering sincerity that, oddly, made me feel a little better. "But it *is* what your village needs."

"I know. In the future, though, if you're going to give me advice, I'd like to know not just what you think, but how you *feel*."

He squeezed my hand, and a tiny smile teased the corners of his lips. "So, we're going to have a future, then?"

"Again. Hypothetical," I said as I gently pulled my hand from his grip and started down the path. "Come on. It's late, and—"

A shriek shattered the night, and I realized we were closer to the village than I'd thought. I took off at a run, and Max's steps hurried after me, light from the lantern casting swinging shadows on the path ahead.

"Someone catch that thing!" a woman's voice shouted as we stepped out of the woods. "It has my hen!" A streak of white shot out from behind the Rousseaus' barn, and a second later, Madame Rousseau—Elena's mother—followed, holding her skirt up as she ran.

Max and I watched, stunned, as she chased what appeared to be a small dog with a chicken hanging limp from its muzzle.

Only that wasn't a dog.

"Oh *no*," I breathed, just as Grainger raced into view from the other direction, his lantern swinging with each step. His sword clanked at his side, but when he stopped and set down his light, it was his bow that he drew, along with an arrow from the quiver on his back.

He took aim, then his arrow whispered through the darkness,

247

and the little white pup fell to the ground with a pain-filled yelp.

"Did you get it?" Madame Rousseau called, squinting into the darkness beyond the light from her candle.

"Stay back!" Grainger shouted, and she skidded to a stop on the frozen mud, her shoes peeking from beneath the hem of the skirt she still held up. "It isn't dead. And . . . it isn't a fox."

My pulse spiked with a bitter bolt of dread. "Grainger!" I raced toward the wounded pup, tugging my cloak closed to cover my hatchet and leather belt. "Stop!"

"Adele!" Max whispered fiercely, as his footsteps pounded behind me.

"Adele?" Grainger frowned at me in the glow from his lantern. Suspicion knit his brows together when he saw Max behind me. "What are you doing out so late?"

"I was . . . We were—" Panic tightened around me like a vise. I'd been caught out at night with Max, and Grainger had shot one of the whitewulf pups, and I had no good way to explain either of those events.

"What *is* that?" Madame Rousseau demanded, staring at the pup in confusion. "I heard a noise behind our cottage, and then the chickens started squawking. I thought it was a fox, in the dark, but I've never seen a white fox."

"It isn't a fox." Grainger pointedly turned away from me, approaching the wulf pup with his sword in one hand, his lantern in the other, his bow hanging from his shoulder. "Go get more light. Please," he added when Madame Rousseau hesitated, still squinting at the wounded animal.

She gave him a terse nod, then turned and headed back to her cottage, on the other side of the barn.

I exhaled slowly. "Grainger—"

"It's a wolf," he said, his voice cooler than I'd ever heard it. "Only a pup, but—"

The puppy began to tremble just as the light from Max's lantern fell over it. I darted forward, but Grainger put out one arm to hold me back. "A wolf in pain will bite."

Yet surely he had no idea how right he was.

"I've never seen one so white. There isn't a single streak of gray in its fur." Grainger placed his boot lightly on the poor thing's leg, and I flinched when he pulled his arrow free from its shoulder. Blood poured from the wound. "Probably because it isn't yet mature." He frowned as the wolf's trembling became a full-body convulsion. "What's happening to it?"

Before I could figure out what to say, a gruesome popping sound came from the pup, and I realized exactly what was happening.

Oh no.

Grainger jumped back, startled, his lantern swinging wildly as the pup's fur began to recede into its skin. But a second later he knelt close, holding his light high to illuminate the oddity.

"Mon dieu," he whispered. "It's a werewolf. That pup is *loup garou!"*

But I could only shake my head and take a step back, miming

shock and fear, because he had to believe that Max and I were as astonished and confused as he was.

"I've only seen one slink out of the dark wood before." Grainger stood again and glanced back at the tree line, a new wariness evident in the dip of his brow. "And it certainly wasn't a pup. Keep your distance." He spread his arms and urged us back even farther as he drew his sword. "We have no idea what this little monster is capable of."

Horrified by the turn of events, I could do nothing but stand there and watch, feigning shock with my arms crossed over my cloak. Waiting to see which of the little pups he'd just shot. Which one was exposing itself to the entire village.

I didn't have to wait long.

A few seconds after it began, the process was over, and a familiar child lay on the ground before us, naked and shivering, bleeding from a gruesome hole in her shoulder. Her eyes were glazed with pain and shock.

"Mon dieu," Grainger whispered again, staring down at her in utter shock. "That's Romy Paget."

"We don't know what this means," I insisted softly, struggling to find something to say that wouldn't incriminate me or make things worse for Romy.

"It's *devilry*," Grainger declared, his eyes wide as he stared at the child. "She's fallen into the clutch of a monster."

Max gave me an uneasy look over his shoulder, and my

mind raced while I tried to come up with a sensible counter to Grainger's conclusion.

Footsteps pounded toward us as Madame Rousseau returned, this time with her husband, as well as Elena and one of her brothers. From the center of the village came more voices and bobbing lanterns as my neighbors came out to investigate the middle-of-the-night commotion.

"Where's the fox?" Monsieur Rousseau demanded, his legs bare and prickled with gooseflesh beneath the hem of his night tunic.

Though there was no fox to be found, the stolen hen lay a hand's span from the semi-conscious child's head, its neck broken, wounds slowly leaking blood where her teeth had punctured its skin.

"Is that Romy Paget?" Simon Laurent asked, as several other villagers gathered close, his parents and brothers among them. My mother wasn't there—she couldn't have heard Madame Rousseau's scream from across the village—but it was only a matter of time before the ruckus reached her. "What's happened to her?"

"Oh no!" Elena tried to kneel at the child's side, but I lurched in front of her and dropped onto my knees next to Romy, worried that she might bite, though she looked close to losing consciousness as she shivered on the ground. "She's hurt! She's going to bleed to death, if she doesn't freeze first!" Elena took off her own cloak and draped it over the child, when I wouldn't let her get any closer.

"Stay back, Adele!" Grainger pulled me up by my arm, his brows knit low. "That little girl is a *wolf*."

"What the devil is he babbling about?" Elena's father demanded, clearly ready to reclaim his warm bed, despite the tragedy unfolding before him.

"I shot a young wolf with a chicken in its mouth, and it became little Romy Paget," Grainger said. "She's a *werewolf*."

Silence settled over the crowd, and every gaze landed on him.

"That's quite a serious charge," Monsieur Laurent, Simon's father, said at last.

"And yet it's true. That child was a *wolf* a moment ago." Grainger's earnest gaze skipped from face to face. "She only became human again after I shot her."

A sick feeling churned in my stomach, and I let Max tug me back until we were just two more faces among the crowd.

"But that's Romy," Elena said softly. "She's just a little girl."

"A little girl who wore a wolf's skin and fur moments ago," Grainger insisted. "She stole a chicken from your yard."

"Madame?" Monsieur Laurent turned to the Rousseaus, his brow furrowed in confusion. "Did Romy Paget steal your chicken?"

"It was a fox, I think." Elena's mother frowned. "I couldn't see well in the dark, so it could have been a small wolf. But it definitely wasn't a child."

"It *was* a young wolf," Grainger insisted. "Unnaturally white, carrying a hen in its maw. *That* hen." He pointed at the dead chicken, and the crowd eyed the bird as if its existence might clarify the situation. "I shot the creature with my bow. Madame Rousseau went to get more light, and while she was gone, the wolf began to thrash about. A moment later the child lay on the ground, naked as the day she was born, and injured in the very same spot as the wolf."

"Devilry . . ." Madame Gosse whispered, one hand clutched at her breast. Behind her a fearful murmur rippled through the crowd, and hair began to rise on the back of my neck.

"We must find the source of the infection before it spreads," Grainger said. "Has the child been in the dark wood, or is there a wolf among us, right here in Oakvale? We'll have to interrogate her family, and—"

"Grainger, you know the Pagets," I interrupted, desperate to stop a boulder that seemed to be picking up speed as it rolled downhill. "They're good people." I appealed to him as much with my gaze as with my words. "They haven't hurt anyone."

But if my neighbors truly believed that Romy had been infected with lycanthropy, they would soon realize the only bite on her had come from little Tom. And if her family tried to defend her, the entire Paget household could be declared witches, protecting their own. Just as Max predicted.

"They may well be good people," Grainger said. "But Romy hasn't been in the forest, that I know of. She hasn't been

253

attacked by a werewolf, which means we don't know the source of this infection. But the village watch has an obligation to root out corruption from the dark wood wherever it may roost, and if that leads back to the Pagets, then this village will have a duty to perform, unpleasant though that might be. For the good of all of Oakvale." His gaze locked with mine. "A wolf is a wolf, whatever face it may wear in the daytime."

Whatever face it wore. Including mine.

The ground suddenly felt unsteady under my feet. As if the world were crumbling beneath me.

Max gave me a sympathetic look, but he didn't seem surprised by Grainger's declaration. In fact, he seemed almost relieved to hear it spoken aloud. As if he'd been waiting for Grainger to say those words—for me to hear them—since the moment he'd arrived in the village.

"Grainger . . ." Elena began, her words halting, her tone cautious. "Let's think about this for a moment. Romy is just a child, and you're right; she hasn't been anywhere near a werewolf. So how could she be infected?" She let her words sink in for a heartbeat. "The hour is late and you haven't slept. Surely your eyes were deceiving you. Maybe you were dreaming, on your feet."

"You think I dreamed it? You think I shot a child in a *dream*?"

She shrugged, and Simon stepped closer to her, standing

protectively by her side as he spoke. "There's no other sense to be found in this."

"Sense or not, it's the truth." Grainger stood taller, secure in the accuracy of his report. Determined to do his duty. "They saw it, as well." He turned to Max and me, and with his expectant gaze came the attention of the entire gathering.

"I . . . I'm not sure what I saw," I stammered. "As Madame Rousseau said, it was very dark."

"Romy!" Madame Paget cried. A second later, she forced her way to the center of the crowd with her husband on her heel, carrying a lantern. "What's happened?" She gasped when she saw her daughter, then she fell to her knees at the child's side.

I let her stay, because Romy had fallen unconscious and couldn't bite her.

"What is *wrong* with you?" Madame Paget stared up at the crowd, accusation written in every line of her face. "She's injured! Why is no one tending her?"

"She's right. Let's get Romy inside," I said, eager for the opportunity to break up the crowd before people could grab pitchforks.

"No!" Grainger blocked my arm again, when I reached for the child. "It isn't safe to touch her, and as cruel as it seems, we have no choice but to put her out of her misery."

"He's right," Madame Gosse said, and my heart dropped into my stomach when an uneasy murmur of assent rose from the crowd. "'Suffer not a witch to live!' We all heard it in church, not a month ago!"

"What are you saying?" Madame Paget demanded, pressing her hand over her daughter's wound. "What happened to her?"

Grainger's hand tensed around the handle of his lantern. "Madame, you should move back, for your own safety. I shot a wolf pup, but what lies in its place is your daughter." He looked around at the crowd again. "Everyone, step back." He threw out his arms, to push back the crowd. "Romy Paget has been infected by a werewolf, and she's a danger to us all."

"Lycanthropy is a curse from the devil . . ." someone murmured from the crowd, as the circle slowly expanded away from us.

"Unnatural . . ."

"It's witchcraft!"

"Nonsense!" Madame Paget shouted as she glared at them, still applying pressure to her daughter's injury. "She's only a child!"

"I'm sorry, Madame," Grainger said. "But I saw it with my own eyes. So did Adele. Tell them, Adele."

Panic flooded my veins, burning like fire beneath my skin. "I—"

"That's nothing more than frivolous superstition!" Monsieur Paget roared, lifting his lantern high, so that shadows fled from his face. "She's just a little girl recovering from an illness."

"Grainger Colbert is telling stories to cover his own guilt!" his wife declared, tears shining in her eyes. "For firing an arrow at a child! You should be *ashamed*!" she added, aiming a distraught look at him.

Another murmur rose from those gathered, and I could feel the crowd's confusion. Its shifting sentiment.

Grainger turned to Elena's mother. "Madame Rousseau. You saw me shoot the wolf. Tell them."

"I . . ." Eyes wide, her nose red from the cold, she glanced around at a crowd still swelling as more people gathered. "It was dark. I thought I saw a fox. The one that's been killing hens all over the village. But I see no fox now."

"Are you saying there *was* no fox?" Monsieur Laurent turned to me, obviously expecting a verification.

I could deny what I'd seen—what I knew—and let our neighbors believe Grainger had shot a child in cold blood, or out of negligence. In which case he would surely stand trial. Or I could admit the truth and condemn the Paget family to accusations of witchcraft. In which case they would surely be burned.

"It was a wolf," Grainger insisted. "But now—"

"It was—" My voice broke, and I cleared my throat as a dozen different gazes settled on me with an unbearable weight. "It was a wolf," I said, and I saw Grainger's tense grip on his lantern ease. "A young one."

Grainger exhaled slowly, relief flooding his features. "It is

257

as Adele says. She would never tell a lie."

"But a natural wolf, not *loup garou*," I continued, and a gasp went up from the crowd, as Grainger stared at me in shock. "It was just a wolf pup that stole Madame Rousseau's hen. Monsieur Colbert fired an arrow at it. But he missed and hit little Romy instead. It was an accident. Right, Max?"

"Of course." Max nodded decisively. "He was aiming for the wolf and hit the child instead. The wolf was startled and dropped the hen, then it fled into the forest. Monsieur Colbert is not to blame. It was just a tragic misfortune."

Monsieur Laurent turned to Grainger. "Lad, was it an accident?"

"No!" Grainger insisted, his eyes still wide and stunned by my betrayal. "There was no child. I shot a wolf pup, white as a fresh coat of snow, and she transformed into Romy Paget. The Paget girl is a werewolf. Why else would she be out at night, in the cold, without a scrap of clothing?"

"Because that's how she sleeps, as do half the children in the village!" Madame Paget said.

"Since the fever hit, she's been walking in her sleep," her father added.

Max knelt to lift the unconscious child. "I'll help you get her home," he said. "I only hope it isn't too late." But I could tell from the look he gave me that as tragic as that would be, he believed Romy's death at Grainger's hands would be a blessing for the two of us. And for the entire village.

Numb, I took the lantern from him and tucked Elena's cape around the little girl.

"Someone fetch Monsieur Colbert," Madame Gosse said, pliable as ever to the shifting will of the crowd. "And tell him his son has lost his mind."

"Take his bow!" Another voice shouted as Max carried Romy down the dirt path, with the Pagets and the rest of the crowd on his heels. "Before he shoots someone else and calls them cursed!"

"Adele." Grainger grabbed my arm, holding me back with him. His gaze pleaded with me to come to his defense. To confirm his account by damning the Paget family as witches.

"Just tell them it was an accident," I begged him softly. "They'll believe you if you take it back. Say you were tired and confused. Say you were mistaken."

"I know what I saw." His hand clenched around my arm, hard enough to hurt. "*You* saw the wolf, Adele. I know it."

"I saw a child." Fighting tears, I pulled my arm from his grip. "And if you want to maintain your good name—your position—you need to have seen the same." Shaking with guilt, I left him staring after me in astonishment while I hurried to catch up with Max.

My mother met us in the village square, and I could tell from the alarm on her face that she'd only just heard the commotion of the procession toward the Pagets' cottage. "What's going on?" She lifted her candle so she could see the small form in Max's arms. "Romy! What happened to her?"

"Grainger shot her with an arrow," Madame Gosse said. "He's lost his mind."

"It was an accident," I told her as Monsieur Paget took his daughter from Max. "She got between his bow and the wolf that stole Madame Rousseau's hen."

"Take her inside." My mother turned Madam Paget by her shoulders. "Get her warm. I'll prepare a poultice. Max, Adele, will you stay with Sofia and Jeanne?"

"Of course," Max said.

"Where's Colbert?" Madame Gosse demanded again. "Someone wake the captain of the watch and tell him his son has lost his mind."

"He hasn't—" I exhaled, guilt and frustration making my head pound. "It's very dark tonight, with no moon out. Grainger was tired and confused. It would be easy to mistake one shadowy shape for another, under those circumstances."

"Adele." My mother nodded toward our cottage, and Max took my arm, half-leading, half-dragging me toward my home.

As the door closed behind us, I heard Madame Gosse make one more terrifying declaration. "We'll convene the village tribunal in the morning. Anyone who shoots a child should face trial."

SEVENTEEN

———▶

J ust before dawn, my mother returned to the bakery, her skin
pale and drawn, her dress stained with blood. I'd gone to
the Pagets' cottage twice during the night to help with Romy's
wound, but twice she'd sent me home.

The second time, she'd sent Tom with me, with whispered
instructions to keep an eye on him and to keep him apart from
Jeanne and Sofia. But that proved easier said than done.

As it turned out, the little blond boy who was so calm and
docile during the day wanted nothing more than to play—and
likely to hunt—in the dark. Which made sense, considering that
he and Romy had probably been hunting chickens at night all
week.

Max and I had taken turns playing with him, staying well
away from his mouth, to keep him occupied and inside the cottage. We couldn't tell if he was aware at all that Romy had gone

chicken hunting without him, and he seemed completely unconcerned by his little friend's injury.

My mother exhaled as she closed the door, then leaned against it. "Well?" I demanded, standing from the table. "How is Romy?"

"I think she'll make it. There was a lot of blood, of course. But it's been hours now, and there's no sign of fever. Possibly because she's no longer human. Though her mother is more inclined to attribute that miracle to a higher power." She took off her cape and hung it on a hook by the door. "The girls?"

"Still asleep, and completely unaware," Max told her.

My mother sank onto the stool next to his, and I scooped some broth into a bowl for her from the pot I'd hung over the fire an hour before. She blew over the surface of the bowl, then sipped from it. "Romy's parents are distraught and unclear on exactly what happened, but what I've gathered is that Grainger shot Romy, believing her to be a fox, and now he's accusing her of being a werewolf?"

"He saw her change from wolf form, after she was shot," Max said in a whisper, with a glance at the back room, where the girls were still asleep.

"The whole thing is unthinkable." I blinked back tears before they could fall. "I had to lie to protect Romy, and now Grainger hates me."

My mother sighed. "I know how upsetting that is, but maybe it's for the—"

"Do *not* say it's for the best," I snapped at her. "You were right, okay? I can't marry him. But that doesn't mean I want him to *hate* me. And now . . ." I sucked in a deep breath. "Now there's talk of a trial. All because I lied."

"It seems you had little choice in the matter," my mother said. And she did look sorry about the turn things had taken. "But it's a little more serious than that. The Pagets are accusing him of crying witchcraft to cover up his own carelessness, and right now, people seem to believe them. But if Romy transforms again, or if she wakes up and says anything that supports his claim, the Pagets will be condemned as witches, which will unleash a plague of paranoia on the village that will eventually come to roost beneath our roof."

"I know." Half the town already thought we were cursed. "That's why I lied." Why I'd betrayed the man I'd once intended to marry.

My mother cradled her bowl in both hands. "Can you convince him that he's wrong about what he saw? That he was dreaming, or that the shadows played tricks on his eyes?"

"I tried, but he doesn't have any doubt about what happened, and he seems determined to protect the village. Not to mention his own honor."

"You *have* to convince him that he was mistaken," my mother said as she lifted the broth to her mouth for another sip. "And we have to deal with Tom and Romy before they become proof that he wasn't." She sighed. "It would have been a bizarre mercy for us all, had Grainger's aim been truer."

"I'm surprised you didn't just finish her off, while you were tending her," I muttered.

"If I'd had a moment alone with her to give her a peaceful end, I would have." To my mother's credit, the confession seemed to weigh heavy on her. "What did your grandmother say about the pups?"

"She agreed with you, that they should be 'put down' humanely and quickly, for the good of the village. But that was before Grainger shot Romy. People are paying a bit more attention to the poor girl, now, which will make that more difficult."

My mother's brows rose. "And yet, her new injury will make her death easier to believe."

"There's no guarantee of that. Let me release them into the dark wood." I lowered my voice, unsure whether or not Tom would understand what we were saying, should he wake up. "With any luck, people will think they had another nighttime adventure and wandered into the woods."

"That's still a death sentence for two small children," Max insisted. "But instead of giving them a quick, peaceful end, you'd be condemning them to starve to death in the forest— assuming they don't get eaten."

I turned on him, anger burning like flames in my chest. "*You* have no say in this. You have no *part* in this. You aren't married to a guardian, and you're not going to win my hand by default, just because I can't marry Grainger."

"Adele!" my mother whispered, horrified.

"I'm sorry." I shoved hair back from my face and exhaled. "It's just that a month ago, I thought my future was going to include Grainger and our children, and a little cottage on the edge of Oakvale. Instead, I got a hatchet and a crossbow, and nights spent hunting monsters, followed by mornings when I can hardly keep my eyes open. And that's fine. At least, it *was* fine, when I thought that would all be for the good of the village. And that I could perform this new duty and still have my marriage and my little cottage next door to Elena. But now . . . Now my duty has led me to betray Grainger in front of the whole village, and Max seems to think he can just step into his place. What was the point of ruining everything with Grainger—of turning the entire village against him—if Romy and Tom are *still* going to die? I sacrificed Grainger for *nothing*."

"No." My mother took my hand and refused to let me pull away. "You were protecting the rest of the Pagets. And us. If people think some malevolent force has been at work in the village, how long do you think it would take their suspicion to land on us? And if they turn against us and we have to flee Oakvale, there will be no one left to protect this village from its own superstitions. Much less from the dark wood."

"And, if it makes you feel any better, I never intended to just step into Grainger's place," Max added. "I want my *own* place in your life. Not his."

"I know. I'm sorry." And yet despite their obvious sympathy for the position I'd been put in, neither of them had changed their minds about the children. "Mama, *please* let me take the kids into the forest tonight."

She shook her head slowly. "We're supposed to be culling the population of the dark wood, not adding to it."

Max nodded. "The safest thing is to deal with them now, once and for all. Otherwise, the blood of anyone they grow up to kill is on our hands."

I bristled. "On *my* hands, you mean?"

He exhaled slowly. "Yes."

"Adele, they have to be dealt with . . . *permanently*."

"I know. But if they both die here in the village, their deaths won't seem natural," I pointed out as rationally as I knew how. "Especially considering that Tom isn't sick or injured. However, if they wander into the dark wood, when they already have a history of roaming at night? No one will question that. So let me do it. I'll take them into the woods tonight. And I will do my duty."

My mother frowned. "*You* want to—"

"No, I don't *want* to. But it's as much my responsibility as it is yours, now, and I'm offering to . . . handle it. Permanently." *My way.* "Away from the village, where none of us will come under suspicion."

She studied my face, trying to understand why I would make such an offer, when I'd been trying to save the children from the beginning.

I shrugged. "I'm a guardian now, and I have to start making difficult choices. Isn't that what you both said?"

Finally, she nodded. "Okay. You can take them into the woods tonight. But take Max with you."

"Fine." That didn't fit into my plan, but I could work around it.

"You're doing the right thing, Adele," he said softly.

"I know." That much, at least, was the absolute truth.

My mother stood with her empty bowl. "I'm going to go sit with Romy, to relieve her mother. You two need to get some rest. You can sleep in shifts, with one of you watching Tom at all times. Do *not* let him play with the girls. And, Max, stay away from his mouth."

"I'll watch him. You sleep."

Max's insistence felt like an apology for disagreeing with me, yet he did not actually apologize. Not that I expected him to. He and my mother were right about what Oakvale needed. But I was right, that Tom and Romy deserved to grow up. The hard truth was that there was no good option for what to do with the pups. All of our choices were horrible.

Letting them believe I'd come around to their perspective was the only way to keep my mother from killing poor little Romy in her sleep.

Yet somehow I felt worse about lying to Max than about lying to my mother. Despite what I'd said, I knew he had no intention of simply stepping into Grainger's place in my life. He didn't want to disagree with me. In fact, he probably wanted to tell me that I'd never made a mistake in my entire life. The fact that he'd spoken his mind, even knowing I'd be mad at him, told me I would always be able to trust him to tell me the truth, even when that wasn't what I wanted to hear.

So I gave him a sad smile, to let him know things were okay between us. Then I headed into the back room and settled onto my mother's bed, where I'd just fallen asleep—at least, that's what it felt like—when Sofia pounced on me.

"Oof!" My eyes flew open, and I found myself staring up at my little sister, her red hair wild from slumber. "What's this?"

"Wake up, sleepyhead! Can we have honey with our bread? And milk?"

"Only if there *is* milk. Go tend to the cow." I sat up, running one hand through my own tangled hair. "And take Jeanne with you."

"I'll take Tom too."

"No!" I grabbed her arm before she could make it off the bed. "I have another job for him." I followed her into the front of the cottage, where Tom was stacking split logs against the wall near the hearth.

"We kept ourselves busy," Max said, looking very proud of himself. "And the girls have already fed the chickens and fetched fresh water."

"Thank you. I . . . Do you want to sleep?" I asked. "I can watch them."

Instead of answering, Max studied my face. "It's okay. Go see him," he finally said.

"Who?"

"Grainger." He stepped closer, lowering his voice. "As little as I care for him, I know what he still means to you. And I know how difficult it was for you to do what you did last night." His voice was disarmingly kind, after the argument we'd had a couple of hours before.

He seemed sincere.

"What did she do last night?" Sofia asked.

I spun to find her watching us from the doorway into the back room. "Go milk the cow!"

"I'm going!" she shouted. "But what did you do to Grainger?"

"Nothing. Go milk the cow."

"Then why is he locked up?"

I glanced at my sister, then turned back to Max, my stomach pitching. "He's locked up?"

Max nodded. "He spent the night under guard in the shed behind the church. Madame Gosse came by while you were sleeping, with her jaw flapping faster than a bird's wings. She said his father took him into custody, and he was shouting about Romy being a wolf and you being a liar."

I groaned.

"Madame Gosse says he's lost his senses," Sofia offered sagely, as Jeanne joined her in the doorway. "What happened?"

I closed my eyes for a second, trying to decide whether or not to tell her. Then, with a sigh, I sank into a chair at the table and I waved my sister and her friend forward. They were going to hear it from someone; best it came from me.

"Grainger shot Romy with an arrow last night. It was an accident," I added, when Sofia's eyes widened, and Jeanne's filled with tears. "And Mama thinks Romy's going to be fine, *chère*. There's no sign of another fever."

Yet as true as that was, it felt like a lie; Romy would not, ultimately, be fine.

"Why did he shoot her?" Jeanne asked.

"He was aiming for the wolf that stole Madame Rousseau's hen," Max explained. "But it was dark out and difficult to see."

"Is that what happened to our hen?" Sofia asked. "It wasn't a fox?"

"That's likely." I exhaled slowly and brushed a wild crimson lock back from her face.

Jeanne frowned. "Then why is Grainger in jail, if it was an accident?"

Sofia suddenly looked worried. "What's going to happen to him?"

"I don't know," I told her. "But I'm going to go talk to him and see how he's doing. I'll be back as soon as I can." Then I put on my everyday cloak and headed out the door.

The village was buzzing with a tense energy, despite the fact that most of us had gotten little sleep. Madame Gosse and several other women were gathered in the village square, gossiping, and based on what little I caught as I pointedly passed by them without a word, the story was growing with every retelling.

To my relief, there were no guards at our makeshift jail when I arrived. It was a small two-room shed, one room of which had been fitted with a lock by the blacksmith long before I was born.

Outside of the cell there stood only a single stool and a key hanging on the wall. Through the window cut into the door, I could see Grainger lying on a straw floor that badly needed freshening.

I cleared my throat, and he opened his eyes. When he saw me, he sat up, scowling, but he made no move to stand. "Have you come to damn me with more lies?" His voice was hoarse from the cold air, his gaze hard.

Grainger had never looked at me with anything other than kindness shining in his eyes. For years, he'd made me feel safe and loved, and this change in him left me aching. Struggling to breathe through a suffocating cloud of guilt and regret.

I deserved his anger. But wallowing in my own guilt wouldn't solve anything, and admitting that I'd lied would only make it harder for me to convince him to change his story. To save himself.

"Grainger, I'm *so* sorry," I said at last. "But I can't say I saw something I didn't."

Finally, he stood. "You saw it."

"I saw an injured little girl," I insisted, determined to help him—to atone for what I'd done to him—even if he couldn't see that's what I was doing.

"I *know* you saw it, Adele." His intimate focus pierced me, a blade drawing fresh blood. "You know Romy Paget isn't human."

"What I know is that you didn't mean to hurt a child, and I will go to my grave telling people that." I took a deep breath and met his gaze, steeling myself for yet another lie. "But the wolf got away, Grainger. You shot a little girl, and whatever you think you saw was simply a trick of the shadows. It was exhaustion playing with your mind. You'd been up all day and all night, out in the cold on patrol. If you tell them it was an accident, you might be forgiven—"

"I can't do that. I can't lie and ignore such a grave threat to our village. To our *home*."

"—but if you keep telling this story, they're going to think you're mad. Or that you're covering up your own negligence. Which might lead the tribunal to decide you're a danger to the village."

"*I'm* the danger?" Fury reddened his face, and my heart ached for him. For us. For what could never be. If I hadn't told a lie about him now, he would have told a truth about me later, and I'd be the one in that locked room, awaiting trial. Understanding the inevitability of this moment—of this cell door between us— didn't make it any easier to accept.

"That child is a beast concealed in the body of a little girl, Adele. She's brought evil from the dark wood directly into our village, and the only way to protect Oakvale from such a corrupting influence is to purify her soul by fire. And if you can't admit what you saw—what she is—that can only be because the devil has gotten to you too."

"Grainger—"

"Maybe Lucas and Noah Thayer are right about you," he spat, and my face flamed as if he'd slapped me. "Maybe you're protecting this devil-child because you're just like her. And the timing of these revelations is no coincidence."

Oh no. I backed away from the bars, my heart pounding. "Tom has nothing—"

"Tom?" He shook his head, frowning. "I'm talking about Maxime Bernard. Everything was fine in Oakvale before he arrived. That isn't chance, Adele. He's a stranger and we know nothing about him. He must have brought this evil—"

"Max has *nothing* to do with this," I snapped, as fresh fear swelled in the pit of my stomach. Like a disease, suspicion was a threat to anyone it landed upon, and strangers were especially susceptible. I'd heard tales of accusations being passed from neighbor to neighbor around small villages, the accused each heaping blame onto someone else in their own defense, until no one could be trusted. Until the entire town fell into chaos and violence. That could *not* happen in Oakvale. "And Romy—" I bit off my own words, before I could say too much—before I could admit that Tom had likely killed my hen the night *before* Max had arrived—because there was no need to tell him more than he already knew. "I'm trying to help you, Grainger. I—"

"Help me by telling the truth. You and Maxime saw the same thing I did. Why would you hold your tongue in the presence of such evil?"

"Mademoiselle Duval!" A deep voice barked my name and I spun to find Grainger's father standing in the open doorway, his sword at his hip. Seeing him sent a fresh ache throughout my bones.

I'd thought he would be my father-in-law. I'd thought I would live on his land. That he would bounce my children on his knee.

"What are you doing here?" he asked.

"I . . . I'm trying to help him, Monsieur."

His expression softened. "There is little you can do for him, child, and I'm afraid that association with him will do you no favors."

"Adele." Grainger's voice cracked halfway through my name, and when I turned, I found him staring out at me from the window in the door. "*Please* tell the truth. Don't do this to me."

Tears filled my eyes, blurring his face.

"You should go," Monsieur Colbert said. "My son is not well. He is incapable of listening to reason and advice." The fatigue in his voice said that he had made his own exhaustive efforts in that regard.

"What's going to happen to him?" I asked as I reluctantly followed Monsieur Colbert out of the building.

"I'm meeting with Father Jacque and Baron Carre's estate

manager at noon, since the baron is not here to complete the tribunal in person. The charge from the Pagets is the attempted murder of a child, and for a crime that serious, the village is not willing to wait for the thaw, to take him to court. We will decide his fate today."

"He wasn't trying to kill her, Monsieur Colbert." I grabbed the watchman's arm, and with it, I captured his full attention. "I swear it on my life. He just . . . missed."

"I believe you." The pain on Monsieur Colbert's face broke my heart. "But if he won't say that in his own defense, I'm afraid there is little hope for him."

"How is he?" Max asked the moment I stepped into my home.

Instead of answering, I glanced around the front room, pleased to see that there were several fresh loaves of bread in the oven. My mother had obviously been home. In fact, it seemed I'd just missed her.

Tom was curled up on his pallet again, sleeping, as he often seemed to do during the day.

"Where are Jeanne and Sofia?"

"Playing in the bean field on the edge of town. I reminded them not to go near the trees."

Such a reminder shouldn't have been necessary. We all grew up with the threat of the dark wood hovering at the edge of every thought. Every action. But now that I knew the woods held a special draw for future guardians, I worried that Sofia might give in to the dark lure of a destiny she couldn't possibly understand yet.

It was that same concern for me that had lured my father to his death.

"Thank you. Grainger is . . . stubborn. I tried to convince him that he saw a trick of light and shadow, but he believes his eyes. And he won't lie to save himself, as long as he believes that would mean putting the rest of Oakvale in danger." And the fact was that, as terrifying as his insistence was, I respected his devotion to the village and to his job, especially considering that it had landed him in jail.

"He believes that evil from the dark wood has infected Romy Paget, and that she will, in turn, infect all of Oakvale, unless she's burned alive to purify her soul." Flashes of my father's execution roared to the surface of my memory and sent chills crawling over my skin.

Max exhaled, still watching me carefully. "What do *you* believe?"

"I know she's been infected, of course. But I can't believe that either of the children are actually evil. They haven't tried to hurt anyone."

"Yet."

"Shouldn't that count for something?"

Max sighed. He stared into my eyes, as if he were studying them. "Does this have anything to do with your father?"

"What do you mean?"

"If you believe that Romy and Tom can be saved—that they aren't evil—then the same would have been true of your father, right? I know it must be tempting to believe that he would never really have become a monster."

"That isn't tempting at *all*!" I snapped softly at him. "That would mean my father died for *nothing*."

"And if Tom and Romy die before we know they're a threat, that could be true for them too. Is that what you're thinking?"

"I'm thinking that all we really know so far is that they are *loup garou*. As am I."

"They are *not* the same as you. But I'm the only one who will believe that."

"I know. Grainger believes that you and I know what Romy is, and that the only reason we would lie for her is if we are also corrupted."

Max's jaw clenched, his gaze narrowing beneath a furrowed brow. "And the rest of Oakvale? Which side of this do they fall on?"

"They believe he's lost his mind." I'd taken a long, slow walk through the village on my way home, to listen to the gossip and get a sense of the town's mindset. "His father, included."

"Unfortunately, that's probably for the best." Max stirred the pot still suspended over the fire and scooped up a bowl of broth for me.

"I don't even know what 'for the best' means, anymore," I said as I settled at the table with my bowl and a hunk of bread.

"Grainger told the truth, and now he's being punished for it. Romy and Tom haven't hurt anyone, yet. . . ."

"You don't have to do it yourself, you know." Max sank onto the stool next to mine. "I'll be with you out there. I can—"

"Thank you, but no. This is my mess." I sighed as I stared down into my bowl. "I have to clean it up."

EIGHTEEN

That afternoon, I pushed my way carefully through the crowd gathered in front of the church until I stood at Elena's side, my full basket heavy on my arm. Simon stood on her other side, with two of his brothers.

Max had stayed at the bakery to keep Tom away from Jeanne and Sofia. And to avoid reminding a village balanced on the razor's edge of paranoia that there was a new face in town.

It would take very little for the crowd to decide Grainger was right. A blood moon. A bad batch of ale. A moldy sheaf of wheat. Such minor disasters were regularly attributed to an evil influence, and with Grainger's accusations so fresh, any one of them might be enough to change the minds of most of the village.

"Have you heard anything?" I whispered. My fear for Grainger had kept me from getting any further rest. He could be pilloried and whipped, or he could just be fined. Or, if the tribunal believed that he intended to kill Romy, he could face execution. Likely a hanging.

But it wouldn't come to that. Not even the village gossip accused Grainger of intending to murder the poor child.

"Nothing yet," Simon said with a frustrated frown. "I can't understand how all this came about. Grainger is a good man, and I can't fathom him making up such a story, with no cause."

"And yet, here we are." Elena sighed. "The tribunal has been in there for nearly an hour."

I adjusted my basket in the crook of my elbow, trying not to choke on my own guilt. "Has the crowd been waiting that long?"

"Only some of us," she whispered, nodding toward Grainger's mother, who was wringing her hands hard enough to turn her fingers purple. I couldn't imagine how hard it must be for her, with her husband sitting in judgment of her son. "I don't think anything like this has happened in Oakvale since—" Elena's mouth snapped shut, but I knew what she'd been about to say.

Since your father.

But my papa's situation was very different from this. Grainger wasn't suspected of being a werewolf. They wouldn't be tying him to the post in the center of the square and piling fuel around him.

No matter what the tribunal decided, we wouldn't have to watch Grainger burn.

I could only hope the same remained true for Tom and Romy.

"This must be so hard for you," Elena whispered, and I nodded. "Have they called you in to stand witness?"

"No." And they probably wouldn't. Grainger's guilt would be determined entirely by the judgment of the priest, the captain of the village watch, and the local lord's estate manager, acting in his stead. None of whom had been present during the event. None of whom had spoken to anyone about what happened, except Grainger, and possibly his mother, as a character witness.

I found it agonizing to know that though I'd gotten him into this, I had no way to help him without damning the entire Paget family.

"I'm sure he'll be fine," Elena added, but her typical optimism was belied by the worried crease of her forehead.

Simon must have heard that same concern in her voice, because he turned to give her a reassuring smile, which warmed my heart even as it triggered an ache deep in my chest.

Grainger used to look at me that very same way.

"I have to make deliveries," I told Elena. "I'll be back." Though it looked like most of the people I'd be delivering to were assembled in that very gathering.

"Are you okay?" she whispered, clearly not fooled by my excuse.

"I'll be fine," I lied, though I wanted nothing more in the world than a return to the days when I could confide my deepest, darkest secrets to her. To a day when those secrets would have nothing at all to do with the dark wood.

I made my way through the village as quickly as I could, delivering the loaves I'd pulled from the oven that afternoon, taking payment in the form of smoked meats and winter vegetables like turnips, cabbage, and potatoes from those who were actually home. I dropped my full basket at the bakery with Max—my mother had gone back to the Pagets' to check on Romy—and returned to the gathering outside the church just as the doors were being opened.

Elena reached for my hand as the priest stepped forward and began to speak. "We have gathered here today to hear evidence against Grainger Colbert on the charge of attempting to murder a small child. Monsieur Colbert was given every opportunity to admit his guilt and beg the tribunal for mercy, but he insists that his aim was true. That the child he fired an arrow into is actually a wolf, capable of changing its appearance into that of a little girl in order to corrupt the good souls of Oakvale."

Monsieur Colbert and the baron's representative stood on either side of the priest, and while Father Jacque spoke, Grainger's papa stared at the ground with one hand on the pommel of his sword.

"It is our judgment, absent any witness to support his claims, that Monsieur Colbert is feigning madness in order to excuse his carelessness and ineptitude in the position of village watchman. He was appointed and armed in order to watch over the village—trusted with our very lives—and he has betrayed that trust by gravely wounding one of our most defenseless citizens. We therefore demand the removal of Monsieur Colbert from the village watch—along with the removal of his right hand."

A gasp went up from the crowd.

"Oh no . . ." I whispered, as dread sat heavy within me. "No, no, no."

"At least they don't want his head," Elena whispered in return, her hand tightening around mine.

But that was little comfort, considering the reality.

With only one hand, Grainger wouldn't be able to work at the sawmill. He would have trouble mounting a horse, plowing a field, or even swinging an axe, which meant it would be very difficult for him to provide for himself. To maintain his own dignity.

"The sentence is to be carried out immediately," the priest announced, drawing silence from a crowd determined not to miss a word. "Please gather in the village square."

"No, no, no . . ." I moaned.

"*Adele,*" Elena whispered, a warning for me to be quiet as the crowd began to flow around us like the current of a river.

My mouth snapped shut hard enough to jar my jaw, and I could only stare as two members of the village watch pulled Grainger from the church. His father stood by, watching stoically, while his mother fought tears.

"No!" Grainger shouted, pulling on the rope that bound his wrists. "Don't turn a blind eye to evil among us! Romy Paget is *loup garou*! She will be the undoing of this entire village! She and her family must undergo trial by fire!"

The crowd split down the middle, and I stared at the ground like a coward as Grainger was hauled past me toward the massive stump at the near end of the village square. A man was beheaded there once, before I was born, but that stump hadn't been bathed in blood in my lifetime.

"Adele!" Grainger shouted, and I flinched. Then I made myself meet his gaze. "Tell them the truth! Tell them what you saw! Don't betray your neighbors amid the threat of corruption from the dark wood!"

Eyes turned my way, and I felt the gazes on me like bugs crawling over my skin.

Elena slid her arm through mine and held me close. "Don't listen," she whispered. "He's just desperate to save his hand. None of this is your fault."

But this was *all* my fault. Guilt was a ball of flames burning in my gut, scorching me from the inside. My own personal trial by fire.

Grainger kept shouting as they dragged him toward the stump, where another member of the watch already stood, holding an axe. The tribunal must have alerted him of the verdict before it was announced.

They untied Grainger's wrists, then they forced him to his knees and pulled his right arm forward so that his hand lay over the chopping block.

"No!" Grainger shouted, flailing so that the watchmen had to press down on his shoulders to keep him in place. "To hell with you all!"

I couldn't watch. But I couldn't let myself leave. I couldn't spare myself entirely from the painful spectacle, because it was my fault. Because the very least I could do was remain present for the injustice I had heaped upon a man I'd hoped to marry. A man I would probably always love.

I knew the axe had been raised by the gasp of the crowd, and a second later, I heard the gruesome thunk of a blade into wood.

Grainger screamed, an agonized sound like nothing I had ever heard. Tears filled my eyes, and I opened them to see his mother wrapping the end of his right arm in cloth.

His hand lay on the ground beside the bloody tree stump the axe was still embedded in.

"The devil take you all!" Grainger shouted, while his mother tried to make him hold still, so she could wrap his wound.

His father turned and walked away.

"Adele?" Max stood in the bakery doorway as I approached my home, his face pale and drawn from lack of sleep.

Tom sat at the table, rolling a ball across the surface, from one hand to the other. He seemed anxious, glancing frequently toward the open door, as if the tension in the village were setting him on edge.

Behind him. Jeanne and Sofia played with dolls, seemingly unaware of the gruesome event going on right outside the door.

"Not now." I brushed past Max into the cottage, and on my way into the back room, I realized that my sister and her friend were reenacting the tribunal's sentencing announcement with their dolls, having evidently heard the event through the open window.

My stomach lurched, and I struggled to hold down my lunch. "Stop that," I snapped.

Sofia looked up at me, her eyes wide and scared, and I realized that the girls weren't acting out what they'd heard for fun. They were trying to understand. "Was Madame Gosse right?" Her chin quivered. "Has Grainger lost his mind?"

"No." I sank onto a stool at the table, facing the girls. Aware that Max was listening. "He's just . . . confused."

"And he's lost his hand, because he shot Romy?"

"It's complicated, but yes." I glanced at Jeanne and found her listening closely, her lips pressed firmly together.

"And you're not going to marry him now?" Sofia asked. "Because he's lost his hand?"

"That's not . . . That's not why I can't marry him, *chère*. It's complicated. At the moment, things are very . . ."

"Complicated?"

"Yes." With a sigh, I stood and brushed hair back from her face. "I'll explain it all as soon as I can. For now, just . . . stay away from the forest. Okay?"

She rolled her eyes. "I *always* stay away from the forest."

"Good. I love you."

"I know. Love you too." Then she picked up her doll, and I headed into the back room.

"Adele." Max followed me through the curtain.

"Please don't. I can't look at you right now," I told him. "I know that's not fair. This isn't your fault. But Grainger's lost his hand—he's lost *everything*—and you're standing there whole."

"I—" He exhaled slowly. "That's true. And I'm sorry."

"That you still have both hands?"

"That he doesn't. That my arrival wasn't the joyful occasion I'd hoped it would be."

And he did look sorry. Though he'd done nothing wrong. He also looked exhausted.

I sighed as I sank onto the edge of the straw mattress Sofia and I shared. What happened to Grainger was not Max's fault. It was mine.

"Have you slept?" I asked him. "You can sleep here for a while, if you want. I'll watch the children."

"Thank you, but if you don't mind, I should go to Monsieur Girard. I'm sure he understands my absence, considering the day's events, but I *am* supposed to be helping him."

"Of course. Go. And give him my best."

"I'll be back tonight," Max said as he put on his cloak.

When he'd left, I went back to the main room to get started on the next day's bread orders. As I worked, I watched Tom. He played with a ball for a while, rolling it across the floor until it hit the wall and rolled back to him.

Once I'd covered the unbaked loaves of bread and left them to rise, I sat next to the boy on the floor, determined to pull some information out of him. I needed to know how much he understood and whether he could speak. I *had* to know what it was like to grow up in the dark wood—half human, half wolf—and whether a whitewulf pup could be taught not to kill humans.

After all, aside from biting Romy out of frustration, he hadn't attacked anyone in Oakvale.

"Hi," I said, and though he looked up, he didn't otherwise acknowledge me. "Are you hungry?" I asked, but he only blinked at me. "I'll get you something to eat if you tell me you're hungry. Or even just nod your head."

Tom picked up the ball and rolled it across the floor again.

"Please say something. Just tell me that you can understand me." Had he stopped speaking after the trauma of losing his mother? Or were whitewulf pups mute?

Despite her transition, Romy could still speak.

The front door opened, letting in a frigid gust of wind, and my mother stepped inside. The bags beneath her eyes had grown dark and puffy from lack of sleep.

"Sofia, bundle up and take Jeanne outside to play," she said as she took off her cloak.

"Okay!" My sister stood, her doll forgotten. "Tom, come with us!"

"No, Tom needs to stay here," my mother said.

"But—"

"Go, before I change my mind and give you chores."

Sofia and Jeanne pulled on their cloaks and mittens and disappeared outside.

"How's Romy?" I asked as my mother sank onto a stool at the table.

"She's doing very well. Too well."

"What does that mean?" I set a tankard of ale in front of her.

"Her wound is healing too quickly, and there's no sign of fever. I don't think her mother has noticed yet. She's as occupied with praying as with tending the wound, and she's inclined to believe her prayers are being answered. But I fear there's another cause."

"Do whitewulfs heal quickly?"

My mother shrugged as she lifted her cup. "I don't know anyone who's ever studied a whitewulf, beyond the lay of its fur as trim or lining for warm clothing. But the pace of the child's healing is not natural. Her parents will notice that soon." She exhaled slowly. "Are you still determined to handle this yourself?"

I nodded.

"You're certain? It must be done tonight."

"I'm certain. I'll leave with the pups as soon as I'm sure the rest of the village is asleep."

Her left brow rose. "With Max."

"Yes, with Max."

"Adele, I know this isn't what you want—"

"This isn't about what I want. I understand that."

"I know. I'm just saying . . . This won't be easy, and once you're out there, you might be tempted to just . . . leave them."

I blinked, trying to hide my surprise. To hide my intention.

My mother sipped from her tankard, then she set it down and took my hand. "I know that would be easier for you to bear, believing you'd spared them, but Max is right. If you leave them out there, you'll just be condemning them to slow starvation at best. While that might be easier for you, it won't be for them. And if they *were* to somehow survive . . ."

Any consequence from my decision would be my fault. My guilt to bear.

That's what she was saying.

She took another long gulp of ale, then she met my gaze frankly. "*Chère*, I need to know that if I send you out there, you'll do the right thing."

I swallowed my guilt and doubt and gave her a firm nod. "Mama, that is *exactly* what I intend to do."

Max returned for dinner, and Jeanne finally went home, insisting she could help her mother care for Romy. We had no excuse to stop her, so Mama and I let her go, hoping that Romy was no longer in enough pain to make her lash out and bite.

Max joined us at the table for stew made from the last of Gran's venison roast, but Tom wouldn't move from his pallet, so I took a bowl to him.

"Why won't he go near the hearth?" Sofia asked as she tore a chunk from the fresh loaf my mother had set on the table. "Isn't he cold?"

"Tom doesn't like fire," my mother told her. "He seems to be scared of it."

Sofia turned to him with a curious look while she chewed a bite of rye bread. "You don't need to fear fire unless you stick your hand into it, silly goose. Or unless it catches on cloth, or on the walls."

Or, unless you're tied to a stake in the middle of the village square. Not that Sofia had any memory of our father's death.

Tom blinked at her. Then he poured stew straight into his mouth from the bowl.

We ate in silence after that, and when I looked up from my food, I realized that Max and my mother were both staring at the table, evidently mired in the same guilt and dread that had stifled my appetite.

Nothing would be the same after tonight. Not for the village, and not for me. And certainly not for the Pagets, whose only mistake had been to take in the little boy I'd found in the woods.

I forced down the rest of my dinner and cleared the table, and I was headed into the back to rest until Sofia made a happy little sound. When I turned, I found Max pulling his sketch book from his pack. "Oooh, are you going to draw? May I watch?"

she asked, scooting her stool closer to his.

"I thought I might. And yes you may." He gave her a somber smile that didn't quite touch his eyes, and I realized he was looking for a distraction. Because he was as bothered by what we were going to be doing in a few hours as I was. By what he *thought* we were going to be doing, anyway.

"What's that?" Sofia asked, as I crossed the small space to look over his shoulder.

"It's a crossbow. I saw some soldiers carrying them a few months ago, and I asked one if I could sketch his weapon. He was kind enough to oblige."

The page in front of him held a detailed sketch of the crossbow he'd given me, with dimensions and materials carefully labeled, and as I stared at it, I realized that Max had intentionally hidden this page from me when he'd first showed us his sketch book. Because he hadn't yet given me the weapon he'd made.

He turned the page, and I found myself looking again at the little cottage he'd drawn. Presumably the cottage he'd built for us. And suddenly I couldn't look away.

Max's cottage seemed so perfect. So peaceful, when my life in Oakvale was rapidly descending into chaos and violence. The temptation to chase such an ideal was almost overwhelming.

But escaping to Ashborne with Max wouldn't be leaving those things behind. The violence—my destiny—would follow me, wherever I went.

Max turned another page, and my sister's eyes widened as her gaze caught on the next drawing, the last one in the book.

It was incomplete, but I recognized the forest scene immediately.

"Oooh, what's that? Some kind of beast?" Sofia frowned. "It just looks like a snake with spines down its back."

"See the lady next to it?" Max leaned over to point at the figure. "She's there for scale. That snake is twice as long as she is tall." And though the snake was just a suggestion made of several long, faint lines so far, the woman was fully detailed, including her hooded, fur-trimmed cape.

"She looks like you, Adele!" Sofia squinted at the drawing, and when she tried to bring a candle closer, I blocked her arm, afraid she'd drip wax on the book. "It looks like you're fighting the snake!"

I glanced at Max, and for the first time since I'd met him, he seemed . . . embarrassed. As if he were nervous for me to see that page. "It isn't done," he said. "I'm not sure what that giant snake really looks like." Because we'd extinguished the lantern in order to tempt it toward us.

But he knew exactly what I looked like.

I looked fierce, in the drawing. Strong and confident, as I faced down a beast reared up to my own height and nearly twice my width, with its broad, thick neck.

"Perhaps Adele might have some ideas," my mother said softly. "About how a basilisk should look."

For a moment, I could only stare at the drawing. Was that how he saw me? Did I seem so confident to him? So ready to charge into danger? Had he not seen my fear? Had he not heard the race of my pulse, with his well-trained ears?

The girl in his drawing could do anything. He believed that, and his belief had come through in the sketch. The girl he'd drawn could walk into the dark wood and sacrifice two small children to save an entire village, and she could come out of that experience stronger. Tougher.

More monstrous, in the way a guardian should be.

I did not feel like that girl.

"I'd guess that the spines should be longer," I said at last. "Longer than my arms. And the fangs should drip with venom."

"Thank you," Max said, his gaze holding mine.

Sofia glanced back and forth between us. "Draw me!" she demanded, throwing her arms out. "I want to fight a troll!"

I grabbed the candle before she could overturn it. "Paper is in short supply, and it's *very* expensive," I told her.

"But you're even more precious," Max insisted. "As soon as I finish this one, I will start another. 'Sofia and the Hideous Troll!'"

She beamed adoringly at him as she returned to her seat at the table.

NINETEEN

➤———————————

At the end of a day of baking, our back room was the only room it was comfortable to be in, caught, as it was, between the heat of the oven in the front room and the frigid air leaking through cracks in the walls now that the sun had gone down.

My mother put Tom to bed on his pallet on the floor, then she and Sofia curled up on her bed, and I insisted that Max sleep in the one Sofia and I normally shared, so he'd be alert enough to help me with our middle-of-the-night task.

When they were all softly snoring, exhausted by the events of the past couple of days, I lit a lantern and bundled up, then I trekked across the village square to the Colberts' cottage.

Grainger's mother answered my knock on the door wearing a cloak over her night shirt. "Adele," she said by way of greeting. Her eyes were rimmed in red, and she looked wide awake, in spite of the hour.

"*Bonsoir*, Madame Colbert. I'm sorry to bother you so late. I just wanted to check on Grainger."

"That's kind of you, *chère*, but he's finally asleep. I think he's developing a fever so I'd rather not wake him."

"Of course. But would you mind . . . I mean, can you tell me how he's doing? How he seems? Is he still saying . . . those things?"

Madame Colbert glanced over her shoulder into the warmly lit cottage. Then she stepped outside with me and pulled the door closed, huddling close to the wall to block the wind. "He has not veered one bit in his telling of the incident. His father and I thought that with his fever, he might be frightened into telling the truth. Or, at least, he might be incapable of maintaining the fantasy he's woven, in the grip of illness. But he is steady in his assertion that Romy Paget is a werewolf, and that she is a corruption that will spread through this village like the plague, if no one listens to him."

I exhaled slowly. "Well, that is very . . . unfortunate."

"I have to admit, I can't entirely bring myself to dismiss his claims," she whispered. "After all, the great deceiver is known to work in such ways. And how better for the devil to insinuate himself in a village like ours than to target an innocent? A child, at that? You were there, *non*? Is there any chance you're mistaken in what you saw? Can you think of anything that might have given Grainger such certainty, in such a frightening occurrence?"

296

"No, I'm sorry to say." It pained me to lie to his mother almost as badly as to lie to Grainger. "The only way I know of to account for his insistence in this matter is that he truly believes what he's saying, mistaken though he is."

"And you're certain he's mistaken? That we have no reason to suspect the Pagets?"

"I'm quite sure they are innocent." Saying that was a risk. If Romy bit someone or exposed herself in some other way, Madame Colbert might accuse me of covering up her corruption. But I owed the Pagets as much as I owed Grainger. Maybe more, considering that they were about to lose their daughter. "Please give Grainger my best, when he wakes. And tell him I'm sorry I couldn't be of more help." I could feel Madame Colbert's gaze on me as I crossed the square again.

In my own cottage, I sat at the table for a long time, looking at Max's sketch book by candlelight while I listened to my sister snore, trying to pass the time until I was sure the rest of the village was asleep. Trying to distract myself from a consuming plague of guilt.

A month ago, despite my fear of the dark wood and the monsters that inhabit it, I'd been exhilarated by the idea of my newfound destiny. My pulse had raced every time I'd stepped into the forest, and every beast I felled had felt like an accomplishment. Like both a service to my village and a personal triumph.

I'd never in my life felt so needed—so *intrepid*—as I had

when I'd stepped out of the woods with Tom, convinced that I'd saved him. That I'd found my true purpose.

But now . . .

I'd thought protecting Oakvale would feel rewarding, even if I could never take credit for my efforts. I'd expected to feel noble and courageous, content with my bruises and exhaustion because I knew I was making a difference.

I didn't expect the guilt. I hadn't understood, when my mother told me how difficult my role would be, that she wasn't talking about the hunt. She was talking about the secrets. The lies. The impossible choices.

The sacrifice of one life for another.

That's what made us monsters. It wasn't the fur, or the claws, or the teeth. It wasn't the speed, or the strength, or the eyesight. It was the *choices*. Brutal decisions that often had to be made in the heat of the moment.

Decisions I would have to live with for the rest of my life.

When the moon rode high in the sky, I blew out my candle and stuck my head out the front door. The village was quiet. Nothing was moving, and I couldn't see a single candle lit in a single window.

I was supposed to wake up my mother, to say goodbye and listen to any last-minute advice. I was supposed to wake up Max and bring him with me. Instead, I said a silent goodbye to them both as they lay sleeping. Then I knelt next to the little boy asleep on his pallet between the beds.

"Tom!" I whispered, shaking his leg gently.

His eyelids fluttered, but once they were open, he focused on my face almost instantly. The child clearly had no difficulty seeing in dim light.

"Wake up, *mon cher*. We're going to go for a walk."

Tom sat up, his eyes bright and alert, despite the late hour. When I handed him the worn pair of shoes the Pagets had given him, he put them on without hesitation, though he was still clad in nothing else other than the borrowed tunic he slept in, which came to his knees.

I put on my red cloak, settled the strap of my crossbow over my shoulder, and slid three bolts into my quiver. Then I led Tom outside without bothering to take a lantern, because without Max's company, we wouldn't need it.

"We're going to get Romy," I whispered, and though he didn't say a word, I swear his eyes shone brighter at the mention of his friend's name.

Tom followed me down the path and around to the side of the Pagets' cottage. "Stay here," I whispered, squatting to put myself at eye level with the child. "And do *not* go after their chickens. Okay?" But when he only blinked at me, as usual, I realized I'd have to take the chance that he'd understood. And that he wasn't hungry.

I snuck back around to the front of the cabin and quietly opened the door. The fire had been banked for the night, but I could see well enough in the dark to know that Madame Paget lay on the floor beside Romy on a makeshift pallet, beside a bowl of water and a cloth bag of herbs probably used for a poultice. It was no doubt easier to nurse an injured child in the main room in front of the fire than up in the loft, where I could hear her sister snoring softly.

For a moment, I stood quietly watching mother and daughter sleep, debating the best way to remove Romy without rousing Madame Paget. Should I try to lift her and hope she didn't wake up screaming? Or should I shake her gently and hope she didn't wake up screaming?

Finally, I knelt at the child's side and lightly shook her shoulder, hoping Madame Paget was exhausted enough to sleep through my interruption.

Romy opened her eyes, and I shushed her with one finger laid over my lips. Then I grabbed the small pair of shoes drying on the hearth and motioned for her to follow me out the front door.

It was frighteningly easy to get her out of the cottage.

"Where are we going?" she whispered as I led her around the side of her home. But the second she saw Tom, she abandoned me and raced over to throw her arms around him.

She didn't say a word to him, nor he to her, but they held each other for several seconds, and the scene was so tender that I hated to ruin it, despite the urgency of my errand.

"Here. Put your shoes on," I said at last, and finally Romy disentangled herself from Tom's embrace, so she could do as I'd said. There wasn't even a glimmer of distrust in her gaze when she stood again and looked up at me. Romy had known me her whole life, and she would do anything I asked her to.

And Tom, it seemed, would follow her to the ends of the earth.

"Where are we going?" Romy asked again as I took her hand and led the children down the dirt path in the center of the village.

"We're taking a walk." I expected her to object to the late hour, or the dark, or the cold, until I remembered that she'd already been out at night at least twice in the past week, hunting the village chickens.

The hour and the darkness didn't bother me either, but the cold was another story.

When we spotted a lantern ahead on the path, I tugged both children into the Rousseaus' barn, trying not to think about the time I'd taken shelter there with Grainger, both of us soaked from the rain.

We huddled at the back of the small building in a mostly clean pile of hay, while Elena's father's horse eyed us uneasily.

"Why are we here?" Romy asked, and when I shushed her, she repeated her question in a whisper.

"Because we don't want to be seen by the village watch."

"Why not?"

"Because they would . . . make us go home." The truth was much more complicated than that, of course. They would question us. And no good could come of that.

"Are we not supposed to be out?"

"Not really."

"Why are—?"

"Romy," I whispered, deciding to put an end to her questions by asking a few of my own. "How's your shoulder?"

"It aches a bit," she said with a shrug.

"May I see?"

The child pulled down the neckline of her sleep shirt, and I gasped at what I saw. Where there had been a bloody wound the night before—a grisly hole in her flesh—now there was only a shiny red patch of scar tissue. The area still looked swollen, but the wound was completely closed.

I'd noticed since my ascension that my bruises faded quickly, but I'd never seen anything like this.

"Has your mother seen— I mean, what does your mother say about the wound?"

"She says it's a miracle. And she said that I should keep it covered with a poultice. To keep air from the injury."

"It isn't covered now," I pointed out, and Romy frowned.

"There was a poultice on the wound when I went to sleep. It must have fallen off while we were walking."

And if it was found, there would be evidence that the child had wandered off during the night—a habit Romy had already established well on her own. Yet my part in this would weigh heavily on me, even if no one else ever suspected me.

All I could do was take solace in the knowledge that I was giving them as much of a chance as I could.

"Romy, do you remember what happened last night?"

She shook her head. "Jeanne says Grainger Colbert shot me, but I don't remember that."

"Do you remember going out after dark?"

The child nodded slowly, as if she were thinking very hard. "Tom was hungry, so we went to find some . . . meat."

"*Tom* was hungry? Was he with you last night?"

"Yes. We . . . Well, we went out, but I can't remember what happened after that."

"How do you know Tom was hungry? Did he tell you that? Does he speak to you?"

"He doesn't use words. But I know what he needs." Romy's voice carried a note of pride as she glanced at the boy standing mute at her side. "He makes sounds, and I understand them. They just . . . make sense."

Would I understand him, if I heard the sounds? Would a redwulf be able to comprehend a whitewulf's . . . language?

"Romy, do you understand what's happened to you?" I asked, kneeling in front of the children.

Her hand went to her shoulder. "Do you mean the arrow?"

"No. I mean what's happened to you since Tom bit you. Do you remember anything from the nights you've snuck out with him?"

For the first time since I'd woken her in the middle of the

night, she looked worried. "I'm not supposed to talk about that."

"You're not . . . ? Who told you that? Was it my mother?" I asked when she hesitated.

Romy shook her head. But who else could it possibly have been? Who else could know what was happening, yet care enough about Romy to keep her secret? To instruct her to keep *her own* secret?

"Romy, was it *your* mother?"

Slowly, the child nodded.

I exhaled, long and slow, trying to draw my thoughts into line. Madame Paget knew, and she hadn't turned her daughter over to the tribunal. Nor had she told anyone.

"Did your mother tell you to say that you don't remember sneaking out?" I asked, and Romy's lower lip began to quiver. "I won't tell anyone. I *promise*. You can tell me the truth."

Finally, she nodded again.

"But you *do* remember?"

Another nod.

"How did your mother find out?"

"She saw us in the yard. When we were . . ." Romy shrugged.

"When you were *changing*?"

The child's eyes widened as she stared at me. "You know?"

"Yes, I know. And I would never tell."

"I didn't mean to do it. To . . . change." Her eyes filled with tears, and her lower lip quivered. "But I couldn't help it."

My heart cracked open. "It's okay. I'm going to take you

somewhere where it's okay for you to change."

Her frown deepened. "Into the dark wood? That's where Tom wants to go, but he's scared to go alone."

I couldn't blame him. "Do you know why he wants to go there?" I asked, and Romy gave me another wide-eyed shake of her head. "Because that's where he's from. That's where he belongs. He's lost his mother, but he might have other family out there."

"Is his family like him? Are they . . . like me?"

"Yes. Yes, *chère*, they are."

"Will they take care of me?" she asked, and I was startled to realize that she understood more of what was happening than I'd expected.

"I hope so." *I really, really hope so.*

"Can I . . . can I come back, if I don't like it there?"

"No, *chère*. I'm sorry, but it isn't safe for you here any-more."

Her forehead crinkled with worry. "But it's safe in the dark wood? With the monsters?"

"I hope so." I couldn't bring myself to lie to her. Yet neither could I make myself tell her the whole truth. That Tom might not have any family left. That even if he did, he might not be able to find them. That even if he found them, they might not want to add a new pup to their pack.

That I would basically be abandoning both children alone in a forest that was full of monsters and impenetrable to daylight.

Because the alternative was their immediate death.

"I don't want to leave my mom and dad." Romy's chin began to quiver again. "And Jeanne."

"I know, *chère*. And they don't want you to leave. But they don't want you to be in danger from the village, either. So we need to get going. Are you ready?"

Romy turned to Tom and took his hand. Then she gave me a brave little nod. "I'm ready."

"Okay. Let's go." I took Romy's other hand and guided the children to the barn's entrance, where I peeked out, on alert for the glow of a lantern or the echo of footsteps. When I found neither, I led them outside, but this time we avoided the dirt path and snuck through fallow fields, trekking from shadow to shadow.

We continued through the pasture on the edge of the village, then across the dirt path that circled Oakvale. Beyond that was a small expanse of grass—dead and frozen in the winter—then the ring of torches and the edge of the dark wood.

Romy hesitated, tugging on my arm when I tried to cross the path. "It's okay," I whispered, desperately hoping I was right. As small as she was, it was difficult to imagine her ever growing into the vicious, snarling beast I'd fought during my trial, but the possibility that she would infect someone in the village was real and immediate enough to keep me from turning back, when all I really wanted to do was return both children to a warm, safe bed.

Not that my mother would let them stay there for long.

So I took a deep breath and led them into the dark wood.

I didn't have a lantern, and we had no destination in mind, so there was no reason to stick to the path. Yet it felt odd to strike off into the wood itself, even with my hatchet in hand and my crossbow hanging at my back.

Romy clung to my hand as we stepped over exposed roots and ducked low-hanging branches. The children seemed able to see as well as I could in the dark, but while Tom appeared happy—relieved?—to be back, Romy looked terrified to the point of near-panic.

"It's okay," I whispered. "Look at Tom. See? He's not scared."

"That's because we're here with him."

"And he and I are here with *you*," I pointed out.

"Yes, but—" Romy's head whipped toward the left, her eyes suddenly searching the darkness. "What was that?"

I hadn't heard anything other than the ambient nighttime sounds and the constant slithering of vines through the woods. But Tom was staring in the same direction, his entire frame tense and on alert.

Were their ears better than mine?

"What do you hear?" I whispered.

"I don't know," Romy said. "But Tom doesn't like it."

Probably not a family member, then.

A second later, I heard the sound. At first, it was a series of dull thumps, accompanied by a cascade of soft cracks. But with every passing second, the sounds got louder until the foot-steps became thunderous and the cracking sounded less like the crunch of twigs beneath someone's foot than like the splintering of entire trees.

Romy started to wheeze as her breaths came faster and faster, her hand tightening around mine until her grip threatened to break my bones. Tom began to back up, pulling her with him until her hold tugged my arm as well. I tried to let her go as I slid my hatchet back into its loop on my belt, but she clung to me until I had to pry her fingers loose so I could get to my crossbow.

"Get behind me," I whispered as ahead of us, the top half of a tree broke off and slammed into the forest floor, sending a tremor beneath our feet. And finally, I saw it.

A troll. I'd never seen one, but this beast looked enough like the image my mother had described that I recognized it imme-diately.

It was twice my height, its skin an indeterminate shade of gray with an oddly smooth, almost lustrous texture that seemed to reflect what moonlight my redwulf eyes were able to see. Its head was huge, with facial features marred by odd, knobby skin growths.

"Stay back!" I whispered to Romy as she and Tom scurried behind me, arms wrapped around each other, eyes wide.

Bracing the crossbow on the ground, I pulled back the heavy iron lever to tighten the string, then I laid my first bolt in the groove on the stock.

The troll barreled toward us, huffing with each expansion of its massive lungs. Drool dripped down its chin, because its oversized, blunt teeth seemed to prevent its lips from entirely closing. The beast roared as it lunged at me, and my stomach roiled from the odor of rotting flesh, where remnants of its last meal were still stuck between those enormous teeth.

I would only have time for one blow before it reached us, and if that blow wasn't fatal . . .

I sucked in a deep breath and took aim, high overhead. Then I pulled the trigger.

TWENTY

T he bolt flew straight and true. It pierced the troll's left eye with a horrible wet sound that was swallowed almost immediately by his roar of pain.

The beast stumbled to a stop, shaking the ground with every step, and pulled the projectile from its eye, leaving gore dripping down its face as the bolt thumped to the ground, lost in the underbrush.

"Stay back!" I whispered again to the children as I pulled the crossbow's lever, trying to load another bolt. But the troll was already in motion, barreling toward us again. It bent, and its arm shot out, thick fingers grasping for my waist, but I lurched out of the way.

The beast roared, frustrated, and grasped for me again.

That time the back of its hand—half the size of my torso— brushed me, knocking me off my feet. The crossbow fell to the ground, and I rolled to the left, trying to stay out of the troll's grip as I drew its attention away from the children.

I scrambled through the underbrush, my pulse racing, scratching my palms on twigs and roots as I searched for my crossbow. With no luck. But just as the troll's enormous hand wrapped around my waist, my fingers brushed something long and hard. I grabbed a bolt that had spilled from my quiver as the beast lifted me into the air.

The hand squeezed as it lifted me, and I screamed as I felt one of my ribs crack. I was like a rag doll in the troll's grip, my head whipping back and forth as it shook me.

The children screamed, and when the beast shook me again, my teeth snapped shut over the end of my tongue. Blood flooded my mouth, and I spat it at the troll, aiming for his good eye.

He sputtered, startled for a moment, and I sucked in a painful breath, determined to seize the opportunity. I swung the bolt in my right hand, grunting with the effort, and drove it into his remaining eye as fast and as hard as I could. As deep as it would go.

The troll's hand went limp around me. I landed in a bed of dead leaves, and a second later the beast crashed to the ground next to me. Unmoving.

For one long moment, I could only sit in the underbrush, clutching my cracked rib as I sucked in breath after deep breath.

"Adele?" Romy whispered, and I looked up to find the children huddled together at the base of a tree, arms around each other. Trembling as they stared at me. "Is it over?"

I stood on unsteady legs and looked down at the troll.

"Yes," I whispered. "It's over." For now.

Bracing my foot on the beast's forehead, I pulled the bolt from its eye, then I used the hem of my skirt to wipe eye gore and grayish brain matter from it.

"Here." Romy handed me the bolt the troll had pulled from its other eye. "I found this in the leaves."

"Thank you, *chère*." A quick search of the immediate area revealed that my crossbow had fallen into a thorny bush, and wrenching it free resulted in a series of scratches on both of my arms, through the sleeves of my dress.

"Tom's hungry," Romy said as I settled the strap of my crossbow over one shoulder. "Where are we going? Did you bring any food?"

"I—" I hadn't brought any food. I hadn't intended to come this far into the woods with them, but I couldn't just leave them there, alone and hungry. And cold.

Though neither of the children actually looked cold, at the moment. In fact, I'd never seen Tom so much as shiver, and since Romy's fever had broken, she hadn't complained even once about the temperature.

A soft, high-pitched whining sound drew my attention, and I turned, one hand on my injured rib, to find Tom staring into the distance. His nostrils were flared, his eyes intently focused. "He hears something," Romy translated, but I'd figured that much out for myself. And I was pretty sure he could smell whatever he was listening to.

"Can you hear it?" I asked her. Romy followed his focus, and her own nose began to flare.

Slowly, she nodded. "It's food. But not a chicken. I can hear its heartbeat." She sounded oddly calm. Captivated, evidently, by what she was hearing. "I can hear its . . . blood."

Another sound drew my attention away from her, and I found Tom writhing on the ground, on his side, halfway through the transition that would turn him into a wolf pup.

"We're going to eat," Romy said as she pulled her night shirt over her head and dropped it on the ground. Then she squatted in the dirt next to him and began her own change.

"Romy! No!" I whispered. But the children ignored my plea, and as I watched them, I realized they were seconds away from taking off into the dark wood on their own.

I should let them go. That was the whole reason I'd snuck them out of the village. But then my gaze snagged on the corpse of the troll that had very nearly eaten us all, and I couldn't do it. I couldn't leave them. So, as Tom stood on four short, furry legs, I hung my crossbow on a branch and my cloak next to it. Then I knelt on the ground and forced my own body through the same transformation.

Dimly, as I breathed through the familiar pain of disconnected joints and overstretched muscles, exacerbated this time by my cracked rib, I realized that Romy and Tom had both gone. That I could hear the soft patter of their paws headed away from me in the woods.

Their change was much faster than mine, even though I'd hunted on four legs many times since my ascension. I'd endured the discomfort of my transformation while Max turned his back to give me privacy, even though he couldn't see, without the lantern.

As soon as my pain ebbed, I stood and crawled out of my clothes, surprised to note that the pain in my rib had faded to a dull ache during the transition.

I took off across the woods, following the sound of soft breaths and racing paws, relieved that the forest looked brand-new and crystal clear.

WELCOME HOME, the wind whispered as I ran, the gentle breeze rippling through my fur, addressing me like a long-lost friend. Startled, I realized it was the same voice that had greeted me after my trial, the first time I'd taken on a wolf's shape, and that I had not heard it even once when I was in human form.

The words seemed to come from inside my own head, and they felt like the voice of the dark wood itself. Like a caress of my mind. A very intimate intrusion.

I shook off the seductive greeting and raced after the pups.

It didn't take me long to catch up with them, and somewhere along the way, as my paws pushed off against the fragrant earth, my claws digging into the dirt for purchase, I realized I could smell the scent they were following—and I recognized it.

Rabbit.

Like the lush vegetation growing in the dark wood, the natural wildlife seemed unbothered by the unnatural darkness. Deer, rabbits, and other prey evidently saw as well in the darkness as the pups could. As I could. Maybe even better. But since the villagers couldn't see to hunt, no one other than my grandmother and the monsters native to the dark wood had access to the wild game populating the forest.

Armed with longer legs, I pulled ahead of the pups, my nose practically glued to the ground as I sniffed out our prey. My pulse raced, my heart pounding with an excitement like nothing I'd ever felt before.

I'd killed several kinds of monster over the past month during my forays into the woods with Max and with my mother, yet I'd never *truly* hunted them. I'd just kind of . . . let them find me. But this was different. Though the rabbit posed no threat to me, this was hunting, and my lupine form *longed* for this activity. This full-body effort that burned in my lungs and ached in my muscles.

I was made for this, and the satisfaction of the moment I discovered that hole in the ground—the very second I stuck my muzzle into the burrow and found an entire family of rabbits, just waiting to be devoured—was like nothing I'd ever experienced.

My satisfaction—my *hunger*—was so great that it didn't occur to me to be disgusted by the thought of eating raw meat until I'd already pulled the closest rabbit from its burrow. Until I'd already shaken it vigorously, snapping its neck. Until the pups dove in after me, growling and nipping at each other for the right to go next.

In fact, I'd already devoured half of the rabbit—hide, small bones, and all—before it even occurred to me that I was eating raw game. And even once I'd realized that, there was no disgust. Because the rabbit was *delicious*.

My body—in this form, anyway—didn't want burnt flesh or bubbling stew. I didn't want broth or bread. My body wanted meat. Fresh and tender. Juicy. And as soon as I'd finished one rabbit, I dove into the burrow for the next trembling morsel.

After the pups ate their fill, Tom curled up on the ground, tucked his nose beneath his tail, and closed his eyes.

I should go home.

I should have gone back for my clothes, changed into my human form, and headed back to the village, leaving the pups in the woods where they belonged. But I couldn't.

I told myself that we were still too close to the village. That if Romy got scared, she'd find her way back, and that Oakvale might not recover from that.

What if she bit someone?

What if someone—other than Grainger—saw her become a wolf?

What if she told someone that I could do the same thing?

I would have to take them farther into the dark wood, angling away from my grandmother's cabin. From the path leading from the village to the other side of the forest, toward the west. But there was no reason to change back into human form for that. The pups traveled faster and easier on four legs, and though they didn't seem to feel the cold in either form, I was certainly much warmer with a layer of fur between my skin and the frigid winter air.

I yipped and nudged Tom with my nose. *No time to sleep, pup.*

He whined at my intrusion, but I insisted, and finally he stood. Romy rubbed her muzzle against him in an affectionate greeting I understood instinctively, though I'd never seen a gesture quite like it. In this form, I just . . . knew things.

How to track prey, evidently. How to interpret Tom's whines and yips, and how to communicate with him in return, without words. I knew how to track a rabbit and eat it without hands.

These new instincts and abilities were exhilarating. Liberating. They opened a whole new world for me—one I'd hardly even glimpsed in the time I'd spent guarding Oakvale on four legs. Because that's all I'd been doing: guarding. I hadn't ever taken the time to truly get to know my lupine form, because deep down, I'd feared that the more comfortable I was as a wolf, the less human I would feel. The more monstrous I would become.

But this didn't feel monstrous. It felt natural. *Free.*

I yipped at the pups one more time and took off deeper into the forest, and to my relief, they followed me.

It was strange, navigating the dark wood as a wolf. The monsters were still out there, and they were still a threat. But in this form, my ears and eyes functioned so well that I could hear any sign of an approaching beast long before it got to us. In plenty of time for us to get away. And we were *so* much faster on four paws!

Despite their exhaustion, running through the forest obviously felt like a game to the pups. Like village children racing each other across the square or through the fields.

It wasn't a game to me—I was too busy listening for threats—yet there was something undeniably thrilling about moving at such swift speeds. And the sense of triumph—of power—that came with that sensation was seductive.

Soon, though, the pups tired out, and I had to admit that I could use a rest. So when they began to lag behind, I stopped and without being entirely sure what I was looking for, I began to search for—

Shelter.

—some place to stay. Some place safe to sleep. In the dark wood, in wolf form, that place wouldn't be a cottage or a cowshed. Not even a lean-to. It would have to be a—

Den.

—small, safe little hollow. Something like the rabbits' burrow, only bigger. Large enough for the three of us to curl up in, yet small enough to be covered by whatever brush I could drag over us.

I hadn't realized I'd discovered a suitable place until I found myself digging beneath a clump of thorny underbrush. The earth was fragrant with the scent of dead plant life. Of leaf mold and moss.

In minutes, I'd created the perfect little den: a hollow space carved out of the earth, just big enough for both pups and me. I yipped to call them over, and I nudged them into the hole. Then I climbed in with them and clamped my teeth around a clump of brush, to drag it over us.

The plan was to stay with the pups for a little while. To rest up for my trek back to Oakvale. Then to . . . sneak out. To just go home, leaving them in the safest place I could find for them—a place I'd *made* for them—hidden from any casual observer, be it man or beast.

It would be more merciful to tell them, of course. To warn them that they'd have to care for themselves from now on. But if I did, fear might send them into hysterics. They might cry and draw predators, or they might try to follow me. A clean break seemed to be the safest bet; if they woke up alone, they'd have no choice but to learn to fend for themselves. To depend upon each other.

But as I started to dig my way quietly out of the den, I realized I'd overlooked one worrisome possibility. If the pups woke and found me gone, there was every chance in the world that they'd track my scent, the way they'd tracked the rabbits, and it would lead them back to the village. I would have to meander, and I'd need to come up with a way to disguise my scent.

Unfortunately, while I was pondering that new challenge . . . I fell asleep. And I didn't wake up until the pups began to stir sometime later, trying to crawl over me to get out of the den.

I had no idea how long we'd slept. Unable to see either stars or sunshine in the dark wood, I had no idea what time of day it was or how long ago we'd left Oakvale.

Had dawn arrived? Had Max and my mother awakened to discover Tom and me missing? Had Madame Paget reported Romy's disappearance? Had anyone found the poultice that had been on her shoulder?

I needed to go home. To put an end to my mother's fears and assure her that I was fine. And I would, after just a few more—

Food, Romy's whine demanded as she nudged me with her muzzle. *Food*.

Growling, I nipped at her ear. Not hard enough to draw blood. Just hard enough to warn her to let me sleep.

She returned my growl with a cute attempt of her own. Then she huffed into my ear and crawled over me. Tom followed her, his paw digging into my bladder on his way out of the den.

Play! his yip announced, and for several minutes, I listened to them scamper through the underbrush, my eyes still closed. Indulging in a few more minutes of semi-slumber before I'd have to—

Danger.

The thought shot through me like a candle lit in a dark room,

changing everything in an instant. Reframing familiar surroundings with a new perspective. My head popped up and I scented
the air, trying to draw the threat into focus. Had I smelled something? Heard something? Sensed something?

The pups were still playing. Wrestling in the dirt. Whatever
was wrong, they hadn't sensed it yet. So I crawled out of our den
and stretched, trying not to alert them as my ears pivoted on top
of my head, listening for . . . anything. Everything. Cataloguing
grunts, howls, and soft slithering sounds that had been the back-
drop of our existence since we'd first come into the dark wood.

A twig cracked in the distance, followed by a soft sob, and
suddenly I remembered. That's what I'd heard. What I'd only
half-processed, as I'd snoozed. I'd seen a dozen kinds of monsters since I had begun training in the dark wood. I'd fought at
least half that many. But none of them had ever made that sound.

There was only one kind of beast that sobbed.

Human.

Danger.

My low, soft growl alerted the pups to the threat, and they
came toward me, just as I'd showed them the night before.
Heads held high. Ears rotated toward the sides to catch sounds
from all around. And to assure me that they were listening.

The sob echoed through the forest again. It was coming
from the direction of the western path out of Oakvale. And as I
listened, I heard the crack of another twig. Then another. Then
two at once.

No.

The harder I listened, the more footsteps I heard. This wasn't a single human headed down the path, alone and scared. This was a procession of humans. This was . . . a pack.

No. Humans don't form packs. This was a party. A merchant caravan?

Couldn't be. I heard no wagon wheels rattling. No axles groaning. There were only footsteps—lots of them—and soft voices.

This was a search party.

TWENTY-ONE

→

The pups and I were nearly a mile from the path, and though we could hear footsteps and the occasional whispered word of encouragement or warning, there was no way the humans walking the trail could hear us.

But if we could hear them, so could everything else wandering around in the dark wood.

Protect them.

The voice was my own. My human conscience, calling me back to my duty. Complicating . . . everything.

I was honor-bound to protect the people tromping through the dark wood—doubly so, considering that it was my fault they were here. But I couldn't protect the humans from the shadows while I had the pups with me. And I couldn't abandon the pups. Not yet. Not when they could follow the search party home. Or just expose themselves to their human friends and family, here in the forest.

And if there was a search party in the dark wood, chances were good that my mother was out here somewhere, watching them. Maybe even my grandmother. If I came any closer, one of them would hear me. Or smell me.

RUN.

The dark wood caressed me with the thought, comforting me with the possibility. I didn't have to go home, just because they'd come for me. I could stay in the forest, with the pups. I could just . . . stay. After all, I was as much wolf as they were.

No, that was ridiculous. I snorted as I tossed my head, trying to shake off the temptation. I couldn't live in the dark wood. But I could finish the job I'd come here to do. I could find them a safe place, far from the village.

I yipped, calling softly to the pups. Telling them to follow me farther into the forest, away from the path. They both turned to obey. But then that sob echoed toward us again and Romy stopped. She turned toward the sound, her head bobbing as she sniffed the air.

Her posture changed in an instant. Tension and fear melted from her frame. Her ears rotated, focusing on just that one direction to the exclusion of the entire rest of the dark wood—a mistake that could get her killed. And for what?

I sniffed the air, trying to understand what could make her disregard my command. I forced myself to mentally peel apart the scents. It was like unbraiding a plait of hair, separating it into distinct strands until I could distinguish individual smells, belonging to individual people.

Though I'd never before noticed any difference in the scent of one of my neighbors, compared to another, in wolf form I was able to recognize each of them. Monsieur Gosse, the potter. Simon Laurent and his father. Monsieur Girard, the carpenter. Monsieur Martel, the blacksmith, who probably believed he would gain my mother's favor, if he found her daughter alive.

Romy whined and Tom watched her, seated on his haunches, his tail stirring a clump of fallen leaves in his distress. Which was in reaction to *her* distress.

I sniffed the air again, and finally I caught the scents that had upset her.

Madame and Monsieur Paget. Her parents had come into the forest to find her. And suddenly, before I could figure out how to calm her, Romy took off in the direction of the footsteps and soft voices, following her parents' scents toward the only home she'd ever known.

A home that no longer existed for her.

With a scolding yip, I took off after her, racing through the forest with little Tom on my heels. I expected the pup to tire herself out, but her energy seemed boundless, and when several points of light—bobbing lanterns—caught my eye, revealing a line of people slowly, carefully following the path, I forced another burst of speed from my tired legs and finally overtook her.

In response to my soft growl, she only whined, staring over

my head at the lanterns and the backlit forms holding them. And when I wouldn't let her go any farther, she sat on her haunches and threw her head back, then she let loose the most agonizing little distressed howl.

One of the lanterns stopped bobbing. "Romy?" Madame Paget called, and I flinched at her volume. Any beast that hadn't already heard the human procession would have heard that. As would my mother and grandmother, though I could see no sign of them.

"That was a wolf, Alice," Monsieur Paget said. "Don't let Grainger Colbert's mad mumblings get to you."

His wife didn't argue, but when I turned, I could see her staring into the woods in our direction, her lantern raised, her eyes narrowed in a futile attempt to see in the darkness. Next to her, caught in the glow of her lamp, stood . . .

Max.

My heart beat too hard within the cage of my ribs. He'd come looking for me. He'd probably also come to help protect the search party, but there was a sadness in his eyes. A determination in his stance that said he'd come out here for me.

I inhaled deeply, and his scent settled into my lungs with an odd weight, making my pulse race too fast. And suddenly I wanted nothing more than to run through the forest toward him. To apologize for disappearing without a word and tell him about everything I'd learned out here in the dark wood. Living as a wolf, for . . . however long I'd been gone.

I wanted to go home. To see my mother and my sister and assure them that I hadn't lost my mind. To hug my grandmother and chat with her in front of her hearth. To sit next to Max and describe monsters for him as he sketched.

But as I stared at the line of my friends and neighbors, breathing through a wave of homesickness that was strangely at odds with the lupine instinct telling me to run deep into the woods, a devastating realization pierced me like a sword through my heart. Even if I went home—even if I had somewhere safe to leave the pups—things would never be the same for me in Oakvale. If I were found alive and unscathed, people would want to know how that was possible. Why I'd disappeared into the woods on the same night as Tom and Romy, yet had come out without them. There would be more rumors. And I would no longer have Grainger at my side defending me. Balancing out the gossip with his respected status and obvious affection for me.

I'd injured my standing in Oakvale forever when I'd disappeared into the woods with the pups, yet there Max stood, staring intently into the dark, his gaze unfocused. Because he was listening. He had recognized Romy's howl as belonging to a whitewulf pup, and he knew that if the children were still out here, so was I.

The others may have come expecting to find three bodies, but Max knew better. He knew I was still alive. And he wanted me back.

That familiar ache swelled inside me, the conflicting draw

of home and the dark wood threatening to pull me off balance. I felt caught between two worlds, not fully at home in either, and—

"She's out there," Romy's mother whispered, drawing my focus back to the pups sitting on either side of me, their little frames trembling with tension. "Whether that was her or not, *she's out there*, Philip! She needs—"

Romy whined and started toward her mother. Panicked, I lurched after her and bit carefully into the scruff of her neck, then I carried her with me, Tom close on my heels. When she began to struggle, I stopped and set her down, growling a gentle warning. Then I nudged her forward, deeper into the woods, because while I could return to Oakvale if I chose—albeit, under a cloud of suspicion—the pups could not, under any circumstances, go home.

And I was not yet ready to leave them.

As we headed back into the forest, I turned for one last look at Max.

A smile turned up the corners of his mouth. And his lips formed my name in silence, as he stared out into the darkness.

STAY WITH THEM, the breeze whispered to me, as skeletal tree limbs rattled overhead.

Yes. I would just take the pups a little farther. Find some place safer. I had little choice about that, since I wasn't willing to abandon them, but I had to admit, as I raced through the forest with my small charges, that they weren't the only reason I was still out in the dark wood. It was easier to think about protecting and providing for the pups than about what my life might be like when I left the forest.

My home would not be the same as when I'd left it, but Oakvale was not my only option. A clean slate awaited me in Ashborne, along with the Bernards, and I had certainly come to care for Max. And yet, despite the suspicion that would be heaped upon me in my own village, I had no desire to abandon my neighbors. To leave the only home I'd ever known.

In my attempt to help my neighbors, I had put them at risk. I had cost one man his hand and one family their daughter. Didn't I owe them safety and protection now, even more than before?

Romy whined, drawing my attention from my own thoughts. She was upset about having lost her parents all over again, and when Romy was upset, Tom was upset. So I distracted them by making a game of tracking the scent trails left by various monsters. We would come just close enough to identify the beast we'd been tracking, but not close enough to alert it to our presence. I'd once used a similar technique to convince Sofia to keep churning butter, despite the ache in her arms.

By the time the pups needed another nap, I'd caught a familiar scent.

Food.

I hadn't eaten enough the day before, and my stomach felt like a gaping, aching vacuum. So I hunted.

Sleep.

Again, the need couldn't be resisted. The command couldn't be ignored.

Hunt.

Defend.

The hours began to blur together. The demands of my lupine form began to blend into each other, forming an existence I'd never intended to indulge. They became a life I hadn't even realized I was capable of living until I'd killed for the pups. Until I was feeding them and playing with them. Until I was defending them and sheltering them, both awake and asleep.

Until the days passed and I began to forget that I'd ever had another life. Another form. Another . . . option.

YOU BELONG HERE, the breeze whispered to me, in quiet moments. And slowly, I began to believe that.

Then one day—or night? They were much the same in the dark wood—the tired little pups began to snap at each other, fighting over the rabbit they'd found. Worried by their vicious jaw snapping and snarling, I snatched the rabbit and gave them the signal to sit and wait. Then I lay down on my side in a bed of moss and reclaimed my two-legged form.

Human again, I sat up, shivering violently in the frigid air. Without clothing, I would only be able to stay in that form for a few minutes. Hopefully that would be enough time to impart a lesson they needed to remember, in whatever form they took.

"Come here, you two." I waved the pups forward, and they

piled onto my lap, scratching my bare stomach with their claws as they cuddled. We'd slept curled up together for so long that I could hardly remember slumber without two squirming little bundles of fur pressed against my side and splayed across my stomach. I couldn't stand the thought of abandoning them, either to the dark wood or to their own monstrous instincts.

"You two know better than to fight with each other, don't you?" Romy gave me a hesitant bob of her muzzle. I didn't really expect a response from Tom. I rarely ever got one, other than either his refusal or acceptance of my instructions, when I gave them. But to my surprise, his little muzzle bobbed up and down. "Good. Romy is your sister now. You've each lost family, but you've found each other, and I want you to promise me that you'll stay together. No matter what. Okay?"

That time both pups nodded, and Romy whined softly—a guilty sound she always made when I scolded her.

"Good. You're both going to be fine if you stick together. If you protect each other. Do you understand?"

Tom nodded. Romy nuzzled me with her cold, wet nose.

A twig snapped behind me, and I shoved myself to my feet, dumping the pups from my lap, to find a lantern bobbing toward us with each step its carrier took, accompanied by the clank of a sword. For a second, the unexpected light blinded me. Then my eyes adjusted, both to the light and to the ambient darkness my human eyes couldn't cope with as well as my eyes in wolf form could.

The carrier's face came into focus, and I gasped.

Monsieur Colbert. Grainger's father. What was he doing alone in the dark wood?

Confused, I glanced past him and saw the edge of a narrow dirt path. I'd taken the pups deep into the wood—far from Oakvale—but there were several paths traversing the forest in different directions, leading toward neighboring villages.

Had Monsieur Colbert come looking for us? Maybe he was part of another search party and had veered at a less-traveled fork in the path to widen the search. Or maybe he'd come alone, convinced that the captain of the village watch would fare better on his own than with a group of terrified villagers.

Either way, he'd clearly heard us and had ventured from the path, a bold move, even for the captain of the watch.

"Who's out there?" Monsieur Colbert demanded, and I realized that his weak bubble of light hadn't revealed us yet. "Adele, is that you? I heard your voice, *chère*. Is that . . . ? Is that really you, or is the forest playing tricks on me?"

My pulse raced, my teeth chattering in the cold without the furry pups to help warm me. I took a step back, and a twig cracked as it bit into my bare heel.

Run. I could outrun him, but I'd only make it so far, naked and in human form. And running wouldn't make him un-hear my voice. If he reported what he'd heard, would anyone believe him? Would they redouble their efforts to find me or assume the dark wood had stolen my voice from his memory?

If they believed him, would they know there was only one way I could have survived this long, alone?

Romy whined, hiding behind my left calf, and Monsieur Colbert stiffened, holding his lantern higher. Squinting into the dark beyond the fragile fall of his light. "Adele? There's something out there with you. Please come forward. Let me help you."

A rope of darkness slid across the ground near his foot and he jumped, startled when a vine slithered across his boot. He stomped on it, and his lantern swung, casting swaying shadows that he probably couldn't see well enough to notice.

I took another step back, waving the pups behind me with a one-handed gesture. Then I turned, resigned to running—until a vine snagged my ankle and pulled.

I landed on my face in the leaves. My impact with the ground knocked the air from my lungs, stunning me for a second. And as I sat up, pulling at the vine, trying to saw through it with my ineffectual human fingernails, Monsieur Colbert rushed forward . . . and his bubble of light fell over me.

Grainger's father gasped, his gaze quickly raking over my naked form, then snapping back up to my face. "Adele. What's happened? Where is your clothing? Are you okay? Are . . . are you *real*?"

"I—What are you doing out here?"

"Grainger's wound is festering. I'm on my way to Oldefort to bring back a physician." His frown deepened. "What are *you* doing out here all alone? Here, take my cloak." He started to remove his outer layer, and I jerked backward. His eyes narrowed as his surprise gave way to suspicion. "Adele?"

KILL HIM. The order came from the dark wood itself, carried on a viciously cold gust that somehow stoked the flames of a ravenous fire burning in my gut. The forest had never spoken directly to me in human form before, and its command compounded an urge my body already felt—an ache in my bones to let them reassume my wolf form. To sink my claws into his skin and my teeth into his throat.

To taste his blood. To devour his flesh.

No.

Monsieur Colbert had seen me with the pups. He'd seen me unscathed by the dark wood. Eventually, he would understand what he was seeing, and when that happened, he would be a threat to me, and by extension, to my family. Which would make him a threat to the entire village. But that threat had nothing to do with the dark urge burning in me as I ripped the vine free from my ankle.

KILL HIM. NOURISH THE GROUND WITH HIS BLOOD. SATE YOUR HUNGER WITH HIS FLESH.

The dark wood taunted me with unspeakable possibilities. Violent pleasures. Gruesome indulgences. And I wanted everything it was offering.

God help me, I wanted it all.

Tom jumped in front of me, growling fiercely, for a pup, and

334

Romy was right behind him, snapping at the intruder's shins. They'd decided I was vulnerable. That this man was a threat. And the little monsters were determined to protect me.

Startled, Monsieur Colbert kicked out, his lantern swinging again, and his boot slammed into Tom's left side. The pup whimpered as he thumped into the dirt a yard away, and I was on my feet in an instant, snarling at the watchman, my lips curled back from human teeth, spittle flying from my mouth. "Don't . . . touch . . . him," I growled.

Monsieur Colbert's eyes widened as he took in my shameless nudity. As he heard the guttural quality of my command—my defense of a wolf pup. Then he took a single step back, his hand going to the pommel of his sword. "It's true . . ." He started to draw his weapon, and Romy advanced on him, growling bravely.

KILL HIM.

My fists clenched with an effort to resist the command.

"Is that . . . Tom?" The watchman's focus landed on the fierce little pup as he stood, favoring his left side. Then his gaze slid toward the other pup. "And this is little Romy?" His voice cracked, broken by the discovery. "Grainger was right. The devil take you all, he was *right*, and you lied. You let them—"

A flash of guilt sliced through me, and the pain brought with it a moment of disorientation. A brutal doubt.

What was I doing? How long had I been in the forest?

Then he took another step backward and started to draw his

sword, and alarm surged in my veins.

Romy looked back at me, whining. Asking permission to obey the forest's command. To eliminate the threat.

KILL HIM.

"I'll have you all burned in the village square, your ashes sprinkled on unhallowed ground," he swore, carrying his bubble of light with him in his slow retreat. "Your whole family, and the Pagets."

Romy's whining reached a frenzied pitch as my pulse began to roar in my ears. Tom growled, his tiny claws digging into the dirt. They both looked back at me just as Monsieur Colbert turned and ran for the path.

If he made it back to the village, my entire family would die. So would Romy's.

I nodded, my jaw clenched, my fists opening and closing at my sides. And the pups raced after him.

They caught him in seconds, and I closed my eyes as they pounced, driving him to the ground.

KILL. KILL. KILL.

Monsieur Colbert screamed, and both pups snarled. I heard the ripping of cloth and the clatter of a sword still in its scabbard. Then the screaming stopped.

I opened my eyes, and at first I couldn't make any sense of what I saw. Of the blood splattered across trunks and roots. Dripping from branches. Both pups' muzzles were slick with it. The entire forest suddenly reeked of it.

EAT, the dark wood commanded. *INDULGE THE YOUNG IN THEIR VICTORY—A CUSTOM AS OLD AS TIME.*

The pups stared at their kill, heads cocked, as if they were studying it. As if they couldn't quite understand what had happened. Then Romy lunged at Monsieur Colbert's corpse and tore a hunk of flesh from his neck.

"No!" I shouted. My teeth clattered together, and this time my chill had as much to do with what I'd just seen—what I'd just let them do—as with the cold. "No, spit that out!"

Romy turned to me with another curious cock of her head, but she'd already swallowed her bite. She'd already *eaten* part of *Monsieur Colbert.* Of the man whose family I'd expected to join. Whose grandchildren I'd thought I would bear.

What have I done?

Grief crashed over me. Shame burned in my gut.

"Stop! Come away from him." I waved the pups toward me, still shivering, and reluctantly, they came. "We don't eat people," I whispered. "We don't eat people, *ever.* Rabbits. Deer. But no people. Do you understand?"

Romy nodded, but Tom only gave me a confused look. "We aren't just wolves. We aren't just monsters," I told them. "We're people too, and people don't eat people."

Tom glanced back at the body still leaking blood onto the ground—the dark wood seemed satiated by that, at least—and I could hear the question he couldn't ask.

We can kill people, but we can't eat them?

"No," I said in response to his unspoken query. "I shouldn't have let you do that."

Monsieur Colbert had to be stopped. In that moment, he'd been as much a danger to my family—to the entire village—as the dark wood was. But how could I explain that to two young children? To two young *whitewulf pups*, struggling not just with immaturity and inexperience, but with monstrous lupine urges I was just beginning to truly understand, having felt them myself.

Why now? I'd been in the woods several times since my trial, and I'd never felt the urge to kill a human before. Certainly, the forest had encouraged me to kill monsters, but that was my destiny. My responsibility.

Yet it was now clear that the dark wood didn't care what I killed, only that I *did* kill. That I nourish its soil with blood—be it human or monster—in the absence of nurturing sunlight.

I've been here too long. There was no other explanation. Living in the forest had eroded my resistance to its grisly, homicidal urgings. Living in the dark wood had tipped the balance—the scale in my soul, measuring how much of me remained human and how much became monster. In favor of the beast.

With sudden, terrifying clarity, I realized that if I stayed in the forest for too long, in the company of monsters and two pups who demonstrated less and less human compassion with every passing day, I would become one of the very beasts I was charged with protecting Oakvale from. That under the influence of the dark wood, the difference between redwulf and whitewulf might actually be reduced to the color of our fur.

But how was that possible, if my mother was right? If I was a human who also had a wolf form, while the pups were wolves who also had human forms?

So far, the children had obeyed my commands. They'd learned from me when it was acceptable to hunt and what it was acceptable to eat. But if I left them—if they survived, only to be raised by the dark wood itself—I would someday have to kill them to protect Oakvale.

There has to be another way. There had to be some place where they could live without being threatened by the village. Where they could grow up without *becoming* a threat to the village.

"Give me a minute to change," I whispered, my mind racing while I tried not to look at the man they'd killed. The loss I'd just dealt to Oakvale. To Grainger and his family. "Then follow close behind me. Do you understand?"

Both pups nodded. So I knelt in a bed of leaves and let my body reassume a form it had become frighteningly comfortable in. Then I stood and headed for the only sanctuary I knew that might take in three lost wolves.

TWENTY-TWO

Gran's door opened the second I entered the clearing, as if she'd been expecting us. Or maybe she'd heard us coming.

"Adele!" She blinked, surprised for a second when two whitewulf pups followed me out of the woods. But she beckoned all three of us with a wave. "Come in, child. Children," she corrected, holding the cabin door open for us.

The pups scampered inside, and though they seemed to welcome the warmth, Tom shied away from the roaring blaze in my grandmother's fireplace. Romy whined at him, and when he wouldn't join her by the hearth, she reluctantly joined him on the other side of the bed, her head hanging in disappointment.

Gran plucked a long, cracked deer bone from the stew she was making, and the pups licked it clean. And by the time they began gnawing out the marrow, I had changed into my human form again.

"Oh, Adele . . ." But instead of asking the questions I could practically see behind her eyes, my grandmother handed me a clean rag and a bucket of water, so I could wash up by the fire. "Your mother's gone out in search of you every night for the past week. Since the search party came back without you. And without bodies."

A week. I'd been gone a week. Somehow, the time I'd passed in the woods had felt like a lot less—yet also much, much more.

I dipped the rag in the bucket, then wrung it out. "Max was with the search party." My voice was hoarse, either from neglect or from the cold.

"Yes. He told your mother he thought you were out there. With the pups." I followed her gaze to see that the children had fallen asleep in the corner, one end of the bone tucked beneath Tom's left paw. "He said you would come back. He never doubted it."

My hand paused, the rag hovering over the clean spot I'd been uncovering on my arm. Could he possibly know me so well, already? I hadn't been sure myself, at times, that I would come back.

Gran's focus found the pups again, while I bathed. "The girl is little Romy Paget?"

"Yes, and the other is Tom. The boy I found in the woods."

She sighed. "Okay. Finish cleaning up, then we'll talk."

It took a while to wipe off all the grime from the forest, and by the time I was finished, the rinse water was brown. Gran pulled open her trunk and handed me a bundle of cloth. I shook it out while she dumped the bucket and ran fresh water from her well, and I was surprised to realize I was holding my own dress. The very one I'd worn into the dark wood a week ago.

Warm, clean, and dressed, I finally began to process my surroundings, and I was surprised to find my bright red cloak hanging from a hook on the far wall. The arced arm of my crossbow sat on the floor, peeking beneath the hem of the cloak.

"How do you have my things?" I asked as my grandmother came back inside carrying a bucket of clean water.

"I found them." Max stepped into the cabin behind her.

I crossed the room in several steps and threw my arms around him, and my throat felt thick with the effort to hold back tears. "What are you doing here?" I buried my head in his neck, breathing him in, and his arms wrapped around me, holding me close.

"Looking for you," he whispered into my hair. "Which is how I found a beautiful red cape hanging from a tree branch, and beneath that an exquisitely hand-crafted crossbow. Why would anyone leave such nice things abandoned in the dark wood?"

"I'm so sorry. I didn't know what else to do. I couldn't just leave the pups, and we were much safer as wolves."

"You were never going to dispatch them, were you?" he asked.

I shook my head. "I couldn't. And I couldn't let my mother do it either. It isn't right. This isn't their fault."

Max stepped out of my embrace to frown down at me. "That's why you left without me? You thought I wouldn't let you leave them alive?"

I nodded, but the truth was more complicated than that. Some part of me had known from the beginning that I couldn't just leave the children out there. But Max couldn't have survived in the dark wood, stuck in human form and largely blind, his lantern drawing attention to us everywhere we went.

I'd left him behind because deep down, I'd known there was a possibility that I wouldn't be coming back.

Max exhaled and let the question go, as if he could see the answer in my eyes.

"You shouldn't have gone looking for me," I whispered. "Even with your experience, the dark wood isn't safe for you."

"Your mother was with me that night. When I found your things." He brushed tangled hair back from my face and pressed a kiss to my forehead. "And when she isn't, I stay on the path."

"Has this become a habit?" I asked, glancing at my grandmother over his shoulder.

She shrugged, taking two wooden bowls down from the shelf. "Well, someone has to keep an old lady company."

I laughed. And then suddenly I was crying.

"Sit, child." Gran handed me one of the bowls and waved me toward the suspended pot of stew. "Eat something."

I tried to compose myself as I ladled stew into my bowl. "I'm so sorry. I didn't mean to disappear. I just couldn't leave them. And now, because of me, people have been venturing into the dark wood, and—"

"No," Max insisted, taking the ladle I offered him. "The

search party isn't your fault. Madame Paget would have gone out on her own, even if everyone else had refused. They found Romy's poultice on the path leading to the forest, and she insisted that the children had wandered too close. And that you might have gone looking for them."

I sank into my chair. "She knows about Romy."

Gran pulled a chair close to the fire for Max. "Are you sure?"

I nodded as I scooped up a steaming bite of venison. "Romy told me. Her mother told her to keep it a secret. I don't think she'll tell anyone."

"Does she know about you?" Gran asked, pulling a stool closer to the fire for herself.

"No. Not that it matters. Everyone probably thinks I'm dead."

"They don't," Max said. "Your mother told everyone you were staying here for a little while, to help your grandmother in her advanced age."

Gran snorted, but the sound echoed with good humor.

Max smiled. "Your mother was as convinced as I was that you would come back."

For several minutes, we ate in silence while I processed everything I'd heard. Then, finally, my grandmother turned to me, her expression carefully . . . inscrutable. "What are you doing, *chère*? You were supposed to deal with the pups, for the good of the entire village."

"I know. But I can't do it. I can't kill them, and I can't just leave them."

"Adele—"

"I *won't*. And I don't think leaving them out there would truly help Oakvale, anyway." I turned to Max, begging him to understand. "The dark wood . . . it talks to me. To all three of us, I think. I don't mean whatever creature it is that makes us hear the voices from our memories; I mean the woods itself. Have you ever heard it?"

"No." He frowned, cradling his half-full bowl.

"I've felt like it was calling to me for as long as I could remember. But it was always a vague kind of pull before. A feeling that deep down, I might *belong* there. Then, when I started training, that feeling became . . . more defined. As if the dark wood itself were a presence inside me. A part of me. Or at least, as if it knew me. I thought that was a lie. A trick, intended to scare me. To make me careless. But now . . ."

His focus narrowed on me. "Now, what?"

"When I started spending all of my time out there in wolf form, it was as if the voice of the dark wood came into focus. That's when it began talking to me in earnest."

Gran exhaled slowly. "What does it say?"

"It tells me to do things. To stay in my wolf form, and to . . . kill things. That didn't really matter when the only thing around to kill was monsters. But then people started searching for us. And the dark wood wanted me to kill my own neighbor."

"I've heard the voice," Gran said, softer than I'd ever heard her speak. "When the dark wood starts to talk to me, I know I've been out too long. That I've been the wolf for too long. I should have told you that. I should have warned you."

"You had no way of knowing I would just disappear into the forest."

She exhaled, and for the first time, I saw real fear swimming in her eyes. "The dark wood wants to keep us, and when you didn't show up after a couple of days, I worried that it had gotten you."

"It almost did. I was out there too long, and I lost myself. I . . . I let something bad happen." Fresh tears formed in my eyes, and the cabin swam beneath them. "Grainger's father is dead."

"Mon dieu," Gran breathed.

Max set his bowl down, his brows dipping low. "You . . . ?"

"No. It was the pups. Monsieur Colbert was on his way to Oldefort to ask for a physician and he heard me talking. He left the path and saw me with the pups, and he figured it all out. He was threatening to burn our entire family alive in the village square. Along with the Pagets. I couldn't let him do that, and the dark wood was promising me that if I just killed him, everything would be fine.

"I didn't do it, but . . . I let the pups. I think the forest was talking to them too, and I just . . . let them." My voice hitched as a sob clogged my throat. "And then they tried to eat him, and I realized what I'd done. I let an innocent man become a threat, then I let the children dispatch with that threat. Because I was a coward. And now Romy's tasted human flesh. What if she can't

346

come back from this? What if I let the dark wood make monsters out of those children?"

Gran shook her head slowly. "*Chère*, they're already—"

"No, they aren't," I insisted, gripping my spoon so hard that my fingers ached. "They were listening to me. They hunted when I told them to hunt and they stopped when I told them to stop. They didn't attack Monsieur Colbert until I gave them permission. But then the dark wood told them to eat him." At least, that's what I imagined they were hearing. "And now I'm afraid I've lost them."

"Adele." Max sat straighter, looking me right in the eye. "Maybe it isn't that simple. Maybe human flesh isn't a poison apple, and they aren't damned with one bite. Tom almost certainly hunted humans before you found him. Yet he obeyed you out there, right? As if he were a part of your . . . pack."

I hadn't thought of that. Tom was born a whitewulf, in the dark wood. Surely Max was right about his pre-Oakvale subsistence. Yet . . . "Yes, he obeyed me. And both pups backed away from their kill as soon as I told them to. So . . ." I stood, as the power of my conclusion drove me to my feet, my food forgotten. "Maybe it's not true," I said, my focus shifting between Max and my grandmother. "Maybe whitewulfs are no more monstrous than we are. Maybe they've just been in the dark wood for so long that it's eroded their humanity. Tilted their inner balance in favor of the beast."

Gran frowned. "I don't think that's possible—"

"It *is* possible. I know, because it was happening to me. The longer I spent out there, the less I wanted to go home. The more I wanted to hunt. To spill blood. I think . . . I mean, yes, there are differences between whitewulf and redwulf, but I think the only *important* difference is where we've chosen to live."

"You think Tom and Romy can be redeemed?" Max asked.

I nodded firmly. "I really do. I think they can be taught to hunt monsters, rather than villagers. To eat deer, rather than people. I think they can be guardians, Gran." I turned to her, capturing her gaze and holding it. "I think we owe them a chance, at least. Because the alternative will only lead to more death. More destruction. If we abandon them in the dark wood, someday we will face them again, when they've become a threat to the village. When it's too late to save them. And if we kill them now, we'll never know if they might have been enlisted in Oakvale's defense. If they might have saved lives."

"Okay . . ." she said, clearly thinking it over. "It's certainly worth a try. But what will you do with them? You can't take them back to the village. They seem to have accepted your authority, but if Romy goes back to her family . . . ? If Tom winds up living in another household . . . ?"

"I know." I shrugged with a glance at the sleeping pups. "I was hoping I could keep them here. Safely away from the village, yet not in the dark wood."

"Adele, I'm too old to raise pups," she said.

And though I had my doubts, I nodded. "I'll raise them. I

thought . . . maybe I could stay here with them. I can protect the village from out here, just like you have. And I can teach the pups to do the same."

"Well, you've obviously given this some thought." Gran stood and laid one hand on my shoulder. "I have some wood to chop and some saplings to clear. Why don't you let me think about this while I do my chores?"

"Of course." I'd certainly sprung the whole thing on her.

My grandmother took her maul and headed outside, leaving Max and me alone with the sleeping pups. For one long moment, I stared at my hands and he ate stew, while we tried to figure out what to say to each other.

"I thought I'd never see you again," he said at last, and the ache in his voice triggered an answering pain deep within me. "I worried that you'd chosen the dark wood."

"I thought you were *certain* I'd come back," I teased softly.

"I was. And yet I still worried that you wouldn't."

"I would never choose the dark wood," I assured him. "But it isn't that simple. I don't think anyone ever consciously makes that decision—not even whitewulfs. Because it isn't a decision, really. The dark wood takes a little more of you every day that you're out there, until things that seemed unthinkable a week ago suddenly seem acceptable. Or at least unavoidable. I don't think the dark wood is just a home to monsters, Max. I think it's the *source* of monsters. And I'm worried that it's made one out of me."

He set his bowl down again and took both of my hands.

"No. Adele, *no*. What happened to Monsieur Colbert—I know that wasn't easy. And I know you think there must have been some other choice to make. But there wasn't. What the dark wood wanted you to do is irrelevant. You would have had to make that same choice if he'd found you and the pups here in the clearing. Or in the village. You would have had to do your duty, regardless of what the dark wood whispered into your ear. Because the loss of an entire family of guardians would have been more damaging to Oakvale than the death of one watchman. As cruel as that sounds."

He was right. But I should have done it myself, rather than letting the pups take a human life.

Gran came in then, carrying an armload of split wood for the fireplace, and Max jumped up to help her. "Adele," she said while he stacked the wood. "I need to patrol the path to Oakvale. Will you come with me?"

I hesitated for a second. I'd spent so much time in wolf form lately—I'd lost so much of myself—that I wasn't eager to let go of my human shape. Of the ability to speak. But I wasn't in the habit of saying no to my grandmother.

"Sure," I said at last. "Max, will you stay with the pups?"

"Of course."

"If they wake, tell them to change and give them each a bowl of stew. It's been a while since they've had anything other than raw meat."

He nodded.

"Adele, why don't you change and meet me outside?" Gran said on her way out.

"When you and your grandmother return, I'll head to Oakvale to tell your mother that you've come back. I'm sure she and Sofia will want to see you."

"Sofia. We're going to have to tell her something. If I stay here with the pups, we're not going to have the option of waiting until she's sixteen. At the very least, we'll have to tell her about her betrothal." Surely Mama and Gran would see that.

"I agree. And maybe with that much time to get used to the idea, it won't hit her quite as hard—or as suddenly—as it did you."

"I hope so. Why don't you finish your stew? I'll change, and I'll be back as soon as I can."

So Max returned to his bowl, turning his back, as always, to give me privacy while I took off my clothes and reclaimed my four-legged form. But before the transition was complete— when I was still stuck in the middle of it, unable to even rise from the floor—I heard a lupine snarl from outside.

Max rose and lifted the wooden shutter to look out at the front of the clearing. "Adele," he whispered, closing the shutter. "Hurry. We have company."

TWENTY-THREE

M ax headed outside, leaving the door cracked open so I could follow. "Monsieur Laurent!" he called, his voice calm and even, yet loud enough to be heard easily. "Don't make any sudden movements, or you'll spook the wolf. Just slowly lower your axe and put it on the ground."

Oh no . . .

I tried to reverse my transformation so I could help Max reason with our uninvited guest, but the tension in my grand-mother's growl made it clear that there would be no time for that. So I pushed through the familiar pain, and seconds later I stood on four paws.

I peeked through the crack between the door and the wall, expecting to see Simon's father. Instead, I found Simon him-self, my friend and my best friend's fiancé, with his back to me. He was gripping an axe and facing my grandmother, who stood snarling at him in wolf form.

What on earth was he doing out here?

"Maxime?" Simon was clearly surprised to see him. His frame was tense, his axe raised and ready to wield. "Where's your bow?"

"I have it right here." Max slowly patted my crossbow, which was slung over his shoulder. "But I'm not going to need it, just like you're not going to need that axe. Wolves are common out here, and sometimes they wander into the clearing. That one looks well fed. If you show her you're no threat, she'll go on about her way. So please put the axe down, slowly, and everything will be okay."

And it would be, if he let Gran retreat into the woods to hide until he was gone. But Simon's tight grip on the axe spoke volumes.

He was terrified. And he was *not* going to put down the weapon.

I nosed the front door open slowly, so that it wouldn't creak. Though Max and my grandmother saw me sneak out of the cabin, Simon still had his back to me, and he did not hear my approach.

"That is no ordinary wolf," he insisted, and my heart dropped into my stomach. "I was on the path, just inside the forest, when I saw her—Adele's grandmother. She came out of the cabin. Then the wolf just . . . *consumed* her."

Max frowned. "*That* wolf?" He pointed at Gran, who maintained her defensive stance, still growling softly. "You're saying that wolf *ate* Madame Chastain?"

"No, it consumed her *form*." Simon spoke so quickly that his words tumbled over one another, but his grip on the axe never weakened. He never took his focus from my grandmother. "She *became* that wolf. She is *loup garou*. Grainger was right." Simon shook his head, fear and astonishment seeming to overwhelm him. "Oakvale has been corrupted by evil from the dark wood—evidence of the devil's grip on this world—and the infection has spread beyond little Romy Paget. We have to contain it." He raised his axe, as if he'd throw it, and Gran's growling grew sharper. Louder.

My pulse raced so fast the world started to lose color.

Max frowned. "Simon, surely you are mistaken."

"I'm not. Grainger tried to warn us, and we didn't listen, but we can no longer turn a blind eye to the truth. Draw your weapon. We must save Oakvale from this witch. And her family . . . Adele is staying here, isn't she? Elena was worried, so she asked me to come check on her, but she's probably infected as well." Grief flickered across his face. "This will *devastate* Elena."

Fear and anger warred inside me as I snuck toward him, my paws silent in the dirt.

"You've misunderstood," Max insisted.

"Draw your bow!" Simon ordered, as dread stormed inside me. Like Grainger, he was an innocent man, trying to do the right thing. He didn't deserve to die. But also like Grainger, he was a threat to my family, and by extension, to the entire village.

Slowly, Max lifted his weapon, pulling back on the lever with a bolt notched. But instead of pointing it at the wolf, he aimed right at Simon's chest. "Put the axe down. You don't understand what you've seen."

Please, please believe him . . . Maybe if Simon backed down, he could be spared. Maybe he could be made to understand. Maybe he and Elena could still—

Simon's brows furrowed. A desperate shout burst from his throat, and he pulled his arm back.

"No!" Max shouted, as Simon threw the axe at my grandmother.

Gran leapt at him as I raced across the clearing toward them, watching in horror as the axe flew end over end.

It struck the center of my grandmother's torso. She hit the ground with a whimper, unmoving, and terror flooded me like fire flowing through my veins.

I pounced on Simon, driving him to the ground, where he screamed and twisted, trying to throw me off. Pleading for his life, even as he promised to see my family burn.

Suddenly, the chaos rioting in my head went still. Quiet. And everything became clear. I had no choice. So I lunged at him and sank my teeth into his neck. Then I tossed my head and tore his throat out.

Blood arced over me. Simon gasped, then he started choking. A second later, his blue eyes dulled, and his hands fell to ground.

Numb, I backed off of him and sat on my haunches, waiting for guilt to wash over me. For the horror of what I'd just done to sink in.

What came instead was grief. A complex feeling of mourning not just for the man—for the friend—I'd killed, but for the girl I'd been. The girl who didn't have to choose between her family and her neighbors. To sacrifice the few for the good of the many.

"Adele!" Max shouted, and I turned to see him kneeling at Gran's side. She lay in human form—pain having caused her to change, just like an arrow to the shoulder had for Romy. The axe was still buried in her stomach. "Adele!" he called again. "Come help me!"

But there was nothing I could do for her without hands, so I changed into human form again, as fast as I could. And when I finally stood on two legs, I dropped onto my knees next to him, staring into my grandmother's eyes while she blinked up at me, sucking in short, pain-filled breaths.

"Adele," she whispered. "Take care of them." I wasn't sure whether she was talking about the pups or the villagers, but it didn't matter.

Tears filled my eyes as I took her hand. "I will, I promise."

Her gaze shifted to Max. "And you take care of *her.*"

"I'll never let her out of my sight again," he swore. And as I knelt on the cold ground, crying while I held my grandmother's hand, she took her last breath.

A sob tore free from my throat as Max tugged me to my feet, wrapping his arms around me. Over his shoulder, I saw Simon, still lying where I'd killed him.

I pulled out of Max's embrace. "You still don't think I'm a monster? I've killed an innocent man. My best friend's fiancé."

He took my chin and tilted my face up until I was looking into his hazel eyes, rather than at the carnage. "I think it takes a monster to answer your calling, Adele. There's just no way around that. Your destiny is *made* of brutal choices. But try as the dark wood might to make you forget your humanity—to make you abandon it—I will try just as hard to help you cling to it.

"You asked me once what I bring to this union, and I had answers for you at the time. And those are still true. But I think the most important thing I can do for you is to *remember* you as you are now, no matter how hard the dark wood tries to change you. I will remind you of who you are, when you start to forget. If you will have me."

Crying again, I pulled him into another embrace. "I will," I whispered into his ear. "Of course, I will have you."

His exhalation seemed to carry the weight of the world.

"But I can't go to Ashborne, Max. I'm needed here. With the pups." Especially now that Gran . . . I shook off that thought, not yet ready to confront the reality of my loss. "Will you stay here with me? Will you help me raise them and protect Oakvale?"

"I will." He said it without hesitation. He chose me, over his own village. "But first, I'll have to return to Ashborne to explain to my family. I'll ask my brother to come visit, when he's older, to get to know Sofia. To see if they are a match, and if she might like to see Ashborne. Someday."

"She's always wanted to travel," I told him, sniffing back more tears.

"Adele?" Romy said. Startled, I pulled away from Max to find her looking up at me. Behind her, Tom stood—also in human form—in the doorway of the cabin. "You're shivering." Romy held up a familiar bundle of cloth, and I took my dress from her, then pulled it over my head.

A second later, Tom tugged on my skirt, and I looked down to see him holding a bright red bundle of material. "Thank you, Tom," I said as I secured the cloak over my shoulders. "You two must be freezing. Go back inside, and I'll come bathe you, then we'll find you something to wear."

But mostly, I didn't want them out there with Gran and Simon. They'd seen enough death. They'd heard enough from the dark wood.

The children obediently headed into the cabin, and Max knelt at my side to help me with my grandmother. But before we could lift her, a twig cracked from the forest, and my head snapped up at the sound. My vision narrowed on a form in the shadows, as a man—had someone accompanied Simon?—took off down the path, headed for Oakvale. To tell them what he'd seen.

To tell them what we were.

"Adele." Max handed me my crossbow with a solemn frown. "It takes a monster."

I nodded as I accepted the weapon.

Then I pushed my red hood back and aimed into the shadows, at the shape still fleeing down the path. And I pulled the trigger.

ACKNOWLEDGMENTS

This book was a special challenge for me, despite the return to my shifter roots. But I had fun with every single word! However, as usual, it takes an entire village to turn a story into a book, and some special thanks are due.

Thanks to Maria Barbo, the original editor for this story, whose enthusiasm for my "little army of red riding hoods" idea got the ball rolling. And to my agent, Ginger Clark, who makes things happen.

Thank you, especially, to Catherine Wallace, whose vision made *Red Wolf* the book it is today. Your guidance has been invaluable, and I could not be more pleased for the opportunity to work with you.

A huge thank-you to the HarperCollins art department, for one of the most beautiful covers ever to bear my name. I love this art. Seriously. I *love* it. Front and back.

My gratitude also goes to the HarperCollins editorial and

production departments, for their incredible eye for detail. For catching the balls I dropped.

And, most important, a huge thank-you to everyone who will read this book and find a place in their heart for Adele and her little monsters. May she keep you safe in your dreams.